May everyone you work with have wonderful pedicures!
Thanks for all your help Dr. Goldberg!

Worthy of a Pirate's Love

Always live your fantasy
CD, [signature]

Amanda Broadbeck

PublishAmerica
Baltimore

ISBN: 1-4241-9335-4
PUBLISHED BY PUBLISHAMERICA, LLLP
www.publishamerica.com
Baltimore

Printed in the United States of America

This book is dedicated to my baby sister,
who's been with me every step of the way.

I love you, Ames.

Acknowledgments

I would like to acknowledge my family for everything they've done for me: my dad for his hidden support; my mom for not putting my written manuscript in the box (despite it laying out untouched for several weeks at a time); and my brother for not reading it. I would also like to thank Chris Gruin for buying every pirate book that exists and listening to me talk endlessly about plot lines and character flaws. Lastly, I want to thank my preliminary readers, Paul, Scott, Ashley, Vicki, and Carrie.

I love you all…

Prologue

March 1741

Lightning penetrated the black sky, with thunder chasing after in an endless love tryst that knows no time. Rain fell in violent chasms, drenching the earth below.

A lone horse and rider tore through the pounding rain, braving the storm above them. The man kicked the horse, urging him to go faster to get them to their destination. He'd come a long way for an opportunity like this—across an ocean to be exact. And now that he had one, he was not about to let a little inclement weather stop him.

He briefly thought about his ship, the *North Star*, anchored at the British port about seven miles or so northwest. He wondered how his men were managing in the storm, and if the ship would receive any damage. For a moment he thought about what would happen if his identity was discovered, but he quickly pushed it out of his mind. For now he needed to concentrate.

In a flash of light, he saw the tavern up ahead, steadily growing bigger as he approached. *Faster*, his head screamed over the pounding of hooves on the ground. In moments, he brought his horse to a sudden stop in front of the tavern.

With a grunt, he dismounted and tied his steed to the post nearest the entrance. He caught a glimpse of his reflection in the window as he moved toward the door. The man staring back at him was barely visible against the black sky. He was dressed in his usual attire: black boots, black shirt, open at the chest to show his patch of chest hair, and black breeches. As always, his sleeves were pushed up to his elbows, displaying his tanned forearms. His shirt clung to his torso like second skin, presenting his muscular chest and broad shoulders. His near-black hair was slicked back, with a few individual strands stubbornly dangling in front of his sky blue eyes, water still dripping from them. He shook his head, letting his hair return to its natural position. As he turned toward the door, the cutlass at his side gleamed in a flash of lightening. He pulled open the heavy door and stepped inside.

As he stomped his feet on the wooded floor to remove the mud from his boots, his eyes slowly scanned the crowded room, looking for any familiar faces. Last month, when he stumbled upon this tavern, he found it empty except for the three men he had returned here to meet. Although he didn't know their names, their faces were etched in his mind. Looking around now, the place was packed, perhaps in part due to the storm that was still hammering above them. Seeing no one he recognized, he marched to a table in the far, dark corner and told the four men sitting there to move.

One of the men slammed the drink he was holding to his lips on the table in protest. As he stood up, the man in black moved his hand to the handle of his sword. The men at the table grumbled to each other as they stood up and moved across the room. The man in black thanked them kind-heartedly and sat down. He ordered himself a plate of hot food and stared at the door as he waited for the other men to arrive.

It was almost two hours later before the other three men stepped through the doorway. The man in black eyed them carefully over the rim of his mug as his colleagues shook off their wet cloaks.

The man closest to him stood almost six feet tall, with the build of a man who had experienced hard labor early in his life. *Farmer, more than likely*, the man in black thought. As the man turned, the man in black noticed the man's protruding stomach, indicating that he had moved up in society. In the candlelight, his hair looked grayer than what it actually was, even though it was wet. His dark blue eyes searched the room for the man in black. They landed on him for a moment, but the blue-eyed man did not see him.

The man next to the blue-eyed man took a step forward and said something to a passing waitress. She shook her head and gave him a small smile as she walked away, adding an extra swing to her hips. His bright green eyes followed her as she moved about the tables. The man in black noticed how his wet clothes molded against his body, making him look sickly thin. His hair matched the color of red clay, a mixture of browns and reds, and ran away from his forehead several inches. He turned and looked at the third man standing behind him.

Must be his son, the man in black decided. The third man looked like a younger version of the green-eyed man, with matching hair and eye color. The only difference was that the young man had more hair on his round baby face, making him look like a child. The brown freckles along his cheeks and nose enhanced the child-like look. The man in black watched as his bright green eyes eyed every wench in the room. As one blonde-haired waitress passed him, the young man leaned against the wall in a nonchalant stance. He watched her as she moved to the corner and served the man in black.

"Remember, do not give your name," the young man whispered to the other men as he stepped around them and moved toward the man in black. He gained the attention of a passing wench with a slap on her posterior and commanded her to get them all mugs of warm ale. With a smile, he pulled out the bench across from the man in black and sat down.

The four men huddled close together around the small table, drinking their mugs of warm ale. The tavern was noisy with dirty sailors and smelly beggars attempting to escape the storm. The smell of body odor, blood and smoke filled the room. Occasionally, a tavern maid would approach the table to refill their drinks and bring them a fresh plate of warm meat, but before she could offer further services that involved retreating to one of the back rooms, the man in black would send her away.

"And you can do this for us, Captain?" asked the blue-eyed man to the man in black.

The man in black nodded. "Yes. If you can get the money together, I'll bring you all the supplies you need."

The blue-eyed man turned to the man with the green eyes sitting next to him. "Six months?"

His friend nodded. "Of course. Is that all the time you need, son?"

"Son" was busy winking at a passing waitress. His dark green eyes and red-brown hair made him look like a child in the candlelight. The man with the green eyes shook his arm and repeated the question.

"Yes, that'll do just fine. I'll get the money. Don't worry about that," the young man mumbled without taking his eyes of the wench as she served the other men in the tavern. His green eyes showed no mercy as they traveled along the curves of her body.

The man in black rolled his eyes in disgust. With a grunt, he pushed back his chair and stood up. "I wish you goodnight, gentlemen. I'll see you in London in six months from today." He pulled a few coins from his purse and dropped them in the center of the table. "Don't forget."

"No, of course not," said the blue eyed man.

The man in black nodded and took his leave without another word.

"Who do you suppose that was?" asked the young man returning his attention back to his companions.

"Don't know. But I got a plan," said the man with the green eyes, smiling. The blue-eyed man smiled in return. "Good. I knew you would."

The young man folded his hands on the table. "Jonathon," he said, turning to the blue-eyed man. "If I do this, I want to marry your daughter. She's a pretty little thing and…" his voice grew deeper, "I think it'll be the right thing to do."

The blue-eyed man sighed, hearing the unspoken threat. "You're a good man. It's only fair." He paused. "She'd be lucky to have you."

"And her dowry?" the young man asked, eyes boring into the blue-eyed man. "I'd like to have it as soon as possible."

Jonathon glanced down at his pale, wrinkled hands, then looked at the man with the green eyes. Gritting his teeth, he turned back to the young man and nodded. "I'll have it to you in a fortnight."

The young man stood up. "It's a deal then. Tell me the plan in the morning. Right now I could use a good toss with a wench." He smiled, avoiding Jonathon's eyes as he turned to face the nearest woman. He dug in his pockets for his coin purse and, with a smile at the woman, shook out several coins. The woman eyed the coins, counting them in her head. With a grin that displayed her missing front teeth, she nodded.

"Bra—" Jonathon began.

"Goodnight, gentlemen," the young man said as he reached for the woman in front of him. She giggled as he cupped her bottom in one hand and her breast in the other. He picked her up in one strong swoop and placed her over his shoulder as he headed to one of the back rooms.

"This had better work," one of the men said behind him.

Chapter One

January 1742

"One...two..." counted Adelina, using a slender finger to point out the falling snowflakes lit by the meager moonlight. Adelina Ellingsworth sat in front of the large window overlooking the empty streets of London, listening to her mother play the piano. Adelina's younger brother Christopher sat in her lap.

"Remember, it's not snowing unless you reach ten," their father instructed from behind.

Christopher looked back for a moment and let out a long, agitated sigh. Upon returning his attention to the window, "three...four...five...six seven eight nine ten!" he shouted, bringing laughter from everyone in the room.

On the other side of the room, Brandon Wexford leaned against the mantle of the fireplace. His dark maroon suit made him look taller than he actually was. He was thin, with diminishing freckles on his face and arms. The red in his brown hair was brought out by the glow of the fire behind him, making him appear even younger. His green eyes danced as he watched the Ellingsworth family enjoy the late winter evening.

In the large green chair facing the window sat Lord Jonathon Ellingsworth, father of Adelina and Christopher. He wore dark breeches and an open waistcoat that displayed his white shirt. His dark blue eyes were focused on his children. His hands rested on his round stomach, holding a small glass. As he laughed, he could feel his belly ripple in delight.

Lady Elizabeth Ellingsworth withdrew her fingers from the ivory keys. She stood up and walked to the small cabinet standing next to the piano. She withdrew a bottle of brandy and filled a short glass. With grace, she walked to where her husband sat and handed him the drink. She looked down at Lord Ellingsworth with big, honey-brown eyes that sparkled with love. She was tall, with wavy brown hair, with hints of gray in it, that almost reached her knees when worn down, hugging her slim waist. Women of her class looked at her with envy, for she still held onto her youthful beauty that men still yearned for, even after having a child in her late age. She smiled warmly at her husband as her fingers toyed with his gray hair. Her fingers grazed the back of his neck before she returned to the piano and began playing a light melody.

Being just over five years old, Christopher's head barely reached Brandon's thigh. Christopher had medium blue eyes, blonde hair, and a face spotted with red freckles. But Brandon wasn't interested in looking at Christopher.

His gaze landed on his betrothed, Adelina, a full woman of eight-and-ten. He admired how the evergreen gown she was wearing revealed her slim waist and ample bosom. He noted how the shade of green offset the color of her creamy skin. How he longed to feel that silky skin against his own, to feel her soft hair, a sea of tumbling curls tickles his chest as she pleasured him.

Just as his gaze was slipping downward to the curvy bosom and hips, Adelina looked up and caught his stare. With a slight blush of embarrassment, Brandon blinked and made contact with her honey brown orbs. Turning a slight shade of red, he turned to add another log to the fire.

Adelina forced herself to smile at her fiancé. After knowing him for barely a year, it was still hard for her to accept that they were to be married. *Why did Father have to take on a new partner—William Wexford. No, I can't blame Father. But why did we have to invite his family for dinner, him and his son.* Adelina sighed. *I could tell that Brandon was completely taken with me. I actually thought of accepting his courtship at the time. He was really sweet and charming, always making me laugh. But there was something about him that I didn't trust. I still can't put my finger on it. A week after that, Father and the Wexfords went on a business trip. Upon Father's return, I was engaged to Brandon.*

"It all happened entirely too fast," Adelina muttered. Christopher glanced up at her, face scrunched with curiosity. She gently squeezed his nose, leading him into a series of giggles. She nudged Christopher off her lap and strolled over to Brandon's side.

"Father has informed me of tomorrow," Adelina whispered. Earlier that morning Lord Ellingsworth had told his daughter that they would be traveling to Wexford Manor near the city limits of London for an overnight business conference. Lord Ellingsworth and Adelina were to leave just after sunup to reach their destination by noon. "Besides," her father had added, almost reluctantly, "he's to be your husband. You might as well get to know the man."

Brandon smiled. "Well then, good. If you'd like, we can do some shopping in town. Maybe even sit and read all afternoon."

Adelina nodded.

"I'll see you tomorrow, my dear," Brandon said. With a nod, he gave his farewells to the rest of the family and left the house to return to his home.

Adelina waited for Brandon to leave before she said her goodnights and went upstairs to her bedroom, closing the door to her bedchamber with a sigh.

"Good evening, Mary," Adelina greeted her servant as she stepped into the room. Adelina sat down in front of her vanity, studying her face in the mirror as Mary begun pulling pins from her hair.

Her face was long, giving it an oval shape. Her eyebrows were long and thin, arching high over her brown eyes. She hated how her nose was long and ended with a slight bend upward, making her look as thought she was overly proud. For that, she held her head slightly tilted downward so that no one would notice. When she smiled, her whole face lit up, turning her cheeks a hint of pink above her dimples. On those pink cheeks, slightly below her right eye was a mole—or a freckle—she was unsure of which. Men have often told her that she was the most beautiful woman in all of London. But she didn't see it.

Adelina looked up from her reflection to study Mary's. She was four-and-ten, and a tiny girl with blonde hair and tiny blue eyes. Adelina's father had found her wandering the streets several years ago and offered her a home so long as she would serve Adelina as her lady's maid. Because Adelina didn't care for the conceited attitude of other girls her age, Adelina had quickly made friends with the reserved girl.

Mary smiled. "Did you have a good night with Sir Wexford?"

Adelina nodded. "Father and I are going to Wexford Manor tomorrow."

"That is nice. Your hair is done, mum," Mary said, stepping back.

"Thank you." Adelina smiled. She stood up, and with the help of Mary, changed into her nightclothes. With a yawn, Adelina crawled between the silken sheets.

"Night, mum," Mary whispered as she opened the door to let herself out.

"Goodnight, Mary."

Mary returned shortly before sunup and gently nudged Adelina awake.

"Mmmm," Adelina moaned. "Go away."

"Now, now," Mary scolded, "you've got to get up and get to the Wexford place with your father now."

"Mmmm," Adelina moaned again. "Oh, alright."

Less than an hour later, Adelina came downstairs in an elegant dress that matched the color of dark red wine. It was one of her favorite gowns because it only hinted at her slim waist and bosom, preventing any unwanted attention. Her wavy hair was pulled loosely back with a few curls left to dangle over her shoulders.

"Daughter, you look wonderful," Lord Ellingsworth said as she reached the final step. "Hurry up and eat so we can get on our way. We're late as it is."

Adelina went into the kitchen and picked up a few biscuits. Grabbing a cloth napkin, she wrapped the muffins and gave her father a smile. He grabbed his jacket and helped Adelina put on her cloak. Outside, Benjamin was waiting with the carriage.

"Hello, Benjamin," Lord Ellingsworth greeted the horseman.

"Morn'n, Master, Miss Adelina," Benjamin said, tipping his hat to her. Adelina gave him a warm smile as he helped her into the coach.

The ride to Wexford Manor was long and uneventful. Lord Ellingsworth shuffled through the papers on his lap while Adelina napped under a heavy fur blanket. Just after noon, they passed through the iron gate with the large, scripted WM in the center. The Wexford butler, George, waited for them at the steps with a young foot servant to carry their luggage. Without looking at anyone he announced that lunch would be served as soon as they were settled.

Wexford and Brandon were already in the dining room sipping brandy. Brandon greeted Adelina with a light kiss on the cheek and pulled out a chair for her to sit. With a smile, he took the seat next to her. Wexford was at the head of the table, with Lord Ellingsworth to his right and Brandon to his left. In moments, Wexford and Lord Ellingsworth were already engrossed in a conversation about politics and the economy.

Brandon moved in his chair so that he could be nearer to Adelina. "You look completely wonderful," Brandon whispered in her ear. "Beautiful. I can't wait until we can get away from here. I just want to hold you and put kisses all over you."

Adelina leaned away from Brandon's hovering presence. "Brandon, please. My Father shall hear you."

As soon as lunch was cleared, Brandon escorted Adelina to the parlor.

Brandon came up behind her and encircled her in his arms. "Adelina," he whispered, "I love you so much."

"Oh, Brandon. You're so silly." Adelina laughed as she placed her palm on his shoulder.

Brandon's smile dropped, as he pulled her against him. "But do you love me?"

Adelina took a ragged breath. "Yes, I do, Brandon," she forced herself to say. *I'm not* in *love with you*, she thought. *But I do love you. Maybe one day I'll feel the same way for you that you do for me.*

To ease the anxiety that was slowly filling the air, Adelina laughed and stood on her toes to place a kiss on Brandon's nose. She stepped out of his arms, spun in a circle and sat down on the couch. Brandon, once again in good spirits, took the seat next to her.

After a moment, Brandon put his arm around Adelina's shoulders and began to play with a loose curl that dangled over her shoulder. He pressed his body against her, feeling her warmth flow through him. He sucked on her earlobe. "How often do you think about me?" Brandon whispered.

Adelina fought to keep from shuddering. She leaned forward and lifted a book from the table and in her movement, she moved a few inches away from him. She thought about him constantly; about the upcoming wedding and being married before she reached a full score. "I think about you every day. Why?"

"Just wondering. I can't stop thinking about you," Brandon whispered. He moved closer to her and placed a hand above her knee. It lingered there for a moment, but then it began to creep upward, fingers toying with the soft material of the gown. "What I want to do with you…to you."

Adelina's virgin mind began to race. His hot calf pressed hard against her thigh, radiating heat through her body. His hand slowly moved up her thigh, pulling the gown with it to expose her legs. She took a deep breath, feeling a brief moment of panic flow through her. "I better go see how Father is doing." She got up and quickly left the parlor before Brandon could say another word.

Lord Ellingsworth and Wexford were still in the dining room. She gently pushed the door open a crack, but stopped at her father's booming voice.

"I thought you said you took care of it!" Lord Ellingsworth yelled, slamming his fist onto the table.

"I did! We have the money *and* the supplies," Wexford yelled back. "But he escaped. I'm telling you, Roark escaped."

"He's supposed to be dead!" Lord Ellingsworth yelled.

Wexford didn't say anything for a moment. "I know."

"If he finds out it was us, he'll kill us," Lord Ellingsworth moaned.

"He won't. We were careful," Wexford assured him.

Lord Ellingsworth said something that Adelina didn't hear.

She heard Wexford sigh. "I know. Believe me I know. We should have known not to cheat a damn pirate."

Adelina gasped. The men stopped talking and turned in her direction. Wexford knocked over his chair as he raced to the door. He threw it open and found Adelina trembling in the doorway. Upon sighting his daughter, Lord Ellingsworth stood up to greet her. He waited alongside Adelina while Wexford corrected his chair.

Lord Ellingsworth placed an arm around Adelina's back and gave a worried glance at Wexford. "What's wrong, my dear?"

Adelina thought for a moment about what she had just overheard. *Why would Father cheat a pirate? Surely Father would never do such a thing. Who is Roark? Is Roark the pirate? Father would be mad if he knew I had listened to his private conversation.* "I was coming to ask you something and I stubbed my toe on the door. I'm sorry. I never meant to disturb you." She made an effort to turn around, but Lord Ellingsworth held her firm.

Lord Ellingsworth relaxed and gave his daughter a warm smile. "It's all right, dear. Why don't you sit down and we'll have a look at your toe."

Adelina stammered, "Oh, um, it's alright now. I'm fine, Father."

Lord Ellingsworth let his arm drop. "Now, what did you want to ask me?"

Adelina looked at Wexford as he sat down. "Oh, I forgot. You know me," she said, giving a little laugh. "If I remember I'll come find you." She left before she could be further interrogated.

"Dinner is served," George announced.

Once seated, Wexford turned to Lord Ellingsworth. "Are you still planning to stay the night?"

"Yes, William. Thank you for your hospitality," Lord Ellingsworth answered.

"Yes, indeed. Thank you," added Adelina.

While waiting for the main course to be served, Brandon boldly placed his hand firmly on Adelina's thigh. "I talked to Father. He said I can give you the room across from your father's," Brandon whispered.

"Thank you." Adelina smiled. She shifted her legs around and his hand fell away from her leg.

Brandon moved a few inches closer so that only she could hear him. "That way, you're next to mine."

Adelina sent a glare to her betrothed, but after catching the lust in his eye, she blushed. "Brandon, please. Show some respect before we are wed."

"You are mine now, and you'll still be mine ten years from now. What will be the difference if you give yourself to me tonight?" Brandon whispered as his hand crawled up her thigh. He could feel his groin fill with heat at the thought of the prospect of penetrating Adelina. *I've never had a virgin before.* "I promise you that no one will know."

Adelina blushed a deeper shade of red and calmly brushed Brandon's hand off her thigh. "Stop," she commanded.

Dinner continued with barely another word. After the dishes were cleared, conversation began again.

"Brandon, will you please have George bring in Adelina's luggage and show her to her room? Have him bring in Jonathan's too. We will remain in here a while more," Wexford said. "Finish some business and such."

Brandon presented his arm and Adelina cautiously accepted. Quietly, they climbed the stairs and walked down the hall to the room that was prepared for her. Brandon pushed the door open to display the grand bedroom. A bed that Adelina could swim in was covered in red silken sheets and equipped with a canopy. The large fireplace across from the bed was already lit and making the room warm and cozy. Elaborate maroon curtains were pulled over the large windows to prevent the morning sun. And, wherever possible, there were lit candles.

"It's beautiful," Adelina whispered. Her own room was nowhere near this large or decorated.

"And you have your own bath," Brandon added. He crossed the room to the adjoining door that opened into a huge bath chamber with a tub and a small fireplace. "You'll have a servant when you awake to assist you."

While Adelina admired the bath chamber, Brandon moved to shut the door that opened into the hallway. When she returned to the bedroom, Brandon wrapped his arms around her waist, pulling her as hard as he could against him.

"No one will know. I'll make sure of it. Please, Adelina? Oh, Adelina, please?" Brandon whispered into her ear. He never gave her a chance to answer for he placed a crushing kiss on Adelina's mouth, preventing any sound from escaping.

Adelina tried to turn her head away, but Brandon pushed harder against her lips, invading her mouth with his tongue. In a desperate attempt to end the brutal kiss, she put her palms against his chest and pushed as hard as she could. He stood fast, pressing harder against her bruised lips. Determine to break herself from him, she balled her hands and repeatedly punched his shoulders and chest.

Yet, Brandon was not dissuaded. His mouth opened wider, his tongue vandalizing hers. His hand moved from her hips to squeeze her breast. Adelina gasped against his mouth in painful agony. Then, he pulled her against him so that he can feel her against his demanding manhood. Groaning, he pulled the strings the supported the bodice against her body so that the gown could lean forward and expose her breasts.

Brandon all but threw Adelina onto the bed. She held the front of the dress against herself as she tried to scramble over the pillows that prevented her from escaping. Brandon ripped his shirt over his head and sneered as he pulled Adelina back to him by her ankles. He loosened the strings on his trousers and pushed his pants down over his buttocks, exposing himself.

Adelina froze at the sight of Brandon's throbbing manhood, red from being ready. He went to cover her with his body. Just as he did so, her knee came up and hit him squarely in the loins.

"Humph," was all Brandon could muster. He fell onto his side and lay still for several moments, watching Adelina as she ran to the fireplace and grabbed the fire poker. She held it over head, ready to strike.

"Get out!" she shouted through clenched teeth.

Brandon stared at her for a long time. After almost a full minute, he got up, although hunched over and holding himself. Without looking behind him, he sauntered slowly out of the room. No sooner did he leave did Adelina lock the door and climb into bed, still gripping the weapon.

It was some weeks later before Adelina could be in the same room with Brandon. At first, she refused his visits altogether, instructing the servants not to even open the door to him. One afternoon, Adelina attempted to speak with her father about terminating the engagement. Lord Ellingsworth shook his head and simply said, "I doubt there is anything I can do."

The following morning, Wexford had stopped by to see Lord Ellingsworth and Adelina overheard him tell her father "it was Brandon's right to bed Adelina."

With the wedding less than a month and a half away, Adelina decided that she needed to swallow her pride and accept that she would have to settle with Brandon as her husband. To prevent her thoughts from turning to Brandon and her dim future, Adelina focused on the wedding itself. She was thankful when the Towson's annual winter ball was announced and she had something to further distract her from thinking about Brandon.

Adelina had forgotten about the Towson ball until she stopped at the seamstress shop to see about the details on her wedding gown. The plump seamstress greeted Adelina as she entered.

"Miss Adelina. How are you this morning, my dear?" asked Christine Montgomery.

"Oh, I'm just fine," Adelina responded. Truthfully, the woman got on her last nerve. As nice and cheerful as Mistress Montgomery appeared to be, she could and would spread vicious rumors about the slightest bit of gossip. If it wasn't for the fact that Mistress Montgomery was well known as the best seamstress and gown designer in all of London, she would have been well out of business. "How is my gown coming along?"

"Oh, it's almost done. I have one of my girls finishing the last details now," Mistress Montgomery said over her shoulder as she went to one of the back rooms.

Adelina sat down on the stiff couch against the far wall, letting her eyes drift over the shop. There was an oval coffee table and two wooden chairs on either side of it in front of her. To the left were two display windows with four model gowns displaying the latest fashion in England. The clock standing on the far wall struck eleven, filling the air with its loud chimes. The air smelt thickly of heavily perfumed women, making Adelina sniffle. She watched her mother as she looked at the paintings hanging on the walls before she joined Adelina on the couch.

"Miss Adelina, it's ready," Mistress Montgomery said nearly thirty minutes later. She instructed Adelina to follow her.

After Mistress Montgomery finished securing the dress, Adelina looked at her reflection in the full length mirror. The gown was shimmering dark lavender that came off her shoulders with a thick neckline that went around her bust and upper arms. The neckline was of a slightly darker shade that drew attention from the dress to her face. The bodice was comfortably tight along her torso, and it seamed at her waist before it spread to the floor. The style revealed her slim waist and was modest with her bosom. She could feel herself falling in love with the gown.

Lady Elizabeth came in and smiled warmly at her daughter. "Oh, Adelina."

Mistress Montgomery would not miss the opportunity to gloat. "Her wedding gown will be the same design, but with pearls. Oh, and they are both made of the finest silks."

"Thank you, Mistress Montgomery." Adelina smiled as she began to undress.

"My pleasure," the woman said, rubbing her palms together. "Now tell me…you and Brandon Wexford…the latest I heard…"

The first time Adelina permitted Brandon into her presence was when he came to escort her to the Towson ball. After an awkward greeting, Brandon led Adelina to the carriage. He has been nothing but a gentleman, persistently sending her flowers and jewelry. Adelina guessed it was because he didn't want to upset her in fear that she would prohibit the marriage whether or not Lord Ellingsworth gave his consent. But it didn't stop her from giving his gifts to the servants of the household.

The ride to Towson Manor was quiet. Brandon tried to begin a conversation about the weather, but Adelina quickly shrugged him off. After his third attempt, he gave up, succumbing to the growing silence in the coach. When they arrived at Towson manor, Adelina gave him a sympathetic smile. In slightly lighter spirits, Brandon escorted Adelina down from the coach and led her to up the building

A servant greeted them with a smile at the door. Without a word, he ushered them through the long interior of the house. Briefly, Adelina caught a glimpse of the elegant tapestries and paintings that hung in the long corridor.

They entered the room, and Adelina was amazed to see herself entering above the celebration. A large staircase expanded to the floor below them where countless guests socialized. Brandon gave their names to the young man waiting at the top of the staircase, who momentarily shouted their names over the festivities, announcing their arrival to the company below.

Lord Alfred Towson welcomed his guests after they descended down the flight of steps that ended in front of him. With a kind voice, he introduced his wife and only daughter, Juliet, who stood alongside him. Upon seeing Juliet, Adelina sighed.

"Why, hello Adelina," Juliet almost sneered as she stepped forward and rolled her shoulders. She wore a pale yellow gown with lace trimmings and styled, her pitch black hair was piled high on the crown of her head. Since Juliet lacked natural volume, she relied on fancy barrettes to accent her hair. Her dark eyes and fair skin became vivid between her hair and dress.

"Juliet! How are you?" Adelina exclaimed with sarcastic squeal that matched Juliet's.

"Good," Juliet said, plainly, feeling that the game was lost. She glanced over at Brandon as he took a step forward. Her green eyes started fluttering and she took a breath to push her chest out so that her breasts were only matters of inches from his chest. Juliet had always believed that she was the most desirable woman in London and was used to receiving visits from many male visitors. As Mistress Montgomery said to Adelina's mother, "She thinks she's God's gift to men." Juliet waited for Brandon to step closer to her. "Good evening, Brandon. It's *so* good to see you."

"Hello, Juliet," he said with a smile.

"Will you save a dance for me?" Juliet asked, ignoring Adelina as she rolled her eyes.

Brandon shrugged. "We'll see."

"I'll look forward to it," Juliet said with a smirk before she turned to the next guest.

Brandon led Adelina to the dance floor. "Would you care for a dance?"

Adelina accepted his offer just as a waltz began.

Adelina danced for almost two hours straight without a moment's rest. Every time she attempted to find refuge in a chair, some other gentleman would ask her to dance. Finally, the strain on her feet became too much. She *had* to sit down, leaving Brandon to dance with Lady Towson.

It's much too hot in here, Adelina thought as she moved about the room in an attempt to find a cool place to sit and rest. The cool air from an open door beckoned her out onto the balcony. Outside, she sat on the wooden bench and began to loosen her slippers. She pulled the hem of her dress back and lifted her feet into the air, smiling at the relief of being able to wiggle her toes.

From behind her came a deep voice. "Feeling better? I think you could use some of this more than me," a man said, handing Adelina a glass of wine.

Adelina gulped the beverage down and blushed as the warmth of the liquid flowed through her. "Thank you."

"You're welcome." The man laughed. Adelina looked up at the man illuminated by the soft glow from the light in the ballroom. The man before her was dressed entirely in black, with the sleeves of his shirt pushed up to his elbows. The neckline of his shirt was open, displaying the hair on his chest. She could tell in the moonlight that the man had a dark tan and muscular shoulders. She gazed into the handsome face of the man in black. Instead of the typical periwig that the other often wore, his hair was pushed back behind his ears. A lock of hair remained in front of his blue eyes, despite his attempt to brush it back. He had a strong, freshly shaven chin. She estimated him to be a few years older than herself.

"My name is Adelina Ellingsworth," Adelina said, her words coming out with a long pause, as though she was unsure of her own name.

"You can call me Henry," the stranger said with a smile. "If you want to put your slippers back on, I'll invite you in for a dance."

Adelina smiled. Without a thought of Brandon, she secured her laces and stood up, surprised to find that the man in front of her was almost a head and a half taller than she was. Smiling, she accepted his arm and allowed him to escort her into the ballroom. The waltz was just about to begin and Adelina watched Brandon lead Juliet onto the floor, oblivious of her presence. Henry pulled Adelina against him, waiting for the music to start.

Adelina's heart sped up as he slipped his arm around her waist. She took a deep breath, forcing herself to breathe as she placed a delicate hand on his muscular shoulder. "I've never seen you before, milord."

"Oh, I've been in London for about a week or two. And, please, call me Henry," he directed.

As the waltz continued, Adelina felt as though someone was watching her. She looked over her shoulder to find a jealous sneer radiating from Juliet. Adelina watched Juliet whisper something in Brandon's ear. A few minutes later, his green eyes looked over and glared heavily at Adelina. But before she could wonder what caused such a look from her betrothed, the waltz picked up speed. Adelina had to quicken her steps and move closer to Henry to keep up with the dance.

The faster the music played, the closer she found herself to him. In moments, she could feel his hard muscles working underneath his shirt and the heat of his body against her own. She could feel her heart beating faster as she moved about the room with Henry holding her close. She couldn't tell if it was the dance steps or Henry that made the blood pump to her checks, turning her skin a slight shade of pink.

The music stopped abruptly, and Henry stopped in his place, leaving Adelina to stumble into him as she fought to steady herself.

Henry looked at her with the bluest eyes she's ever seen. "I'm sure we'll be meeting again soon, Miss Ellingsworth," he whispered. With a sly smile, he kissed her fingertips, sending shivers that rocked through her body. Without another word he disappeared into the crowd.

Before Adelina could blink her mind clear, Brandon grabbed her arm, nearly dragging her out of the ballroom.

"What was that all about?" Brandon asked when they were out of earshot of other guests. *There was something familiar about that man.*

"You seemed preoccupied with Juliet. Besides, what's wrong with dancing with a different partner?" Adelina asked, shocked that Brandon was so angry with her. *I've been dancing with different men all night. Why does he suddenly care now?* "Don't worry, Brandon, I've never seen him before. And I doubt I ever will again."

"Damn it, Adelina, I love you," Brandon said. "It hurts to see you dance with someone else."

"And I love you, too. You don't think it hurt me to watch you dance with Juliet?" Adelina asked sarcastically. "Let me guess, you expected me to just sit and watch with a pretty little smile on my face, didn't you?" She could feel the tears approaching and turned to walk away before Brandon could stop her.

For the rest of the night, Adelina avoided Brandon. She had said the words. She had told him "I love you." Adelina felt dumbfounded at her own words. *Perhaps I fell in love after all*, she thought. *But who was Henry?*

Arrangements have already been made for their future. Wexford moved from his large mansion to a townhouse in the middle of London, leaving the estate to his son. For the time being, the Ellingsworths were to stay at Wexford Manor to help with the move and prepare for the wedding. Wexford had told Brandon that it was time to move to a smaller, more convenient home, where he was closer to the office anyway. "And, besides," he had said with a smile, "a large home would be needed for all the little ones that are soon to come."

The wedding gown was finished and hanging in her bedchamber at the Wexford Manor. Numerous flower bouquets where lined along the walls of the manor for the celebration, making everyone sneeze. Lord Ellingsworth and Wexford hired additional servants to aid in the preparations.

Each night, more and more guests arrived at the Wexford Manor, leading to dancing and drinking in the ballroom. Adelina patiently danced with the male family members and friends of the Wexford family as she met them. By the time she retired at midnight each night, Adelina was sore and exhausted. *What else is there to do?*

It was finally three nights before the wedding. Adelina again descended the stairs to join the excitement in the ballroom. She stepped around the drunken guests that littered the steps and the hallway. She passed by the dining room, where the guests could help themselves to the large buffet. Forcing herself to smile, Adelina followed the music and laughter to the adjoining ballroom.

"Sir, milord, please," cried a frightened voice. Adelina followed the whimper to the far corner. In the shadows Adelina was shocked to find a drunken man fondling Mary.

"You—hiccup—are mine. You see—hiccup—I am—" The man never got to introduce himself to Mary. Right before he passed out, he caught a glimpse of Adelina holding a large candlestick. Then he felt the warm, sticky feeling of blood trail down the back of his neck.

"Mary," Adelina whispered, holding her maid as she trembled. "Go up to my room and lock the door. Stay in my bed tonight. You can use the water warming by the fire to freshen up. There is water warming by the fire."

Mary nodded her thanks and fled upstairs.

Adelina turned to a passing servant and ordered him to have the unconscious man attended to and locked in the shed. Smoothing her dress, Adelina followed the sound of the latest waltz into the ballroom where couples twirled along the dance floor. She wore a red dress accented with lace along the cuffs, bringing stares that came from several of the men when she entered the ballroom. Immediately, she spotted Brandon across the room dancing with a young woman.

A distant cousin, Adelina remembered. She met so many people that she had forgotten most of the names and relationships.

Brandon looked up and smiled at Adelina. He led his partner to the sidelines and escorted Adelina onto the floor. "Three more days, my dear," Brandon whispered.

"Yes, I know." Adelina smiled. He spun her around and she laughed. At this moment, Adelina decided, she was truly happy and meant it when she had told Brandon she loved him.

When the waltz ended, the musicians immediately started playing a new tune. Adelina looked up at Brandon with a smile. "I think I am going to go sit this one out."

"Alright. We'll continue this later, my dear," Brandon said as he kissed her forehead.

While Brandon chose to dance with another cousin, Adelina went to get some fresh air out on the porch that overlooked the garden. She propped her elbows on the railing and arched her neck so that she could gaze at the stars.

A familiar voice sounded near her ear. "Another time, another balcony."

"Henry?" Adelina called out in amazement. She turned around as he stepped from the shadows. Once again, he was dressed in all black with his sleeves pushed up to his elbows.

"Miss Ellingsworth, you failed to tell me you were to marry William Wexford's son," he stated.

"Adelina, please. And, milord, you did not ask," she said with a bashful smile. *Not that I wanted to tell you in the first place.*

Henry chuckled. "All the more pleasure for me." He took one large step to cover the distance between them and grabbed the back of her neck, loosening the curls that Mary had spent so much time in arranging, and heavily kissed her.

She closed her eyes, giving into the way his tongue danced on hers. Adelina felt the stubble on his chin brush lightly against her cheek, sending waves of goose bumps along her skin on this warm night. It made her almost feel something deep inside of her, below her stomach. She could tell that there was more to this feeling—and she wanted it.

This is wrong! Adelina's mind screamed. Her eyes flew open and she tore her head away as she made severe contact to his cheek with her right hand. "Milord!" Adelina hissed. She had all intention to leave and find Brandon, to toss herself into his arms and beg him to escort Henry from the estate. But as she turned, Adelina felt a strong grip on her waist, preventing her escape. Adelina opened her mouth to let out a scream that would disrupt the festivities, but swallowed a gulp of air instead when Henry covered her mouth with his large hand.

25

"No, no. I've worked too hard and too long for this. You don't want to ruin my plans, do you?" Henry mocked in a light tone.

Adelina looked at him squarely in the eye and nodded.

"I'm going to move my hand now. If you scream, my dear, there will be an unwelcome surprise for your precious Brandon," Henry warned. Adelina made a move to run, but Henry strengthened his grip and lifted her onto his shoulder. He ran down the steps and followed the shadows through the back of the property to a waiting horse. Tears came to Adelina's eyes as she watched the soft glow of the ballroom fade, but quickly blinked them away before they stained her cheeks.

Chapter Two

About an hour later Adelina came out of her daze. The scenery of the rich fields flew by as they rode through the night. She found herself on the back of a large, black horse with Henry behind her. He had his arms wrapped around her, holding the reins and trapping her.

Henry sensed that she was awake. "Good evening, my dear."

Adelina turned slightly and looked up into those cool blue eyes. He smiled as his arms tightened around her. "Filthy swine."

Henry tossed his head up as he laughed. "Silly girl. You see, I'm sure by morning your betrothed will find the ransom note I had left in your room. By then you and I will be far away from here. Speaking of which…"

Henry turned his horse, kicking the beast into a faster gallop as he guided him to a tall hill that looked back over the land. Rapidly approaching was a large group of horse and riders. Slightly ahead of them was a single rider. Henry had no doubt that it was Brandon.

Adelina thought for a moment. *I'm being held for ransom? Why?* "I'm sorry. I forgot to mention that I had sent my maid up to my bedroom shortly before you so wonderfully kidnapped me."

Henry expelled a long stream of words and "wench" finished it. He kicked the horse into a breakneck speed and Adelina's laugh died in the wind.

They rode for hours. Henry made abrupt turns and crossed numerous streams and rivers. Twice he guided the horse into a shallow river and traveled downstream for a mile or two to hide his footprints. Eventually, he lost his followers, but still continued to ride further into the night, much farther than he had originally intended to. Adelina attempted to keep her bearings by using the stars, but quickly gave up.

Shortly before dawn, Henry stopped the horse by an old, dilapidated barn alongside a mass of rotten wood that had once been a house. He dismounted and turned around to help Adelina descend. Stubbornly, Adelina refused his help and attempted to dismount herself. Her ankle got tangled in the stirrup, causing her to lose her balance. Henry caught her in his arms and pulled her against him to keep them both from falling over.

"Don't touch me!" Adelina nearly screamed, pushing him away from her.

Henry shook his head and tethered the horse to a nearby tree. Over his shoulder, he caught a glimpse of Adelina shifting from what foot to the other, eyeing the ground for a place to sit. With a half smile on his face, he paused in his work and watched her. She grimaced as she put one leg forward and attempted to kneel, proving the movement to be too painful. Instead, she stood up again and tried to bend directly at the knees which, by the look on her face, proved to be just as painful. She rubbed the insides of her thighs for a moment and attempted to sit again, but her body refused her the relief. With a sigh she gave up and remained standing until Henry returned.

Henry saw her dilemma and almost felt guilty for dragging her out into the wilderness the way he had. She seemed so helpless to the situation. He watched as she tried to use her fingers to brush out the tangles in her hair, but to no avail. Her hair remained loose, and flew in every direction, despite all her attempts to fix it.

Henry couldn't help but notice how it framed her face perfectly. *She actually looks…pretty.*

Adelina stood there feeling awkward and stupid without a brush. She pulled out all the loose pins and simply tossed them to the ground. The lace from her dress was loose, nearly torn off completely. Adelina gripped it and tore it off in one smooth motion. With an aggravated sigh, she used it to tie her hair out of her face. She looked up to find Henry staring at her and dropped her hands to her sides immediately.

"We should get some sleep," Henry said. He lightly touched Adelina's elbow to lead her into the barn, but he felt her tense up. "Don't worry, it won't be together," he assured her.

Adelina cautiously followed her captor, never taking her eyes off him. Henry picked up a tattered blanket from the corner and threw it onto a pile of hay and pointed. With a lack of options, Adelina slowly sat down. Surprisingly, the slight give in the hay comforted her aches and pains. Henry disappeared for a moment and returned with a second blanket and a length of rope.

Hoping he'd leave her alone, Adelina closed her eyes and pretended to sleep. She listened as Henry moved about and then stop to kneel down by her feet. Moaning, she rolled onto her side, ignoring Henry. When he lifted her foot, her eyes flew open. Henry had used a rope to tie a knot around her ankle, securing her to a nearby pillar.

"What are you doing?" Adelina cried as she tried to scramble away. The knot held fast, preventing her from going any farther. She reached for the knot around her ankle and groaned when she discovered that it was too tight.

"We're not far from town. I don't want you to escape and run to your betrothed while I'm asleep," Henry replied. He threw the extra blanket on a bale of hay across the barn and lay down. In minutes, he was asleep.

Adelina attacked the knot again. It was far too tight to untie, and the more she struggled with it, the tighter it became. She attempted to slip it over her foot, but to no avail. Reluctantly, she gave up.

It took a long time before Adelina could fall asleep. At first she just stared at Henry and wondered what he wanted with her. *Why me? Why am I being ransomed?* she thought. She laid back and allowed her mind to drift back to Brandon. *What was he going to do? How can I get back to him? The wedding!* She opened her eyes and rolled onto her side so she could glare at Henry. *Who does he think he is anyway?*

Adelina didn't think she could ever sleep, but she could feel the overwhelming exhaustion consume her. She slept well into the afternoon. When she finally awoke, Henry was nowhere in sight. She looked down to find that the rope had been removed and that her ankle was free. She rubbed the welt that was left behind before she stood up. Carefully, she walked to the opened door.

Henry sat outside, cooking something over a small fire. Adelina breathed a sigh of relief, seeing that his back was turned to her. She closed the door, carefully laying the hook in its latch so it wouldn't make a sound.

This is my chance! Adelina thought as her eyes scanned the inside of the building. *I can escape.*

From outside, the aroma of food filled her and her stomach growled. Adelina thought of her last meal, a bowl of potato soup for dinner the day before. *I do need something to eat*, Adelina thought. *Maybe I can find a way to escape when we come to town or something instead of in the middle of the woods.*

"Hello, my dear. Hungry?" Henry as he offered her a piece of meat on the edge of the knife.

Adelina eyed the knife.

Henry followed her gaze and lifted the meat from the blade and handed to her. "Sorry. I never leave home without it. Used to be my father's."

"Is there a stream or something where I can freshen up a bit?" Adelina asked in between bites. She was dying to get the smell of the horse ride and the grime of the barn off her.

"Yes. Beyond those bushes," Henry answered, lifting his chin in the direction of a group of bushes. Adelina thanked him and moved toward the bushes. Henry got up to follow her.

"Pardon me, but I prefer bathing alone," Adelina said when she got to the water's edge.

"Really?" Henry mocked. "Me too. Guess we'll have to bathe alone together, since there is only one stream."

Adelina turned a shade of red and gave her captor a glare. "Funny," she said as she picked up her dress and began to wade in the water, fully clothed. The water was cold, but it felt refreshing. Giving into temptation, she leaned over and splashed some water on her face with her free hand.

Adelina was just beginning to feel relaxed and clean again when she heard splashing behind her. She knew it was Henry coming to wade in the water next to her.

And she was right—yes, she was right.

Henry walked past her and gave her a grand smile. He was surprised to see her return his smile. He walked a little farther out into the stream so that the water was just past his knees. That's when Adelina noticed—Henry was completely naked! And yet she couldn't tear her eyes away from him. His muscular shoulders and back glistened like bronze in the afternoon sun and his muscles were strong and noticeable. There was a long, jagged scar that was engraved from his right shoulder to the lower part of his back. He dipped his body into the water so his head was just above the surface. He spun around and stood up.

"I don't know about you, but I like to bathe naked," he said with a huge grin. "You get cleaner that way."

Adelina's eyes widened as her gaze dropped to Henry's fully erect member. She gasped. Nearly screaming, she spun around and ran back to the campfire with Henry's laughter following her.

Adelina thought about running away. Henry took a long time to bathe and she was left alone in front of the barn. *From where he is, he can't see me. He said that town wasn't too far off. But in which direction is it?*

Adelina walked to the edge of the woods and looked around. *Everything looks the same. It would be easy to get lost. But if I can find a road or a path—but then there are thieves and bandits to worry about. Then I might never make it home. But what if I don't try?* She couldn't help but think if it was worth it or not. *It is.* Adelina took a breath and gathered up her skirts.

"Don't think about it," Henry commanded from behind. Adelina looked over her shoulder. He was fully dressed and was putting out the campfire. "Town isn't in that direction anyway."

Adelina made a silent curse for procrastinating. "I wasn't doing anything."

"Yeah, right," Henry said sarcastically as he walked to the massive horse to untie him.

"Come, Midnight," he coaxed the steed as he led him to Adelina. He climbed on the stallion and lifted Adelina off the ground, carefully sitting her in front of him. Then, with a brief kick, the beast flew into a brisk run as they entered the forest.

They rode for a few hours, that seemed much longer on the back of the horse. Shortly before sunset, they stopped by a small stream to stretch their legs and have a makeshift dinner of dried meat. But, before long, they were back on the horse to continue their journey until long after nightfall. After the moon rose high over the horizon, Henry slowed the horse and looked around.

"We're here," he said.

"Where?"

"Where we shall spend the night."

Adelina snorted. "You're jesting, right?"

"Nope," he said as he jumped off the horse. He turned and helped Adelina dismount. He led Midnight to a tree and tied him to a low hanging branch. With a snort, Henry removed the saddle blanket and spread it out on the grass. Groaning, he sat down. "We shall sleep here."

"Together?" Adelina asked.

"Since I expected to be much farther than where we are now, and I don't know the area, yes, I suggest we sleep together," Henry said sarcastically. "I will be the perfect gentleman. Promise."

Cautiously, Adelina sat down. Henry got up to retrieve the rope.

"Not a chance in hell, sir," Adelina said standing up.

"Adelina, do you really think you are in a position to challenge me? I'm not taking any chances," Henry said. Adelina took a step backward. Henry sighed. "I promise that I am an honorable gentleman and would never force a lady into something she didn't want to do."

Adelina's lips drew in a thin line. With a heavy sigh, she sat back down and allowed him to tie her to the tree. Henry laid down with his back to her and immediately fell asleep. Adelina leaned against the tree and reluctantly closed her eyes. *What else can I do?*

It was early morning and, once again, they were on the horse. But this time, Henry kept the pace at a brisk walk. There was little conversation, mostly about Midnight and the weather.

"Shortly after nightfall we'll be there," Henry estimated.

"Be where?"

"On the *North Star*."

Adelina glanced back. "What do you mean, the north star? Like the one in the sky?"

"Not at all," Henry said, looking down at her creamy face. His face beamed with pride as continued. "My ship."

Lord Ellingsworth sat beside his wife on the couch, while Wexford stood behind them, gulping down his glass of whiskey. Brandon was carving a hole in the floor with his pacing.

"We made a mistake—William and I," Lord Ellingsworth muttered, listening to Brandon's advice and keeping him out of it. "And now he has her and is holding her for ransom," Lord Ellingsworth said, finishing the story to his wife. He hung his head in shame now, for hearing the story told out loud. Cheating a pirate out of supplies and then having him arrested wasn't the brightest scheme to make money that he's ever come up with. "Elizabeth, love, he's a pirate. I'll not give in to a bloody pirate."

Elizabeth sat calmly by her husband throughout his whole story. She often wondered how her family was kept from the poor house when her husband's law office never seemed to accept new clients. She believed he owned some sort of trading investments. But now she knew—and in the worst way. She didn't make eye contact with any of the men throughout the tale, but simply stared at a random book on the shelf, thinking about her daughter and the danger she was in.

"Elizabeth—Bethy—please say something," Lord Ellingsworth pleaded. He reached for her hand, but she pulled it away.

Elizabeth stood up. "Jonathon, you damn well are going to give into that bloody pirate. He has my baby girl and I want her back. If she is harmed in any way, I will hold *you* responsible. And so help me God, I will kill you," she hissed. Fighting the oncoming tears, she left the room, slamming the door behind her.

Lord Ellingsworth sucked in his bottom lip as he went over his thoughts. *There is no way in hell I will give into a pirate. I haven't given into anyone when a plot went bad astray.* Lord Ellingsworth made a fist. *And I'm not about to start now.*

Adelina rode Midnight while Henry walked along his side. For the past few hours, there was minimal conversation, except for an occasional yawn, groan, or cough that would escape their lips. Adelina stayed mindful of the setting sun. She wanted to determine their direction in case she found means to escape. *We are heading in a southwest direction. Home must be northeast from here…somewhere.*

The group of trees ended abruptly and Adelina found herself on a white beach. They were in the middle of a giant cove with crystal blue water that stretched out to the horizon, with trees swaying in the gentle breeze along the edge of the sand. Several rowboats lingered in the shallow waves just off shore. In the distance was a large sailing ship with *North Star* inscribed on the back in big, black lettering.

The fully equipped schooner stood unpromising in the diminishing light. It had three tall masts reaching toward the sky. The white sails were raised, making the ship look almost like a skeleton. There were four squares outlined in the wood on the side of the ship where large cannon hid, ready to be revealed in battle. Moreover, there three smaller saker cannon peeked through the converted gun ports that were engraved in the railing of the deck. For good measure, when under attack, four swivel guns were strategically laid out on the quarterdeck for easy access. Looking at such weapons, Adelina knew that the same extent of armaments were on the other side of the ship, facing out to sea.

"Isn't she grand?" Henry asked. Adelina nodded, still in awe over the scenery.

"Cap'n? Hey, men, it's the cap'n!" someone shouted. A short distance off was a group of forty men lying on the beach. Several of them remained standing where they were, while others ran toward the horse.

"Hello, men. How are you, Patches?" Henry asked giving a pat on the back to a man with an eye patch made of a piece of rusty metal. Adelina noticed that the man's good eye was dark green, shining brightly as he looked around. He had two black teeth, very thin hair, and a crooked nose. He looked up at Adelina and gave her a bashful smile as he bowed. Adelina returned half a smile and felt herself shudder.

Never before had Adelina seen such creatures. Other than Patches, Henry introduced each of the men around him, beginning with his quartermaster, Billy. Billy, with a wide frame, stood a head and a half taller than Henry. On the horse, Adelina could almost look him in the eye. He was darkly tanned and quite handsome if he hadn't had that red scar etched in his cheek. Adelina cringed as he took her hand to kiss her fingertips. Behind him was John, who lacked front teeth, and had long hair; Ink, who had at least fifty tattoos on his chest and upper arms; Phil, with a handsome smile, and dozens of other men who had missing body parts, scars, tattoos, and a need for a good wash.

Henry turned to Adelina and lifted her off the saddle. He nodded to one of the younger boys standing off in the distance, and the lad approached to lead the horse into the forest. "Now, men," Henry began, "I would like you all to meet Miss Adelina Ellingsworth, daughter of Jonathon Ellingsworth and the betrothed to Brandon Wexford, son of William Wexford."

There was a brief moment of stunned silence as the men digested what they had just heard. A whisper began to travel throughout the crowd and cheering soon followed. Two of the men before her linked arms and began to dance around in a circle, laughing as they did so. Adelina looked up at Henry and noted the grin on his face.

Looking around, Adelina felt a sudden dread inside, as if everything inside of her died. She knew what these type of men wanted, and she knew there was nothing she could do to stop them. *But I will die trying,* she vowed.

As two of the men stepped forward to get a better look at her, Adelina couldn't help but step back into Henry. He saw her fear and uncertainty and placed a comforting arm around her waist. "Don't worry, my dear. They are all loyal and good men," Henry whispered near her ear.

Adelina was not convinced that what he said was true, yet she still found comfort in his arms. "They look so…different. What merchant do they work for?" Adelina whispered as Henry began to lead her to a rowboat.

"Me—I'm their captain."

Adelina nodded faintly. "I didn't realize you were a…businessman, milord. Or is it that you're military?"

Henry cocked his head and smiled. "A little bit of both, I guess."

"What do you mean? What is it that you do…exactly?" She already knew the answer, but prayed against it.

Henry took off his boots and threw them into a waiting coxswain. "Well, my dear," he started as he began to help Adelina into the boat, "we are entrepreneurs, creating our own business agenda."

"What!" Adelina exclaimed. She instantly froze, forgetting to grab the boat's rim for support. She fell away from Henry and landed on her posterior in the shallow water.

Henry smiled and several of the crewmen fought back their laughter by disguising it as coughing. "I said that we are pirates."

Adelina stood up in the water and looked at the men around her. They all refused to meet her eyes. "I know what you said," Adelina hissed through clenched teeth.

"Then why ask?" Henry smiled and patted the coxswain. "Come now, into the boat."

Adelina stood her ground. "No," she paused a moment to build up courage. "Not with you awful pirates. I'm going home," she said as she turned around and marched back toward the forest where they had just come. She heard his forced laughter and was suddenly unsure of what to do. So, she kept walking.

"Do you really think that you can get away from a band of pirates, missy?" Henry called after her. "We'll even give you a head start. We'll find you by morning," he said, expecting her to stop.

She didn't. She didn't even bother to slow down.

"Damn it, Adelina. I'm not in the mood for this," Henry mumbled, jogging after her. Without warning, he scooped her up in his arms and gently tossed her over his shoulder. Adelina repeatedly punched his back and pulled on his pants until they were obviously uncomfortable, but he refused to put her down. He placed her in the boat with a soft thud and straightened to fix his pants. But before she could move, Henry sat down next to her, firmly holding her down. Adelina grumbled and cursed as the men rowed back to the ship.

After struggling to get Adelina aboard the ship, he led her to the captain's quarters, with her fighting every step of the way. He paused outside a cabin door and gave the orders to raise the sails and set course.

Adelina sighed, knowing there was nothing left for her to do.

He opened the door and led her inside the room. Immediately to her left, almost within reaching distance, was a dining table with three chairs. A few feet behind it was a desk half hidden underneath a pile of papers and rolled maps. Against the wall was a bookcase, overly-crammed with books, folios and additional charts. To her right, she saw an old dresser with a full length mirror next to it. On the other side of the dresser, hidden in the corner, was a wooden tub.

Reluctantly, Adelina's eyes rested on the unmade bed that extended into the center of the room across from her, with four tall posts reaching almost to the ceiling. The sheets were a deep, royal blue with white pillows. A couple of discarded shirts were piled in the center, completing the man's domain. Adelina noticed that the size of the bed would easily accommodate two.

"I, uh, I can't, I mean…" Adelina stammered, taking a step into Henry.

What does she think this is…a bloody inn? "Seeing that you don't have much of a choice, my dear, you can and you will," Henry commanded as he put his hands on her shoulders.

Adelina immediately gasped at his touch and moved away from him. She wheeled around and faced him, eyes narrowed and jaw set. "No. You can't force me into anything. I will not permit it."

"You're on a pirate ship, milady. What do you think you're gonna do?" Henry asked, crossing his arms.

"I will not have…relations with you," Adelina hissed. Even as she said the words, she did not believe there was anything she could do to stop him.

"Have relations?" Henry repeated, mouth agape. *The wench thinks I am going to rape her.* "I assure you that there will be no relations to have."

Adelina cocked her eyebrow. "I have your word?" *Not that a word from a pirate means anything.*

"As a gentleman," Henry promised. "I will sleep on the hammock."

What else can I do? she thought. She watched as Henry straightened the room, removing discarded shirts from the floor and tossing them onto the bed. A knock came on the door several minutes later. A boy of about six-and-ten, with blonde hair and freckles entered.

"Adelina, this is Thomas. He'll be at your beck-and-call while you are here aboard this ship," Henry said.

"It's ready, Cap'n," Thomas said softly.

"Good then," Henry said. "Bring it all in."

It took five men to carry in pails of hot water, a trunk, and a plate of food. They sat the food on the table and the trunk at the foot of the bed while the other men poured the hot water into the tub. With an approving nod from Henry, the men left.

"This is for you," Henry mumbled as he tapped the trunk with his foot. "Something just to make you a 'lil more comfortable while we wait."

Adelina looked at him for a moment, uncertain of what was in the trunk. Cautiously, she moved to it and lifted the lid.

"Oh, my!" exclaimed Adelina as she pulled the contents from the trunk. Inside were two lavender scented soap bars wrapped in brown paper. Under the soaps were four gowns, the colors of deep blue, aqua blue, evergreen, and yellow. There were also two new slippers, a brush, a variety of ribbons, and a modest sleeping gown. "Thank you, milord."

"You're welcome," he said as his cheeks turned a slight shade of pink. *She keeps calling me milord or sir. You'd think in the intimate situation we're in, she'd use my given name.* "Please, just call me Henry."

Adelina didn't respond. *He has full control over me and expects me to call him by his first name.*

"Make sure you lock the door behind me," he said as he turned to leave. "My men may be good and loyal, but they are by no means beyond temptation."

She did as she was instructed and rapidly undressed. Quickly, she ate the fresh bread and the apple but left the salt pork to cool. Almost smiling, Adelina climbed into the steaming water and lathered her body and hair with the lavender suds. After drying herself with the towel and putting on the dark blue gown, she brushed her hair until it shone bright and soft. She glanced behind her at the bed and decided to correct it. She removed the shirts and pulled up the sheets, smoothing out the wrinkles as she did so. Then Adelina folded the shirts and laid them neatly in a pile on the bed. When she was satisfied, Adelina sat at the table to finish her meal.

After devouring the meat, Adelina slouched back in her chair and allowed a small burp to escape her lips.

"Adelina?" Henry called through the barred door. Adelina thought about leaving the door locked and remain in the safety of the room the entire length of the voyage, but she decided it was foolish. She got up, reluctantly, and turned the key in the lock.

Henry came in and with one glance, suddenly felt like jumping overboard. *The dark blue gown looks all too wonderful on her*, he thought. The neckline was as modest as it was seductive, hinting at the bosom beneath it. He enjoyed how the gown hugged her hips just so that it moved with her every step. He felt a sudden surge of heat flow through his manhood as he realized his body ached for the woman in front of him.

"Damn," Henry muttered.

"Did you say something?" Adelina asked. She smiled and it was apparent that she was in a much better mood.

"No," Henry lied. "Would you care to go for a walk, see the stars and taste the sea air?" Adelina gave a quick nod and placed a shaking hand through Henry's arm. Her light touch sent shivers through his body, exciting him. He fought the urge to pull her closer, to comfort her and let her know that he would protect her. But he knew he couldn't do that, it would make everything worse.

Once they stepped out on deck, Henry unconsciously placed an arm around Adelina. She moved into its warmth to escape the chilly night air.

"Sir?"

"Yes?" Henry looked up. *Will she ever call me Henry?*

Adelina bit her lip. "Why me? What did I do?"

Henry looked down, and for a split second felt guilty for his actions. Kidnapping Lord Ellingsworth's daughter was never part of the original plan. He had seen her at the Towson ball as nothing more than a beautiful woman and toyed with the idea of possessing her for one night. When he had learned of her name, he began to work out a plan where he could seek revenge on Lord Ellingsworth using his daughter. When he discovered who she was being wed to, it made the kidnapping more idealistic. He knew she was beautiful from the first moment he saw her on the balcony, but he never imagined that Adelina would float into his dreams at night and haunt his thoughts during the day. "It wasn't you," Henry said, honestly.

Adelina didn't respond.

"Your father, your betrothed, and his father stole from me and tried to have me killed. I don't take kindly to that and I plan to get my revenge," Henry said quickly in one breath.

Adelina took a step back. "No…no…that's too…simple."

Henry shrugged.

"You…kidnapped me because of Father? Brandon? And William?" Adelina asked, shaking her head. *Henry was telling her a lie, a complete, dirty, disgusting lie.*

"I have proof—records," Henry said. "In my logs."

Adelina shook her head. "No! I will not believe it! My father is a good man."

"Adelina…" Henry began coaxing.

Adelina didn't give him a chance to explain. She pushed past Henry, picking up her skirts as she ran to the safety of the captain's bedchamber.

Where is his proof then? Adelina locked the door and began searching the bookshelves. She pulled random books out and carelessly tossed them to the floor. She loved books and treasured them dearly, but she didn't care right now about any damage she might have caused. All she could find on the bookshelves were novels, folios, poems, picture books, maps, notebooks, and loose sheets of paper. *Nothing.*

Adelina went to the desk and found the ship's logs in the bottom drawer. She pulled them out, vaguely noticing Roark engraved on the cover. She flipped through the pages, not as if she could understand the markings inside anyway. She was able to follow the math and the different languages inside, but it was the symbols and the shorthand that stumped her.

She heard a key in the lock and turned to see Henry leaning against the door frame. He looked at the mess scattered around the bookshelves and took a sharp breath. He calmly placed his blue eyes on Adelina as he kicked the door closed and walked to the bed. His eyes never left her face as he sat down while she finished her search.

Adelina made contact with those piercing blue eyes, held out her hand and deliberately dropped the log she held so that the loose pages spilt out. She spun on her heels and returned to the desk. Adelina picked up another log, briefly looked through it and tossed it over her shoulder. She smiled when she heard another heavy intake of breath behind her.

Then Adelina picked up a third book. She flipped rapidly through the first few pages and was about to toss it to the other side of the room when her last name caught her attention. And there it was: J. Ellingsworth; W. Wexford; son?, B. Wexford. Random numbers and a list of supplies were alongside the names. Then she thought of the conversation she overheard some weeks ago and distantly remembered hearing the name Roark.

Adelina turned to face Henry. He saw the confusion and despair in her eyes and knew that she had learned the truth.

"I'm sorry," Henry offered, shocking himself when he realized that he actually meant it.

"Frankly, milord, I don't care," Adelina whispered. "Get out."

Henry shook his head. "I can't leave you here alone. Pirate ship, remember?" He stood up and walked to the dresser. He opened the top drawer and pulled out a hammock. He secured it in the corner above the tub and laid down in it, kicking off his boots. "Make sure you clean up this mess, my dear," he said as he turned on his side, facing away from her.

Adelina bit her lip as she gathered up the books to re-shelf them. She left the loose and torn pages in a neat pile on the corner of the desk. Turning her back to Henry, Adelina changed into her nightgown before crawling into bed. She pulled the covers up to her chin, tasting the blood as she bit harder on her lip to fight back tears.

Although dried eyed, tired, and with a knot in her neck, Adelina's mind was clear. *It makes sense now, why we still managed our lifestyle without Father accepting new clients*, Adelina decided. *I guess Brandon is the kind of person who would cheat a pirate since he tried to do what he did…before.*

"I just can't believe it," Adelina mumbled out loud. *Here I am…sharing a room, on a beautiful ship with Captain Henry Roark of the* North Star. *Of course, Captain Henry Roark is the head pirate of a bloody pirate ship and is currently taking me to the middle of nowhere,* she thought. *Funny how things turned out.*

"Just great," Adelina moaned, rolling onto her side to escape the morning sun, and her thoughts. Groaning, she sat up, realizing that she was alone.

Standing on her toes in an effort to protect her feet from the cold floorboards, Adelina hobbled to the trunk that contained her gowns. She removed her nightgown and dropped it into the chest. She picked up the evergreen gown and tiptoed to the mirror. She looked at the thin undergarments that she had worn since her kidnapping and saw for the first time how tattered they had become.

"One or two days without it wouldn't hurt. Just until it's mended," she mumbled as she stepped out of the material. She hummed softly as she pulled the green gown over her legs.

Henry said goodbye to Billy and softly eased the door open, begging it not to creak and wake up Adelina. He stopped short and moaned as he caught sight of Adelina pulling the dress over her thighs. He could feel his pants tighten when he caught glance of what was in the mirror in front of her. He could make out the dark curls surrounding her womanhood, the flatness of her stomach and her ample breasts. Thanking everything and anything that her attention was elsewhere, Henry painfully stepped out of the room and closed the door behind him. With a groan, he stomped off to find some cold water.

It was mid-afternoon before Henry was able to return to the room. When he finally came back, he found Adelina curled up on the bed with John Milton's *Paradise Lost*.

"Any good?" Henry asked as he sat down next to her.

Adelina marked the passage she was reading with a blue ribbon. "Yeah, it's alright. Very spiritual."

"I enjoy Shakespeare," Henry said with a smile. "I like *A Midsummer's Night Dream* the best."

Adelina shook her head. "He's just a passing trend. I prefer Geoffrey Chaucer."

Henry laughed. "What about Swift?"

"*Gulliver's Travels*? I like it very much," Adelina answered.

Henry nodded his approval. "He's interesting. Lots of symbolism."

Adelina rolled her eyes. *I can't believe I am having this conversation with a pirate.* She took a deep breath and sighed, looking carefully at Henry.

"What?" Henry asked.

"How do you know about literature?" Adelina asked. "I mean, you're a pirate."

"Season your admiration for a while with an attentive ear till I may deliver, upon the witness of these gentlemen, this marvel to you," Henry said with a smile, quoting from Hamlet. "My dear."

Adelina smiled, wondering how Henry come to be such a man. But she didn't want him to see her interest so she changed the subject. "What's happening? I mean, we're going somewhere, obviously, but where? And how will you know…when I can go home?"

Inside, Henry smiled. He was surprised that she actually came out and ask him. It was the last thing he had expected. "We are going to Barbuda—a small island I know of in the Caribbean. We should be there in about eight weeks or so, depending on the weather. As for your return home, I have informants and employees who will contact me when your father or betrothed reaches my demands. I have looked into his records and I estimate that it should take about a year," Henry answered, plainly. "Sooner, if he pulls off another one of those schemes of his."

For a moment, Adelina's eyes grew misty, but she blinked them away before Henry could see her tears. "Brandon will find me," she whispered.

Henry almost didn't hear her. "We have to wait and see, my dear," he said as his went to put a comforting arm around her. He thought he felt her lean toward him, but a knock sounded on the door and Adelina stiffened.

Henry stood up and glared at Thomas as he brought in lunch. Thomas felt his captain's silent curse and was eager to leave the room. Henry led Adelina to the table and sat down next to her, avoiding conversation.

"Would you care for a walk on deck?" Henry asked as Adelina polished off her plate. He stood up and walked to her side.

"Yes, please. That would be nice," she mumbled as she pushed her chair back. She accepted his arm as they left the cabin.

"Have you met Patches?" Henry asked as they passed a man tending the arm of a sailor right outside the cabin door. "He's our ship's surgeon."

He turned, looking at her through his green eye. "Even'n, mizez."

Adelina looked at him carefully, from his bare feet to his razor thin hair half hidden under a handkerchief. Her eyes paused at his eye patch, a rusty piece of discarded metal and she fought not to shudder. Uncertain of what to do, she forced herself to look at his good, green eye. "We've met. How…how did you lose your eye…if you don't mind me asking?"

Patches grinned. "Lost it two years m' go while fighting dem savages up near Bost'n."

Adelina nodded, faintly, unsure of what to say.

Henry saw her wring her hands as the silence grew between them. He said his farewell to Patches and led her to the bow of the ship to meet Savon, one of the ship's carpenter's apprentices. She watched him use a marlinspike to loosen a knot secured around a piece of wood.

Billy approached from behind. "Cap'n, I need to go over a chart with you for a moment."

"Be right there," Henry said. He turned and lightly stroked Adelina's elbow. "But a moment, my dear."

He dropped her arm suddenly and took long strides across the ship's length, leaving Adelina alone with Savon. She touched her arm where Henry had left goose bumps. She looked back at Savon. "So, uh…you work with wood, huh?"

Savon dropped the instrument he was working on and stood up. He was a few inches taller than her, but his shoulders were broad and muscular. "Yup, wood."

Adelina nodded and shifted her gaze, feeling uncomfortable as he took a step closer. She gave a small, uncomfortable laugh. "Guess they need you to keep the boat afloat."

"Yup, wood," he repeated.

Adelina took a step back. He followed her. His greasy hands reached up and braced themselves squarely on her shoulders. She brought her hands up in front of her as an effort to protect herself. "Savon…"

"Yup, wood," he said a third time. He pushed her two steps back so that her back was forced against the railing. She could feel his retched, hot breath on her as he leaned forward to kiss her. She turned her head to the side as she tried to use her palms to push him back.

His filthy hands lifted from her shoulders, only to cup her full breasts. He squeezed the tender mounds and Adelina whimpered in agony. Using the full weight of his body, he pressed her harder against the railing, preventing her escape. He removed his hand and began to lift the hem of her gown, pressing against her with his bulging manhood in a steady rhythm as the dress rose to expose her legs.

Adelina gulped a mouthful of air and screamed with all the airs in her lungs. She moved to the side, barely avoiding his fervent mouth as it attempted to take hers. She tried to use her elbows to push him away, but he only pressed harder against her. Inflamed with lust and anger, he pushed her to the deck.

In a desperate attempt, Adelina crawled on her knees as she struggled to get away. Savon overtook her with his large frame, flattening her stomach to the deck. He used his knees to hold her down while one hand undid the front of his pants and began to search under her dress.

She could feel his dirty hands on her thighs and calves and fought to keep her senses. Through blurred eyes, Adelina looked up, spying the marlinspike as it lay next to the project he was working on. She reached out and made a fist around it. Adelina shifted her weight suddenly, throwing Savon off balance. Before he could react, Adelina took the weapon and sank it deep into his thigh.

He wailed out in pain as he fell to the side. With a groan, he pulled out the marlinspike and began to stand up, ignoring the piercing pain in his leg.

Adelina got to her feet, frantically searching around for another weapon. Finding none, she opened her mouth to scream, only to find Henry standing over Savon with a cutlass to the carpenter's throat.

Henry had heard Adelina scream and turned in time to watch his crewman push up against Adelina. He dropped what he was doing and began to run to her side. But he had tripped over a mop bucket carelessly left out by the stairs. He cursed as he fell, never taking his eyes off the scene unfolding before him. He watched in horror as she fell and Savon mounted her from behind. He stood up; afraid he wouldn't be able to make it to her side in time to protect her from being penetrated. Then he saw Adelina lengthen her body to reach something and moments later his crewman lay on the side with a bloody metal rod sticking up from his leg. He knew he had to reach Adelina before Savon stood up.

"Don't move, scumbag," Henry hissed. He called to one of his other men and ordered chains to be brought. In moments, Savon was secured to the mizzenmast, howling in agony that the wench had wanted it.

Henry led Adelina back to his cabin and closed the door behind him. He watched as she moved about the room, unable to settle and calm herself. He stared at her as she went to sit on the bed, shake her head and stand up. She moved to the dining chair, but couldn't sit there either. She walked to the corner of the bed where it met the wall and pressed her back flat against it. He watched as she covered her eyes with her palms and slid her body down the wall until she could sit with her knees tucked under her chin, making herself as small as possible. In moments, her shoulders shook rapidly and violent sobs filled the room.

Feeling as though his heart was about to rip from his chest, Henry strode to her side and pulled her into his arms. He felt her resist for a moment, but her body went limp as she let her head fall against his chest.

He didn't say anything for a long time, allowing her to cry her tears freely. When her sobs turned into mere sniffles, he lifted her chin and looked into her misty brown eyes. He could see utter pain and hurt in them. "I'm sorry."

Adelina shook her head weakly. "It's not your fault."

"I shouldn't have left you alone," Henry said. "I should have known better."

"They're all pirates," Adelina mumbled as she returned her head to his chest. "All of them. Damn, bloody pirates."

Henry waited for a moment. *They're all pirates. They?* "Who are?"
She sighed, not answering his question.

Henry caressed her check, and when she didn't respond to that either, he arched his neck and looked down at her. She was asleep. With a sigh, he lifted her up and laid her down on the bed.

Looking down at her creamy face on his silk pillow, Henry suddenly felt as though there was something pulling at his heart. He wanted nothing more than to hold her, caress her, and tell her that he'd always be there to protect her. That masculine trait cursed him as he knelt down and stroked her eyebrow with his fingertip. He couldn't help but think that she needed him to protect her from those pirates she was talking about.

Pirates! That word reminded him of Savon, and his body immediately filled with rage. He marched from the room, fighting the urge to slam the door behind him. He walked up to Savon, sitting with his back against the mast with a smirk across his face as he looked down at his manhood, still exposed as it protruded from his body.

Adelina awoke to a piercing scream breaking the air. She sat up with a start and frantically searched the room for Henry. Finding him gone, she stood up and walked to the door. She pushed it open slightly and peered out.

There was no one on deck that she could see. She crept from the room and stopped at behind the mizzenmast. She spied Henry standing on the raised quarterdeck, overlooking the main deck's activities. He stood tall, eyes staring straight ahead. She followed his gaze to where a number of his men stood in a massive line, holding a thick rope among them. The rest of the men stood off to the side, cheering the other men on as they pulled the rope in a fast, continuous motion.

Curiosity held her firm as she watched the men heave the rope. Faster and faster they moved, like one united instrument. A wet thump sounded and the line immediately slackened as the men dropped the rope. Nearly half a dozen men gathered around the object, blocking it from Adelina's sight. She spotted Billy, standing tall above the rest. He looked up at Henry and shook his head. Several of the men that had gathered around began to walk away, no longer finding interest in the event. Adelina strained her eyes as she looked at what they had pulled up from the water.

A mangled, naked body lay on his side against the railing with the thick rope tied about his waist. Much of its skin was removed in large pieces, leaving blood to pour onto the deck from the exposed muscles. Bits of green and white objects were thrust into the body, carved into the bloody mess. She recognized the foreign objects as barnacles but couldn't figure out for the life of her what they were doing in that man's back.

"Remember for the future when you try to take something that is mine!" Henry warned from the quarterdeck.

The man standing next to the dead body nudged the corpse with his boot. The body rolled onto his back and the head reeled to face her, his eyes bulging and his tongue hanging limply from his mouth.

Savon! Adelina gasped. She looked up and made contact with Henry's cool blue eyes.

Keeping the scream in her throat, she wheeled on her heels and ran back into the cabin, locking the door behind her.

Henry sighed. *Women should never see the effects of keelhauling.* He gave orders to have the body thrown overboard before he chased after Adelina.

He wasn't shocked to find the door locked. Although he knew he could open it with the spare key he kept around his neck, he didn't. *She'll have to let me in when she's ready.* He walked away, giving her the time she needed.

The door was kept locked for two days, except for the brief moments to let Thomas enter with provisions, leaving Henry to sleep on Savon's hammock in the crew's quarters. He knew that his men were watching him, curious as to what was keeping him from the wench in the cabin. By the third evening, Henry grew tired of her shenanigans and having to come up with excuses to his men as to why he did not sleep in his own bed. He decided it was time to confront her.

He spied Thomas moving across the main deck with a tray of food set for Adelina. He followed the young lad and stood beside the doorway as the cabin boy knocked on the door.

"Food, miss," Thomas called through the door.

After a moment, the latch clicked and the door opened. "Thank—"

Henry stepped from his hiding place and wedged his boot through the door before Adelina could slam it shut. He turned and took the tray of food from Thomas. He pressed his back to the door and forced it open. "Thank you, Thomas," he said before he closed the door behind him.

"Get out," Adelina ordered.

With a smile, he sat the tray of food on the table. "Hungry?"

Adelina shook her head.

Henry proceeded to take the food from the tray and spread it out over the table. With a grin, he sat down so that he could face her. He picked up a fork and knife and began to cut into a piece of pork. "I can't let this go to waste."

Adelina swallowed. "It won't."

"Here's the deal. This is my room and my food. If I'm not in my room to eat my food, neither will you be," Henry said as he took a bite.

Adelina sat down across from him and took a muffin. Her hunger got the best of her. "Alright," she mumbled.

Henry didn't expect her to give in so easily. "Good."

"Why did you do it?" Adelina asked.

"Do what?" Henry knew what she was asking.

"The other day."

"He tried to take what wasn't his," Henry said with shrug.

"That didn't stop *you*," Adelina said, softly as she toyed with her fork.

Henry cocked his eyebrow. "What didn't stop me?"

Adelina set the fork on the table and looked up at Henry with her honey-brown orbs. "Taking something that wasn't yours to take."

Henry grinned, understanding what she was insinuating. "It's all perspective, my dear."

"I was never yours to take," Adelina said as her eyes narrowed into thin slits.

"Again, perspective." Henry smiled. He sighed before Adelina could open her mouth to retort. *We're just going to keep going in circles until she wins...until I let her win.* "I also don't tolerate abuse to women. My men know that."

Adelina blushed from her collarbone up. She looked down at her plate and bit her bottom lip.

"I admire how you fought back," Henry paused. "Not many women do."

She didn't look up at him, afraid that he might see the tears that were beginning to well up in her eyes. "Thank you."

Henry almost didn't hear her. *Why do I have the feeling that she fought back before?* He couldn't bear to look at her heartrending face any longer. He stood up. "I have to talk with Billy for a few minutes. I'll return shortly."

He came back almost two hours later. He found the door locked again and sighed. Shaking his head, he removed the key from around his neck and slipped it into the lock. He opened the door and stepped inside, carefully closing it and locking it behind him.

From the corner of the room he heard Adelina gasp. He turned and saw her frantically pulling her chemise over her silky thighs and rounded bottom. He saw the curls that concealed her womanhood for a brief moment before it, too, was covered. He watched as the fabric moved over her slender waist and rounded breasts, noting the tightened nipples before the chemise was secured over her shoulders.

"Couldn't you knock?" Adelina hissed.

Henry smiled. "I never will again, that's for sure."

Adelina blushed. "Sir, milord, I was indecent."

Henry's grin grew. "That I know."

"Milord, please, I—" Adelina started.

"Am betrothed, I know. Brandon is a very lucky man to being seeing that every night," Henry said, almost disappointed.

Adelina's jaw dropped and her eyes grew wide. She reached for the nearest object—a pillow—and threw it at Henry as hard as she could. The pillow fell to his feet with a soft thud. "Never."

Henry laughed, finding it hard to believe her. *Come on, wench. I met Brandon.* "It's hard to believe that Brandon's never laid a hand on you. Please you in any way."

Adelina reached for a second pillow. She tossed it about the room, landing a foot away from Henry. "Never."

She's actually defending herself. "I guess any woman would be ashamed to admit—"

"I have nothing to admit!" Adelina hissed, brown eyes shooting sparks at Henry. "I have never *ever* had any kind of relations—especially with Brandon."

"Your fiancé?" Henry said, cocking his head.

"I kicked him in his…when he tried," Adelina snapped. "And I will do it again!"

"I believe that." Henry smiled.

"Stop antagonizing me! I am of good reputation for marriage," Adelina said, searching the room for a harder object to throw.

Henry looked at her carefully. "Meaning you're a virgin."

Adelina swallowed. She nodded faintly. "I'd like to keep it, please."

A woman Brandon didn't try to bed. Well, I'll be damned. He thought of the marlinspike and her determination to fight back. "He tried...didn't he?"

A wet mist grew in Adelina's eyes, but she rapidly blinked them away before they spilled onto her cheeks. The memories were too fresh. Not trusting her voice not to break, she nodded.

Henry felt his heart breaking for the woman in front of him. What started as mere teasing turned out to be a revealing, exposing moment. He had learned who the other pirate was and he suddenly felt the compulsion to take her into his arms and hold her. He wanted to pull her against him, keep her warm and safe. Not let any one else touch her that might bring her harm.

He took a step forward, ready to open his arms and accept her. Henry watched as she took a step back. Feeling a hollow pit in his stomach, he turned and left the room to return to Savon's hammock beneath the deck for one more night.

Henry knew that he wouldn't get a wink of sleep tonight. His first mate had informed him during dinner that there was a storm brewing on the horizon. "Great," Henry grumbled as Billy took his leave. "And it was almost a perfect voyage, too."

Henry sat in front of a map, analyzing possible solutions. *It was possible to sail south of the storm, but then the current would fight us all the way back onto course. Heading north would definitely add another month onto the trip and supplies were already beginning to run low. There was nothing left to do but hope against hope that the storm would simply bypass us.* "Straight it is, then."

After dinner, Henry led Adelina onto the deck for a brief walk. The sun was dipping low behind them and turned the sky a light shade of yellow. Even in the meager twilight, Adelina could not mistake the dark clouds up ahead.

"We're in for a good one, aren't we?" Adelina asked.

Henry shoved his hands in his pockets. "No doubt about it, Sweetheart."

Adelina made a face. "Don't call me that. I'm not your sweetheart."

Henry laughed and escorted her back to the room. He waited outside for a few minutes while Adelina changed, then climbed into the hammock and kicked off his boots. He lay on his side and watch as Adelina climbed into bed and pulled the blankets up around her.

Adelina knew sleep would be impossible. She loved being on ships, and usually the steady rocking of the waves relaxed her and often put her to sleep. But she's never been on a ship in the middle of the ocean with a storm approaching. Henry said she would be allowed on deck as long as she remained out of the crew's way as they prepared for the storm. But once the wind picked up, she would have to be locked in the bedroom.

It's my nerves, Adelina told herself. *The oncoming storm can set just about anyone on edge. It's just being in the middle of an open ocean and stuck in a room like a caged animal is not my idea of a pleasant cruise.*

But Adelina knew that she was lying to herself. She missed her family. She missed the comfort of home. *I miss Brandon*, Adelina thought, almost surprising herself. *Don't I?*

What if I never see him again? Adelina thought. She pictured him on a fast ship with his sword and pistol drawn, and ready to save her from this band of horrid pirates.

Pirates. That word was far overrated. She often heard stories of how these smelly, crude men terrorized towns, vandalized women, murdered little children and stole just about everything they could get their hands on. But the men under Henry's command seemed close to gentlemen. *At least, after the incident with Savon.*

She knew that the men were not used to having a woman on board. Ironically, it seemed as though it made the men feel uncomfortable. Henry made sure that they watched their language and actions when Adelina was present, for which she was thankful. *He had threatened keelhauling,* Adelina remembered. *Whatever that may be.* She attempted to make polite conversation with the crew members by asking about their families and homelands. After a fortnight, she no longer feared the men.

Adelina rolled over so that she could face Henry. He was lying on the hammock, looking at her. She couldn't be sure, but she felt that he was watching her. She squinted, wondering if she could make out those bright blue orbs, but a dark shadow loomed over Henry's face. Ignoring him, Adelina drifted off to sleep.

Adelina saw herself standing on the bow of the ship, watching the distant shore slowly draw closer. In her heart, she knew it was England. Heavy footsteps approached from behind and strong arms surrounded her. She knew who it was—her hero—the man who rescued her. She smiled as she turned into his chest. She breathed deeply, taking in the scent of man and seawater. She closed her eyes against the sun and turned her head upward. A kiss was gingerly placed on her nose.

"Oh, Henry," Adelina sighed.

Henry heard his name and sat up. He looked over at Adelina and saw that she was sleeping peacefully. Confused, he left the room.

Chapter Three

Adelina stretched, kicking off the heavy blanket. Taking advantage of the empty room, Adelina gave herself a quick sponge bath with the water that was provided for her. She dressed in the light blue gown, then brushed out the tangles in her hair. Breakfast was left on the table, but Adelina wasn't hungry. She unlocked the door and stepped out on deck.

It was growing dark outside, but the storm wasn't overhead just yet. She saw Henry helping Billy tie one of the ropes near the stern of the ship. He spied her immediately and stood up, glaring fiercely at her as she moved toward him. He didn't anticipate the storm to approach as fast as it was, causing the sun to disappear behind the dark clouds and the winds to pick up speed.

And here is Adelina, fighting a lost battle against the wind to keep her modesty, Henry thought. She was holding her dress against her to keep it from thrashing around her. Her hair was flying behind her and was constantly whipping Thomas in the face as he tried to secure a rope behind her. Watching Adelina try to overcome the wind and Thomas' distress made Henry forget about how angry he was at her and laugh.

"You need to be inside, young lady. The storm is almost here," Henry commanded, doing his best to sound angry.

"Is there anything I can help with?" Adelina asked, pushing her hair behind her ears. Again.

Is she serious? Henry thought. *Oh my goodness, she is.* He braced his hands on her shoulders and turned Adelina around, leading her back to the cabin. He stopped and leaned against the open doorframe to the room. "It's gunwales under, love. You need to stay in here. Take a nap or something. But you *cannot* leave this room."

Adelina continued a few more steps into the room. She spun around and stamped her tiny foot. "I'll not be trapped in here like some wild animal."

Henry tossed his head back and laughed. His action only seemed to frustrate Adelina even more because she immediately crossed her arms and tapped her foot impatiently. He stopped laughing and looked at her. Her cheeks were red from the wind, her dress had slid off her shoulders slightly, and her hair tumbled down her back in wild waves. *She looks quite astonishing when she is angry.*

"Not an animal, my dear. More like…a captive waiting for ransom."

Adelina's eyes grew large and wide. Henry smiled, and to her surprise, he took the two steps between them and took her mouth against his own. Before she could respond, the door closed and Henry was gone.

Hours later, Adelina discovered that she was thankful that Henry had locked her safely in the room. Had she helped the men, she would have tossed herself overboard long ago.

The storm hit the ship with force and fury. Thomas, wet to the bone, entered for a few minutes with a bucket of water, an empty bucket, and a rag. At first, Adelina was curious as to why he had brought her such items, but before long she figured out their purposes. Within an hour, Adelina was curled onto her side with the cool, wet rag on her forehead and the once-empty bucket beside the bed.

There was nothing to do. Adelina tried to sleep, but the unsteady tossing and turning of the ship prevented her from doing so. She tried to distract herself by reading, but it gave her a headache. The only thing left to do was watch the ceiling above her and listen to the faint yelling of the men in the wind. *He kissed me. Henry kissed me*, Adelina thought as she rubbed her bottom lip, growing excited as her heart sped up. *Why did he do it? What does that mean?*

"Stop," Adelina told herself. "You can't think about that. You're betrothed, remember?" She turned her mind to the future. *What is Barbuda like? What will happen to me? Will Brandon save me?* Adelina pictured chaos: dancing girls, pirates, and inebriated men. *I wonder if I shall ever see England again.*

Nearly ten hours after Henry had condemned Adelina to the room, he entered, soaking wet, shirtless, and with fresh wounds on his body. He closed the door behind him with great effort. Slowly, he walked to the bed and fell on it. Adelina threw off the covers and flung herself off the bed. She spun around, ready to protect herself with the soiled bucket.

Henry never moved. He stayed above the covers and proceeded to fall asleep in his wet clothes.

It took Adelina a moment to relax. She walked around the bed to search the drawers of the tall bureau in hopes of finding spare blankets and clothes. She found extra shirts in the second drawer, several pairs of trousers in the third, and a heavy blanket in the fifth. With a smile, Adelina threw the blanket over Henry and knelt to place his clothes on the floor. As she stood back up, Henry grabbed her arm.

"Waaarrmt," he moaned, weakly. He rolled toward the center of the bed, pulling her against him.

"Milord!" Adelina shrieked. But he was too strong, even in his weakened condition. He molded his wet body against her back and held her close. Immediately, her back was cold and wet, but she could feel his growing warmth. "Henry?"

"I need warmth," he muttered, hugging her closer at the sound of his name. "Body heat."

Adelina, too tired to continue resisting, knew that the battle was lost. She relaxed her body, knowing that Henry needed the heat of her body to battle off the cold. She tried to ignore the warmth of his body against her own. She tried to forget the pounding of his heart against her back and the comfort she found in his arms.

Adelina stayed awake for hours listening to the sound of Henry's breathing. She was just about to fall asleep, when a knock sounded on the door. Thomas cautiously opened the door and took a step inside.

"Captain?" he mumbled.

Henry sat up like a bolt of lightening. He stood up on the bed and jumped over Adelina, landing on the dry clothes. Not remembering when he retrieved them, he shrugged and quickly dressed. He pushed his arms through the sleeves as he followed Thomas out the door, shutting it behind him.

Adelina waited a minute before getting up and retrieving another shirt for Henry. She replaced the wet sheets with fresh, dry ones so that he could be more comfortable upon his return. When the task of remaking the bed was complete, Adelina changed into her damaged red gown.

If he is to ruin a gown, than I'd rather it be this one, Adelina thought as she tossed the wet gown into the heap of drenched sheets in the far corner next to the bathtub. Feeling exhausted, she crawled between the dry sheets, ready for a goodnight sleep. With a moan, she got up to retrieve the bucket.

The storm was finally giving up. It ranted and raged all afternoon, night, and the most of the following day. Henry had all the men work in three hour shifts around the clock so that they could rest and, hopefully, not fall ill. Other than the three-hour rest he had taken near midnight, he saw the storm through. Now that the rain was finally letting up, he could retire and sleep until morning.

Henry entered his bedchamber and was thankful that Adelina was asleep. *She's even beautiful when she's not even trying*, Henry thought as he began to remove his wet clothing. He noticed the wet mound in the far corner and added his clothes to the pile. He grabbed the dry clothes that were waiting for him and walked to the window. Naked and bathed in the moonlight, he studied the cuts and bruises along his torso and legs. He grabbed bandages from the bottom drawer of the desk and wrapped the serious injuries.

Adelina heard a faint curse and it brought her out of her dream. She opened her eyes to see Henry kneeling by the window, struggling to tie something around his arm. In the moonlight, she could see the water droplets on his back shine like diamonds, the scar across his back gleamed even brighter. She couldn't help but lower her eyes to Henry's bare bottom.

A scream caught in her throat. Adelina tried to get up, but couldn't bring her body to respond. She just held her breath and stared as Henry stood up and turned to face her. Adelina couldn't help but let her gaze fall to his manhood. She felt a knot twist below her stomach and a slight aching sensation between her legs. She closed her eyes and begged it to go away.

Henry used the shirt to dry himself. With a soft groan, he bent over to put on the loose pair of trousers. He slowly walked to the bed, unsure of what to do. He knelt in front of Adelina and began to trace her eyebrows with his fingertips. Over the past few weeks he had noticed a small change in this sleeping beauty. *She doesn't talk about Brandon as much as she used to. She's far more relaxed around me that she was when she first came on board.* Henry didn't want to admit it, but he enjoyed being with her.

Tonight, he was sore and tired—the hammock just would not do. He missed his big feather bed and the silky sheets. He needed to be comfortable for just this one night. That's all. *Tomorrow*, he vowed, *I will return to the hammock*.

"Adelina," Henry whispered, his voice caressing and gentle.

"Hmmm?"

"I need the bed tonight. I'm sore and tired and I promise nothing—"

"Alright."

Henry looked up with a start. Adelina fought over everything, especially when it came to privacy and decency. That's what he liked about her. He didn't expect her to give in so easily, if at all. "Are you sure?"

"Yes, I'm sure," Adelina said faintly.

"Thank you," Henry muttered.

Adelina slid over to give Henry more room. "You're welcome," she whispered.

Henry crawled between the sheets and lay on his side, facing her. He stared at her for a long time before he could fall asleep.

The following morning, Thomas knocked lightly on the door as he was ordered to. Henry opened his eyes and made an attempt to sit up, but was shocked to discover that he couldn't move. He looked down and found Adelina nestled into the crook of his arm, with her hand on his chest and her knee across his thigh. The hem of the gown was delightfully pulled up to her hips, exposing her tender thigh.

Henry moaned at the thought of having to move. He could feel his body reacting to her affection and it'd been a long time since he'd felt the pleasure of a woman. Slowly, Henry crept away from Adelina. He left the room, quietly, forgetting to put on a shirt.

Adelina slept later than usual. It was just before noon when she finally stirred. After her morning toiletries, she dressed in the dark blue gown that Henry had given her. She quickly brushed out the tangles in her hair and secured it with a ribbon that matched the color of her dress. With a satisfied smile, Adelina skipped out of the bedroom.

The air was heavy with a dense, gray fog that lingered from the storm. She searched for Henry, finding him talking to Billy at the bow of the ship. He had his normal black trousers and lacked a shirt. Adelina skipped up to Henry and waited while he finished his conversation.

Henry turned to her with a smile. "You're certainly in good spirits."

"Yes, sir. Watcha doing?" Adelina asked, clasping her hands behind her back and lightly swinging her hips from side to side. Billy nodded his greeting and left with a smile lingering on his face.

Henry threw his head back and laughed. "I was just going over the damage report. It's not as bad as it could have been, but we do have a lot of repairs to make when we reach Barbuda."

"Oh," Adelina said doing her best to look interested.

Henry put his arm around Adelina's waist and led her along the sides of the deck. "If you must know, the storm actually pushed us a little bit farther south. It knocked a good couple of days or so off our voyage."

Now that *is interesting.* "Good. So, how much longer until we reach the port? I don't know about you, but my legs really miss being stable," Adelina said.

"Well, about a fortnight, give or take a day," Henry said, cupping his chin.

Adelina stopped walking and leaned against the rail. She looked up into his blue eyes, reflecting the color of the ocean water. "Where did you learn so much about sailing?"

Henry smiled. "You have to if you want to be a pirate."

Adelina rolled her eyes. "Ha ha. That's not what I meant."

"But it's true," Henry grinned, his blue eyes sparkling.

"That it is." Adelina laughed. She eyed him, determined to play his game. "Then what made you want to become a pirate?"

Henry raised his eyebrow. "Why are you so interested?"

"Why not?" Adelina asked.

"I didn't have much of a choice in the matter," Henry paused. Adelina looked up at him with her big brown eyes, waiting for him to continue. "After my father died, I met Captain Maraca."

"*The* Captain Maraca? I've heard of him," Adelina said, remembering the rumors of the man who terrorized towns and ships. She wasn't sure if she was amazed or disgusted to be near a man that served under the dreaded pirate. "You sailed with Captain Maraca?"

Henry nodded, smiling. "Mind you that not everything you heard about the man was true. Most of it *he* made up himself so that other pirates would fear him."

"That's smart," Adelina said with a chuckle. *Nice to know that some pirates aren't so bad. Even this one.*

"It was. He was a good man," Henry beamed. "Taught me everything I know."

"Even literature?" Adelina asked, thinking about the numerous books in Henry's cabin. *He's actually opening up to me.*

Henry shook his head. "That was my father's doing. He wanted me to know everything there was to know."

"Was he a pirate?"

"No. But he was everything else," Henry said with a smile. "A trader, merchant, sailor, scholar, clerk…he couldn't get enough of learning and adventure."

Adelina nodded, desperately thinking of another question to ask.

"What about you?" Henry asked, diverting the attention away from himself.

"What about me?" Adelina smiled. "Seems to me that a good kidnapper would have done some research on his victim and know everything there is to know about his victim."

"I am a good kidnapper," Henry grinned as he pulled Adelina against him. He traced the back of his finger over her jaw line and watched her close her eyes, submitting herself to his touch. Fighting the urge to kiss her, he leaned closer to her ear. "I got exactly what I came for."

Adelina's eyes flew open and she tried to push herself away. "Oh—you!"

Henry laughed and wrapped his arms around Adelina, preventing her from escaping. With her trapped, he started tickling her sides.

"Stop!" Adelina tried to evade his grip, but she was laughing too hard, bringing tears to her eyes. "Henry!"

"I don't think so." Henry laughed.

Adelina was squirming to get out of his grasp, but couldn't. Still laughing, Henry picked her up and made a pretending offer to toss her over the side of the ship.

"No!" Adelina screamed, still choked back with laughter. She knew Henry wouldn't drop her, but she instantly locked her arms around his neck and struggled to hold on tighter.

Henry dangled her half over the edge for a moment, enjoying the way she hugged him close. After a few moments, he stepped back and dropped Adelina to her feet. He felt her press against him and bury her face in his chest, holding him firmly by his trousers.

"I'm sorry. I didn't mean to scare you," Henry whispered as he wrapped his arms around her.

Adelina pulled her head away from his chest and looked up into his blue eyes. "You didn't scare me. I'm just out of breath," she lied.

"I'm sorry." Henry caressed the few tears that had escaped from her honey-brown eyes.

"I'm quite alright," Adelina said, forcing herself to give a small smile. Above her, a bell clanged.

Henry looked up with a start and she felt him tense up as he looked out to sea.

"What is it?" Adelina asked. She attempted to turn around, but Henry pulled her into his chest.

"Nothing. Let's get you back," he mumbled as he began to lead her toward his cabin.

"Alright," Adelina mumbled, confusion filling her voice. She willingly walked next to him, but strained her neck to see what was behind her. Through the mist she could see the vague outline of a ship in the distance. She stopped in her tracks and unraveled herself from Henry's arms, running back to the railing from where she had just come.

"Adelina," Henry called as he chased after her. He reached her as she got to the railing and pulled on her elbow.

With a glimmer of hope, she struggled to get a better glimpse of the ship. The mist cleared for a moment and before her stood a tall barquentine, with colossal white sails. Adelina could see faintly along the port side where a half a dozen gunports were open with daunting cannons sticking out from them. Adelina gasped at the sight, wondering if it meant rescue or torment.

Feeling almost elated, Adelina's eyes traveled up the mainmast, where a skull portrayed on a deep, red flag fluttered in the wind.

"Pirates," Adelina mouthed.

At that moment, Billy had approached from the side. "Uh...Cap'n."

"I know, Billy," Henry grunted.

"What are we going to do?" Adelina murmured as she turned to face Henry.

"That's what I need to figure out," Henry said, trying not to sound irritated. "Please, it is time that you go back to the cabin."

"Sir, they're gaining. We don't have much time," Billy whispered near Henry's ear. "They're flying red."

Henry nodded. "I saw."

"It's a barquentine—easy target, if you want to take it," Billy whispered.

Henry glanced over his shoulder at Adelina, unsure of what action to take. "It'll be hard...they probably out man us."

Adelina heard his comment and her eyes widened. "What? You don't actually mean—"

"Pirate, remember?" Henry said to Adelina. He stepped aside with Billy so that Adelina was out of earshot. "I don't trust it. Why fly red on such a ship?"

Billy nodded. "Aye, aye, Cap'n."

Adelina watched as Billy walked away. "If this is a schooner, can't you just outrun them?"

"You don't want to fight?" Henry asked, sarcastically.

"Not particularly, no," Adelina said, flabbergasted at the notion of her with a sword. She watched with growing fear and curiosity as the men moved around her. She saw them bringing small cannon balls on deck and loading the small swivel guns that lined the railings of the ship. She watched as they loaded the larger cannons with gunpowder and lead balls. In moments, the sea air smelt heavy of the acidic gunpowder. She turned and looked back at the ship. "What are you carrying that they could possibly want?"

"There's only one treasure aboard this ship, milady," Henry said with a smile. "Now, if you don't mind, it's really about time that we get you back to my quarters."

Adelina nodded and allowed Henry to escort her back to his cabin. With the door securely locked behind her, Adelina raced to the window and stared through the fog at the ship that was rapidly closing the distance between them. Adelina gulped, fearing for the worst.

She felt the *North Star* jerk as they shifted course. In minutes, the ship behind them was getting steadily smaller. *Thank you, Henry.*

It took them nearly a day's sailing to lose the ship completely. Henry was forced to steer the *North Star* off course by several days in order to escape the certain bloody attack. He hated fleeing like a coward, but he knew it was for the best. Usually, when he was outgunned and out manned, he stayed to put up a fight, confident that his crew would be the better as they had so many times before.

I just can't take that chance with Adelina on board, Henry thought.

He returned to the room and found Adelina reading *Gulliver's Travels* on the bed. He sat at his desk to report the damages done by the storm and the sudden change in course, calculating the new estimated time of arrival on a large map. Thomas entered a few hours later with dinner. He placed the meal on the table and took his leave.

Henry pulled out Adelina's chair, letting her slide in the seat. Then he gave her a smile as he took his own.

"Are you married?" Adelina asked, surprising them both. She dropped her eyes and began twisting the napkin.

"No."

Adelina nodded.

"But I was once."

Adelina looked up.

"It was annulled. She thought I was a lord at the time of the wedding. I wasn't, and never told her I was," Henry said as he began to eat.

Adelina picked up her fork. "What happened?"

"Like I said, it was annulled," Henry said, growing irritated.

"Did you love her?" Adelina asked taking a bite. She swallowed, afraid of the answer.

"I thought I did. She was wonderful and pretty. Smart and sweet. But when I found out that she was after my title and money…" Henry began to trail off.

Adelina was going to ask more questions, but she couldn't bring herself to. Henry suddenly seemed sad and deep in reminiscence that she thought it was best to let the conversation drop.

After a while, Henry sighed. "After that, I became quartermaster under Captain Maraca. He taught me most of what I know. Only recently did I receive my title," Henry paused, "and start getting visits from Michelle again."

"Even after what she did?" Adelina asked.

"Yes. At first I thought she only wanted what she couldn't have before. But she seems so genuine this time that she could actually be serious," Henry said, distantly.

Henry and Adelina sat on the bed with a deck of cards between them. After losing his fifth straight time in a game of Whist, Henry tossed his latest unsuccessful hand at Adelina.

"Damn it! I hate this blasted game anyway," he exclaimed.

Adelina couldn't hold back her grin as she gathered the cards together. "You just hate losing."

Thomas entered the room with a huge toothy smile that made his head look three times smaller. "Land ahoy, sir!"

Henry jumped from the bed, nearly plowing into Thomas as he dashed from the room. Adelina stood up and by the time she took a step, Henry had returned to her side.

"C'mon, wench," he said as he scooped her up into her arms. He caught Adelina's glare and rolled his eyes. "Adelina," he corrected.

Adelina shielded her eyes from the bright Caribbean sun. Henry set her on her feet at the jib of the ship and smiled as the rest of the men gathered around them to see the breathtaking sight. Even in the distance, Adelina could see the crystal blue water splash up on the white sand that outlined the huge island. Tree-covered mountains and rolling hills grew in the sky. Farther off and to the distant right, Adelina could make out tall cliffs that cut into the splendor.

Henry stood behind Adelina and pointed to the cliffs. "See those?"

Adelina nodded.

"Those cliffs mark the passageway to Barbuda. I didn't think we'd make it there for another day, but it looks like we will be there by suppertime," Henry announced. The surrounding men heard his words and began cheering and laughing. Adelina found herself joining their excitement.

"Alright, men!" Henry shouted after a few minutes. "Let's go. Back to work. You too, Patches." As he grabbed the nearest rope, Henry looked back and saw the smile on Adelina's face as she gazed at the island. He couldn't help but smile himself.

It's still forever away, Adelina complained in her thoughts. She refused to leave the railing for any reason other than for lunch. By mid afternoon, the *North Star* ran parallel to the beach and Adelina watched the scenery glide past. There were so many exotic animals: furry creatures, lizards basking in the warm sun, and vibrant birds sitting in the tree tops. She'd never imagined such animals. Once the ship entered the cove that was hidden between the cliffs, she saw five dark-skinned boys with fishing baskets.

Adelina jumped up and down shouting and pointing at the children. "People! Henry, look…people!"

Henry laughed and strolled over to where she was standing. Smiling, he placed a hand on the small of her back and waved with his free hand. Before long, Henry's men returned to the bow and greeted the children. The boys returned the welcoming gesture and followed the ship, encouraging the men to go faster.

"Yup, we'll be there soon enough," Henry said.

Barbuda was bigger than what Adelina had thought it would be. There were five docks that held the variety of boats in the lagoon created by the passing river. Henry had his men anchor the ship in the shallow water and go to shore in the coxswain. After securing the boats to the dock, he paid the dock keeper and escorted Adelina into town. Billy and Thomas followed behind them with Adelina's trunk.

Looking around, Adelina noticed the numerous bars and taverns along the dirt road. A few shops, restaurants and inns separated the noisy drinking festivities. On one side of the street there was a house of ill repute that had several women sitting on the windowsill fixing their nails. Adelina was almost appalled by the provocative gowns that displayed the length of their slim legs and tanned bosoms.

"Heeeelllloooo, Henry!" one of the girls on the porch called out to him, moving her shoulders rapidly from side to side so that her breasts would bounce with her movement. Adelina looked at her, dumbstruck by the woman's bright red dress that barely reached her knees, covered by netted stockings. The neckline of the gown barely covered her nipples that were dangerously close to coming out if she kept shaking her body in that manner. Adelina noticed that the woman had enough makeup on to cover her age of at least two score. She brushed back her cherry red hair that was obviously made from artificial material.

Henry looked over and waved. "Hello, Annie."

"Who she?" Annie asked, spying Adelina at his side.

"My wife." Henry smiled. With that, Henry encircled Adelina with his strong arms and pulled her into him, molding her against his muscular body. He slipped one hand to the back of her neck and kissed her, with his hot mouth enveloping hers.

Adelina wanted to scream! She wanted to pull away and slap him. But she found that she couldn't. Not because she was trapped in his strong grip, but because she could feel her mouth open and accept his tongue like she had done for no one else.

He pulled back, releasing her.

"Well, let me know if she doesn't please you," Annie said, laughing. A man approached her and a few words passed between them before she led him inside.

Adelina looked up at Henry, questioning what had just passed between them.

Henry shook his head. "Don't think that."

"Think what?" Adelina asked. *As if I care.*

"That was Annie Debnam. She annoys me almost as much as her sister," Henry said with a roll of his eyes.

But Adelina could care less about Annie. Henry had kissed her—passionately. She just couldn't laugh it off as Henry had done. Adelina forced herself to shift her gaze to the other side of the street and forget about what happened.

"Different?" Henry asked as he put his arm around her. He wanted to feel her against him again, the way he had when he kissed her. He wanted to feel how her body fit perfectly against his.

Adelina looked around at the variety of people. The pirates from Henry's command fanned out to find their families waiting in the growing crowd. Some, with happy but sullen faces, made their way through the assembly to the empty taverns that lined the dirt road. Billy and Thomas remained with their captain. "Very."

"I have an estate that's a short distance from here. It's a little ways down the river," Henry said.

"Will we have to walk?" Adelina asked. As happy as she was to be off the ship, the idea of walking any great distance would be unbearable.

Henry smiled. "No, my dear. While we eat, I'll arrange for someone to fetch us a carriage."

Adelina felt the relief travel all the way down to her knees. "Oh, thank—"

"Henry Roark!" came a loud feminine voice from across the street. Adelina turned, expecting to see Annie. Instead, she found a woman of about her own age hike up her skirts and run toward them. She threw her arms around Henry's neck, pressing her body against him as she rotated her hips in a circle. "Oh, Henry. How I've missed you so!"

Adelina took a step back, watching as Henry wrapped his arms around her to return the greeting. Thomas stood next to Adelina and gave her a halfhearted smile and coughed.

"Hello, Michelle." Henry smiled, releasing her.

"Henry, you look absolutely wonderful," Michelle said. She reached for his hand and turned to face Adelina. Michelle wore a white cotton dress that ached to push her small bosom upward, making her look uncomfortable in the hot, Caribbean weather. Her blonde hair was pulled tightly to the crown of her head in a large knot, with several escaping curls left to dangle over her shoulders. Her pale face was round, with a large nose in the center. Between her dress, her hair and her fair skin, Adelina thought Michelle looked like a ghost with dark green eyes. No one could miss the questioning, almost accusing, look she gave Adelina.

"Thank you," Henry said. "Oh, this is Adelina Ellingsworth. Adelina, this is Michelle Debnam."

Adelina could not miss the glare that came from those green orbs. "It's good to meet you," Adelina said with a smile. Her smile dropped when Michelle didn't respond.

Henry caught Adelina biting her lip under the unwanted attention from Michelle. "Adelina? Shall we proceed? I don't know about you, but I'm starving," Henry said, presenting his arm to her.

Michelle refused to be ignored so easily. She stepped between Henry and Adelina and threaded her arm through his. Giving Adelina a smile, Michelle began to lead Henry away. "Me too."

Adelina nodded and fell in step a few feet behind them. Billy carried her belongings and left in a different direction to find them transportation. Adelina was thankful that Thomas had stayed by her side. Smiling, he offered her his arm.

"Why, Thomas, thank you," Adelina gushed, threading her arm through his.

Thomas blushed as Henry glanced backward. "You're welcome, milady," he mumbled.

The restaurant was small and charming, considering its location between two taverns on a small island consumed by pirates. They found an empty table located in the far corner and ordered their meals. Michelle sat immediately next to Henry, leaning on him to caress his thigh as he shared his adventures and travels. Thomas sat next to Adelina and whispered sly comments about Henry's story, sending Adelina into series after series of giggles.

Neither saw Henry's fixed stare coming to them while he continued his account. When the meal was over, Billy was waiting outside with the carriage.

Henry helped Adelina into the coach and turned to say goodbye to Michelle. "Goodnight, Michelle. I shall see you again. Soon, I hope."

Michelle beamed and looked directly at Adelina. "Perhaps I'll stop by in a day or two, after you settle in. Goodbye, my love," she said, giving a kiss on Henry's cheek. She spun around and left, swinging her hips profusely.

Oh, come on! No one walks like that. Adelina crossed her arms and looked at Henry for an explanation. He didn't offer one. Instead, he gave Adelina a quick smile and climbed into the coach, sitting on the seat across from her with his hands fastened in his lap. He looked at her through cool, blue eyes and smiled again. Thomas closed the door behind them and climbed onto the step behind the coach.

I don't know why he's staring at me like that, like he's waiting for a reaction. I don't care that he's courting Michelle. Why would I? I'm only here until my ransom is paid and not a moment more. Besides, I'm betrothed. Why would I care? Adelina thought with a sigh.

Adelina ignored his pressing stare and gazed out the window. The bars, taverns, shops and inns slowly gave way to small cottages and farms as they traveled along the road away from the town of Barbuda. As much as she tried not to, Adelina's mind kept drifting back to Michelle. *How could Michelle invite herself along like she did? And throughout dinner, she kept putting her hand on Henry's upper thigh like no one saw. She even leaned over a couple of times so that he could easily gaze down the front of her gown at* whatever *might be down there. And more than anything, it bothers me how it is Henry that I am thinking about—my captor!*

It was shortly before dusk when the carriage arrived at the Roark estate. The carriage pulled off the main road onto a pebbled drive, hidden behind a group of trees. The rough stones slowly gave way into cobblestone, making the journey to the house more comfortable.

Henry opened the door and helped Adelina step out. She looked up, eyeing the large, bronze statue behind her. It was of a Roman soldier with one hand reaching for the heavens and the other carrying a long sword. He stood in front of the house, in the center of the circled drive, as though he protected the property.

Adelina turned to face the house in front of her. It was yellow, with white trimming, standing two stories tall. It was a large home, with eight tall windows on either side of the porch that led up to the white door in the center. The four columns that supported the porch were white, standing tall in the evening light. Several vines blooming with flowers climbed up the side of the house and one column.

"Adelina?" Henry called. He was beside her, presenting his arm. "Are you back with us?"

She accepted his arm and smiled. "Of course, I am."

When Adelina climbed to the middle of the flight of steps, the wooden doors at the top opened. A heavyset woman appeared in the doorway wearing a soiled apron over her brown dress. Her hair was the color of pewter and pulled back into tight bun on the top of her head. Her wrinkled face was round, with a tiny nose, puckered lips and small mole near her right ear. She smiled. "Masta

Roark! Welcome home," she said with a faint Irish accent. She gave Henry a hug before stepping aside, eyeing Adelina as she moved past her. "Mizz."

Adelina felt the old woman's eyes travel over her. She lowered her eyes and gave a brief curtsy. "I'm Adelina Ellingsworth, madam."

The gray-haired woman relaxed a little, ushering her inside the building. "Me name es Catherine. I am the housekeeper. Come, Mizz Ellingsworth, I shall show ye yer room. Ye must be exhausted."

Adelina paused in the marble tile of the foyer and looked around. The foyer was oblong, with two rooms extending from it, presumably closets. A display of guns and various swords decorated the white walls of the room, easily striking fear into unwanted visitors. Beyond the foyer there was a grand staircase that led to the second floor. As Adelina stepped further inside, she could see entrances to several rooms.

"Have a good night," Henry said, exiting the foyer with Billy behind him.

Catherine led Adelina to the staircase with Thomas following behind them, struggling to carry the trunk. The housekeeper chatted about how the house was built, the Roark family, the different rooms, and other things that Adelina barely listened to.

"Here ye are, me dear. Masta Roark's room is next door to ye in case ye need him. There is also an adjoining bath," Catherine informed.

"Thank you," Adelina whispered. With a grunt, Thomas dropped the trunk at the foot of the bed and followed Catherine from the room. Adelina sat on the bed and looked around. The room was painted in burgundy, with gold trim. Across the room, matching gold curtains with burgundy tassels were drawn over the windows that stood tall next to a glass door that led to a balcony. In front of the door was a small breakfast table with two chairs on either side of it. A closet and a door that led to the bath chamber were on the right wall next to the bed. Extending from the wall was a large, featherbed covered in burgundy sheets and gold pillows. Directly across from the bed was a vanity table and full length mirror. Around the room, candles were lit, but it wasn't enough to add any significant amount of light, making the room look melancholy and cold.

For the first time since Henry placed her on his shoulder and carried her away, she felt totally alone.

Chapter Four

After a good night's sleep and a long hot bath, Adelina left her room. After several trial and errors in attempt to find the dining room, Adelina asked one of the young servant girls for directions. When asked about the layout of the house, the girl explained that the main floor had a parlor and a library to the left of the foyer when entering the building. Under and behind the grand staircase was the kitchen and dining room. Immediately to the right of the foyer was the morning room, followed by the small room which adjoined to the dining room. There were also two small, spare bedrooms for servants or unexpected guests. On the second landing was an office, a study and seven bedrooms, three of which had a bath chamber.

When Adelina made her way to the dining room, she found Thomas sitting in the nearest chair with a plate setting next to him.

"Cap'n Roark has already left, miss," Thomas said as he stood up to greet her. "But, um, I am here to keep you compn'y…if you want. I—I already ate. I was hungry. I'm sorry."

"That's alright, Thomas. I didn't expect to sleep in so late," Adelina lied. *I didn't expect the bath to feel so good.*

With a soft smile, she sat at the seat provided for her. While Adelina ate her eggs and cold meat, Thomas talked about his not-so-distant childhood. His father was murdered when he was a lad and his mother had abandoned him and his little sister a few years later. He worked odd jobs at different ports to support them for a few months, until a wealthy married count took a liking to his sister. When she refused him, he accused her of stealing and Thomas as her accomplice. Thomas ended up going to a different imprisonment than his sister. When he was set free, he heard that his sister had passed away from smallpox. He met Captain Roark outside a tavern and was offered the position of a cabin boy. It wasn't much, but at least he had a place to go to.

When Adelina finished her breakfast, Thomas offered to escort Adelina to the stables.

"You mean there are horses here?" Adelina asked with a wide grin.

"Cap'n has five. It's a great way to explore the land. You can ride the beach and 'long the river," Thomas answered, growing excited.

"Well then, I'm going upstairs to change," Adelina said, thankful for something to do. She left the room, fighting the urge to run upstairs. She found Catherine making her bed.

"Mornin', Mizz," Catherine said as she smoothed the folds in the sheet.

"Hello, Catherine," Adelina said as she moved to her trunk.

Catherine smiled. "The Masta said ye are welcome to use whatever is in the room. There are some nice gowns in the closet."

"Oh—I'll do that," Adelina said, closing the lid to the chest.

In the first chest, Adelina found a pale white gown with a hint of pink dye. It was slightly loose around her stomach, which felt oddly comfortable. It was a little tight around her bosom, pushing the top curves of her breasts almost to indecency. But with the matching shawl she found underneath it, no one would notice.

"I'm ready," she said minutes later when she greeted Thomas at the bottom of the staircase. The stables were a short distance behind the house and two horses were ready and saddled.

"Wow," Adelina said as she was a handed a magnificent gray mare. Thomas helped her mount the animal, then climbed upon a handsome black stallion.

"Your horse is Starfly. And this one here is Buttercup."

Adelina laughed. Thomas didn't. "Buttercup?"

Thomas nodded and led the beasts toward the beach. "Yes. Last year, Catherine's granddaughter came for a visit. She named everythin' she saw and we decided to go along with it."

Adelina nodded.

Thomas continued. "We also have a Rose and Pansy. And a male dog called Sunshine, whom we've nicknamed Sunny."

Adelina nodded again, not sure if she should believe him. Looking past Thomas, she saw a wide dock that extended into the water. The sandy beach narrowed to a broken path made up of grass and rocks. They followed the path for a while in silence.

"Do you want to ride until we find the *North Star*? It'll be here by mid afternoon and Catherine packed us a lunch," Thomas offered, breaking the silence.

Adelina agreed and kicked Starfly into an easy gallop.

"Can we take a short break?" Adelina asked a few hours later. *It is far too hot to be riding a horse.*

Thomas nodded. "Yeah, up ahead a lil' is a good resting spot."

They continued riding for another few hundred yards before dismounting in the shadow of a large tree overlooking the river. While Thomas tethered the horses, Adelina unpacked their lunch of fruits and bread.

"The *North Star* should pass by soon if everything went as planned," Thomas said, taking a bite of his lunch.

"Could we wait here a while?" Adelina asked, dreading the idea of getting back on the horse.

Thomas nodded.

"I think I'll go swimmin' a bit," Thomas said as he finished his meal. He took off his shirt and dove into the sparkling water. Adelina watched him for a few minutes before lying down on the cool grass.

She didn't feel tired. She just wanted an excuse to listen to the noise around her and get lost in her thoughts. It was almost soothing. She could hear at least three different birds calling and singing to each other. Above her, Adelina heard the slight afternoon breeze rustle the treetops. A few feet away, she could hear the bubbling and gurgling of the river as Thomas splashed around in it. The shade protected her like a cool blanket from the hot Caribbean sun. It was paradise!

Adelina must have fallen asleep because it seemed like only seconds had passed by before she felt Thomas nudging her awake.

"The ship is coming," Thomas said gently.

Adelina sat up and started to collect the remaining lunch while Thomas untethered the horses. As she went to mount Starfly, she heard water breaking and men calling to one another a short distance up the river. Adelina and Thomas rode toward the sound of the noise and it wasn't long before the *North Star* was in sight. After reaching the ship, they turned the horses around so that they were all traveling in the same direction, toward Roark Manor.

"How can you be sure it won't hit the bottom?" Adelina asked.

"The *North Star* has a shallower draft than most schooners of its size. The first cap'n had it specially built that way for more speed and easier access o'er reefs. It also allowed it to sail through narrow channels, where he had supposedly hid a lot of his treasure. That way, other pirates couldn't get to it in their ships. Anyway, Henry was determined to build a home that was reachable by ship and still a short distance from the sea. I guess he stumbled across here and tested it," Thomas explained. Then he gave Adelina an uncertain shrug, as though he didn't know all that he said.

Adelina watched as the men climbed on the rope ladders, adjusted the sails and scrubbed the decks and railings. Several of the men noticed her and waved, in which she quickly returned. Adelina searched among the familiar faces for Henry, finding him at the helm of the ship.

Adelina cupped her hands to her mouth and shouted with all the air in her lungs. "Henry!"

To her disappointment, he didn't respond. Several of the men around him turned and waved to her. *But he had to have heard me.*

Adelina turned dangerously in her saddle to try again. "Henry!"

Startled by Adelina's shift in weight, Starfly reared up with a loud snort and punched the air with her two front legs before taking off in a heated run. Adelina screamed and pulled on the reins as hard as she could to stop the charging animal, but to no avail. Adelina was forced to lean forward, hold on tight and hope to avoid any low hanging branches.

Adelina turned her head slightly and saw Thomas a short distance behind her. "Th-Tho-maas!" Adelina cried with the horse's motion. She held onto the reins as tight as she could, causing her knuckles to turn white. In moments, her carefully manicured nails sank into her palms, drawing tiny beads of blood.

Adelina gasped as a protruding branch sliced across her left shoulder, taking the sleeve of the gown and the shawl with it. Immediately afterward, she began to feel every branch and every twig scratch across her bare skin and pull at her hair.

"Ple-le-e-ase s-st-o-op," Adelina begged the animal. A thick branch landed across her brow, sending rivets of pain throughout her head. A tear escaped as she closed her eyes and hunched even closer to the beast. From the corner of her eyes, she saw the dock to her right and realized where she was. She pulled on the reins again, hoping that the mare might recognize where they were and stop. But the horse sped on. "Please," Adelina whimpered.

There were more trees with more branches on the other side of the dock. She could tell because they too whipped across her body, causing her to cry out in pain. She spied Thomas behind her, closing the distance between them.

Adelina turned her head and watched the scenery rapidly fly by. Something wet and cold touched her leg. She glanced down, finding the hem of her gown soaked in mud. She grimaced, thinking of the dark sludge that was being trampled upon.

The horse continued to run, never losing speed. She no longer felt the twigs and branches scrapping against her body. She ached all over like one large bruise. *We probably ran across the whole island by now*, Adelina thought. *Sure as hell feels like it.*

"Gotcha!" Thomas shouted as he grabbed the reins from Adelina. He tried to soothe the animal into slowing, but Starfly refused. She reared up again, and this time, Adelina fell off her back. Thomas released the reins to let Starfly continue her run.

"Oof," Adelina cried as her back and side hit the raunchy mud. Despite the smell, she was thankful that the mud softened her fall and the coolness of it dulled her aches for a moment.

Thomas jumped off Buttercup and ran to Adelina's side. He knelt in the mud and gently pulled her against him. "Are you alright, miss?"

Adelina looked at herself. Her arms and shoulders were covered in red welts, bruises, and blood drained from open cuts. She felt where the one branch had struck her above her eye, leaving a thick streak of mud. There was a definite bump, but no signs of blood. The gown was ruined, no doubt, with mud soaking into the tattered material. She could tell without looking that her hair had completely fallen out of its knot. "Yeah, I'm perfect."

Thomas smiled and helped her up. "Would you like to ride—"

"Hell no!" Adelina spat. Thomas gathered the reins in one hand and helped Adelina up with the other. Adelina was covered in mud, making her dress heavy. Twice, she lost her footing and fell backward, returning to the mud and bringing Thomas into the mess with her.

Adelina shivered in the growing chill, feeling herself growing weak as the sun sank deep under the horizon. Shortly into the darkness, Adelina heard a voice calling out her name.

"Adelina…Thomas!" someone called through the trees. Adelina recognized Henry's voice.

"Here, sir," Thomas hollered in return.

Moments later, Henry appeared on horseback. He jumped off in a large swing and took Adelina into his arms. "Oh, Adelina," he whispered, stroking her hair. "I am so sorry. Are you alright?"

"I'm alright," Adelina mumbled into his chest. She felt the tears well up in her eyes and bit her tongue until they disappeared. She let him hug her close, enjoying the comfort she felt in his arms, letting him support her. Adelina took a deep breath, taking in his smell of sweat and sea water. She felt Henry turn her back the way he had came and moved his arm so that Adelina could lean on him as she walked. Thomas climbed on Buttercup and took the reins of the other horse from Henry so that he could lead them back to the mansion, leaving Henry and Adelina alone.

"It's really not that far," Henry lied, trying to comfort Adelina. *Maybe I should have kept the horse.*

"How did you know where to find me?" Adelina asked.

Henry took a few steps. In truth, he heard her scream and saw the horse take off. To his men's surprise, he left the ship to Billy and jumped overboard. He swam the short distance to shore and took the numerous shortcuts through the forest to get to the mansion as fast as he could. He grabbed the first horse in the stable and didn't even bother to use a saddle. But he wouldn't tell her that. "When I got to the house, I got on the horse and followed your tracks."

Adelina walked for another hundred yards before her legs collapsed beneath her. She fell to the ground and slumped over, too weak to even sigh. "I can't," she murmured.

Henry knelt beside her and rubbed her back, not saying a word. He lifted her into his arms and carried her as though she was a feather. Adelina put her arm around his neck and rested her head on his shoulder.

"I think I fell asleep," Adelina mumbled sometime later.

Henry nodded. "You did."

Adelina lifted her head and saw the mansion growing slowly in the distance, with candlelight in her bedroom and in the kitchen, comforting her. "I can walk from here."

Reluctantly, Henry sat her down on her feet. "You sure?"

Adelina faintly nodded. "I am. Thank—"

"What do you think you are doing, you little wench?" shouted Michelle, who was rapidly approaching from the mansion. Her fists were in tight little balls at her side and her stride was long and determined.

Adelina stopped and weakly shook her head. "What?"

"That is my gown! And look at it—you ruined it! I can't believe…you stole it!" Michelle nearly screamed. "I want you out of this house to—"

"No," Henry cut in.

Michelle turned her anger toward him. "What did you say?"

"I said no. Adelina is my guest here," Henry said, taking a step between the two women.

"Guest?" Michelle repeated. "You let her wear my gown—without my permission—and ruin it and you call her a guest?"

Henry nodded. "Well, considering that I paid for the dress, it is at my discretion of who can and cannot use it. Come," he said to Adelina, "you must be exhausted."

Adelina nodded, as she smothered a yawn with the back of her hand. She reached for his elbow for support and caught the unmistakable glare from Michelle.

"I had the servants draw you a hot bath for your return," Henry said as they entered the building. "And I'll have dinner sent up to your room."

Adelina nodded her thanks. They walked in silence and whispered their goodnights before she slipped into her room.

Adelina couldn't rid herself of the mud-caked gown fast enough and not because of the condition it was in. With a sigh, she stepped into the steaming water. All her aches and pains diminished as she sank deeper into its comfort. The soap was by her side, but Adelina couldn't even bring herself to reach for it. She slid her body deeper into the water and leaned back so that she could wet her hair. Adelina sighed peacefully, feeling some of her energy return. She sat up and grabbed the soap to lather herself. She hummed while she did so and didn't hear the door creak open.

"Wench!" Michelle yelled as she marched to the tub.

Adelina looked up in surprise. "Wh—"

Michelle grabbed Adelina's hair and yanked her backward, nearly dragging Adelina over the ring of the tub. "How dare you be in my room—and in my tub! Catherine!"

The old woman appeared almost immediately. Michelle dropped her grip on Adelina's hair and marched to Catherine. "Who gave you the right to place her here?"

Catherine opened her mouth to speak, but Michelle silenced her. "Quiet, servant! This is *my* room. I want her out *now*. And don't you think I won't take this up with Henry and see that you get positioned somewhere else in Barbuda—if you're lucky enough to stay in Barbuda."

Adelina stood up and wrapped a towel around her. "Oh, cork it, Michelle. This is your room and I am sorry that I didn't realize it," she said as she stepped out of the water. Adelina approached Michelle. "But don't yell at Catherine."

Michelle turned her back on Catherine and faced Adelina. "You cannot order me around, stupid wench."

"No, but I can. And I agree," Henry said from the doorway. He leaned against the doorframe for another moment before stepping into the room. He lacked a shirt and his chest and trousers were wet as though he was called from a bath.

Michelle turned to him with her jaw agape. Never before had she felt so trapped. She swallowed and excused herself from the room.

Catherine smiled warmly to Adelina. "Thank ye. Mizz Debnam has always made me feel nervous," she said. With a smile to Henry, Catherine left the room.

Adelina stood in the wet towel in the middle of the room with Henry staring at her. "Milord, I believe that I am in need of a new room," Adelina mumbled, in an effort to draw his attention away from her body.

"Nay. This one will do," Henry said, taking a step closer.

Adelina shook her head and took a step back. "But this is Michelle's."

"She can be moved," Henry said as he took another step forward. "I'd rather it be back in her own manor."

Adelina stepped back again, unsure of how to distract the man before her. "If you two are to be wed, then—"

"We are not," Henry cut in, adding a step. "She wishes to, yes, but I think it is nonsense."

"Then why aren't you more firm with her?" Adelina asked, taking another step back. She could feel Henry's burning eyes all over her body. And she was sure that the wet towel attracted it.

"I thought I could trust her again. Maybe even grow to love her," he said as he took another step. "Only within the past few weeks I realized that I could not."

Adelina stepped back again. The rim of the tub hit her behind her knees and she fell into the tub, splashing water over the rim. She moaned as pain traveled through her back. Unbeknownst to her, the towel that kept her body concealed fell away and began to sink in the water.

But Henry knew it. God, did he know it. From where he was standing, he could see over her knees and directly to her creamy breasts and the pink nipples. As his eyes traveled downward he could make out her flat stomach in the water and he could barely see the tip of the dark curls that led to her womanhood. It was too much for him.

He took the step between them and picked Adelina up by her arms and stood her on her feet. She felt the cold air against her body, realizing that she lacked the towel. She turned a deep shade of red and reached to pick up the towel. Henry held her fast, preventing her from concealing herself. In a desperate attempt to cover herself, she used her hands, but Henry refused to free her arms.

Adelina looked up with pleading eyes only to discover cool blue orbs pounding into her own, boring into her for an eternity. She opened her mouth to demand him to let her go, but to her surprise Henry kissed her.

Adelina immediately stiffened under the hot kiss. Yet, it was so gentle and caressing that she felt herself soften and give into it. Her lips opened to him and his tongue danced wonderfully on hers, making her heart race. It teased her into joining his and, unconsciously, she moved her arms around his neck and allowed him to pull her against him.

The room was spinning around her—she could feel it. Henry's hands moved from her arms to the small of her back and stopped on her posterior. Then, he pulled her closer and molded her against him so that she could feel his heat, his muscles, and his pressing manhood. She felt strangely pleasured from the force against her abdomen and could feel warm moisture develop between her legs.

He freed her lips for a moment and gazed downward in a dreamlike trance to watch his hand as it covered her breast. His thumb toyed and played with the erect nipple for a moment before he leaned forward and attacked it with his mouth. His tongue pushed against her nipple while he suckled and tasted her. Adelina moaned and arched her back against him, giving him further access to her body. He moved to the other breast and continued pleasing her.

He made a trail of slow, tantalizing kisses from her breast to her earlobe. There, he suckled, drawing out more moans and gasps from Adelina. Finally, he returned to her mouth.

"Henry," Adelina whispered, barely audible.

Henry straightened as though he woke from a dream. He muttered a curse, and without a backward glance or an explanation, he left the room, slamming the door behind him.

Henry left the house, slamming every door he passed through. He knew that he was waking up the household, but at this point he really didn't care. He was livid, and any brave servant who ventured from their rooms saw it and hid.

Michelle is a spoiled brat and is used to throwing mean temper tantrums so that she'd get her way. Henry thought. *I don't want Adelina involved in something like that. And even so, I knew I should have left the room when I saw Adelina in that towel.*

Once outside, Henry headed straight for the river for a cool swim. *And more than anything, I knew I never should have touched her, and sure as hell I shouldn't have kissed her. What the hell did I do?* He needed to clear his thoughts. Badly. The closer he went to the water, the more he longed for Adelina. He needed that cold water—fast. He started removing his trousers long before he hit the sand.

He left his pants on the beach and quickly made his way into the water. It was freezing, but it cut clear to his core. But it felt good against his hot skin and raging thoughts. He gradually walked deeper into the water until it reached his upper thighs. It made him groan with agony, but the pain of sexual gratification immediately vanished.

"Do you mind if I join you?" a soft voice came from behind.

Henry ducked deeper into the water and cursed as the cold water enveloped his member. He turned around and saw Michelle stepping into the water. Henry cursed again when it dawned on him that she was nude and that the moonlight wonderfully accented her faint womanly curves.

"Now is not a good time, Michelle," Henry said. He carefully made his way deeper into the water, cursing every step he took.

Michelle ignored him and waded slowly after him. "It's boring to swim alone, my love. Besides, the water feels too good to get out," she whispered, her voice dripping with sweetness.

"Please, not now, Michelle," Henry repeated, feeling himself growing angry with her. He wasn't trying to hide the tone in his voice now.

But Michelle continued to ignore him. She maintained her steady pace as she walked toward him, slowly and seductively, knowing full well that she had exposed herself to him and it would weaken him. "Oh, Henry."

Henry stood up, thankful that he was deep enough so that the dark water would conceal his member. "Please."

Michelle was only inches away. The water remained just under her breasts and she knew it was seducing him. She wet her fingertips with her tongue and lightly touched her nipple, gasping at her own pleasure. It was her only hope to draw his attention from her eyes. *He knows that he can take me…I will let him and it would be our little secret. He could take me, right here in the water. All he has to do is lift me up and spread my legs around his strong hips. The water would make it easier for him to hold me as he slipped inside of me,* she thought. *Oh, take me, Henry.* She put her arms around his neck. "Do you want me, Henry?"

"Michelle…" Henry whispered.

Adelina stood where Henry left her for several minutes. She tried to ignore the fire that had ignited in her loins and the ache in her breasts. She had never felt such pain within her and curiosity got the best of her. She lightly touched herself, just above her dark curls and felt the fire erupt inside of her, gasping at her own pleasure.

Slowly, she donned the nightgown that had come from the ship and went to stand on the balcony. She heard doors slamming throughout the house before she spotted Henry storm across the yard. His stride was straight and determined, reflecting his anger.

Oh, why did you kiss me? Adelina thought. *You know I am to be married…if I get home. And why did you leave the way you did? You, sir, must be mad! But what did I do to anger you?*

With a sigh, Adelina moved back inside the room, closing the door behind her. She told herself to wait until morning to ask Henry what she had done wrong. In her heart, she knew she ought to wait, but her thoughts kept building. *What happened? Why did he leave without explaining? I just can't sit here and wait for him. I need to find him and ask him what had passed between us.* Adelina put on a shawl and left to find her captor.

Nearly running, Adelina followed the same path she saw Henry take from the balcony. As she moved toward the beach, she could make out the *North Star* in the distance. The pirate ship looked intimidating and menacing in the dark. Amazingly, it still struck fear in Adelina's heart.

She walked carefully in the shadows in hope that Henry wouldn't be able to spot her so that she could build up her courage. The moon slipped behind the few clouds that lingered in the sky, providing her with more protection. Adelina gulped when it dawned on her that she was barefoot in a thin nightgown in presence of a pirate ship. Feeling a cold sense of dread, she picked up her pace to find Henry.

Adelina reached the sand, still hidden in the shadows. The damp, cool sand felt good beneath her feet. She scanned the water but didn't see Henry. *Perhaps he went to the ship*, Adelina thought. She made her way to the dock, unsure of how she would obtain his attention.

"Huh?" Adelina stopped. She had stepped on something. Looking down, she saw that she was standing on a pair of trousers. She picked them up, curious as to how it got on the beach. Adelina cocked her head in confusion. Her eyes went wide when she remembered that Henry said how he preferred to bathe naked.

"I guess I'll just have to talk to him in the morning," Adelina mumbled, looking up. She spotted another article of clothing a few feet away. Adelina walked toward it and saw that it was gown.

"What?" Adelina mumbled in confusion. She looked out into the water as though it would provide her with an explanation. It was far too dark to make anything out in the black water. The moon heard her silent prayer and came out from behind the clouds to illuminate the earth with its soft glow.

Adelina spotted Henry and Michelle in the water, just a few feet from the dock. She couldn't help but stare at the sight before her. Henry was facing Michelle, gazing upon her body. She could see the curves of Michelle's creamy body against the dark water and immediately knew where Michelle's gown was.

Tears sprung up into Adelina's eyes, but she managed to blink them away. Just minutes ago Henry was with *her*, gazing at *her*, touching *her*, kissing *her*. Adelina ached, longing to feel his kisses again. But he is with Michelle now. *How could he do that?*

"Damn pig," Adelina muttered. With tears in her eyes, she ran back to the house, forgetting that she still held Henry's trousers. She remembered them when she got to the kitchen door and threw them off to the side. Adelina ran all the way back to her room, slammed and locked the door and dove onto the bed. She covered her head with the pillow and let the tears fall as hard as they could.

"Well, why the hell not?" Michelle asked. She felt his manhood against her stomach and began to slide ever so slightly from side to side, caressing his member. She was confident that he would change his mind when he realized what he was denying and take her.

Henry reached up to remove her arms and sidestepped her. "No," he said as he began walking back to shore.

"It's that awful wench, isn't it?" Michelle asked, crossing her arms. Her tone softened. "I can make you forget all about her tonight."

"Stop it, Michelle," Henry commanded when he stepped back on the beach. He looked around for his trousers, swearing that he left them where he was standing. With a shrug, he glanced over his shoulder at Michelle. "You are welcome to spend the night here, but I suggest you ask Catherine for another room."

"But—" Michelle started.

"Find another room," Henry instructed. He walked back to the house, leaving Michelle standing in the cold water.

Adelina awoke shortly after dawn and crawled slowly out of bed. After using the toiletries, she peered into the mirror and saw that the woman staring back at her had wild hair that would take much energy to brush out the knots. Her eyes were red and dry as sand and the beginning of bruise showed over her left brow. She used a cold, damp cloth to relieve them and climbed back into the warm covers.

Catherine briefly knocked on the door and entered the room. "Mizz, breakfast will be served soon."

Adelina threw the covers back over her head and crawled deeper into its protection. She was not in the mood to see Henry today. *Not after last night.* "No."

Catherine put her hands on her hips and walked to the bed. "Come on."

"Tell Henry I'm under the weather."

"No, ye're fine. Yer just being lazy."

Adelina peeked out. "Please?"

Catherine shook her head and went to the end of the bed. She grabbed the covers and pulled as hard as she could. Adelina lost her grip and gasped as she saw the old woman fly backward with the covers. Catherine released the covers and began to swing her arms in wide circles as she took a few steps backward to regain her balance. But her efforts were in vain. She fell to the ground with a loud plop.

Adelina shoved a corner of the pillow into her mouth to fight the oncoming laughter. Catherine stood up and untangled herself from the sheets without a word. She went to the trunk and pulled out the aqua blue gown and returned to the bed.

"I hope ye choke," Catherine said with a smile. Adelina pulled the pillow out to let out a long, hearty laugh.

While Catherine fixed the bed, Adelina dressed. With Catherine's help, she tied her hair back in a loose knot so that her curls fell down her back. She dabbed a little perfume on her neck and wrists and gave the housekeeper a weak smile. Reluctantly, she descended the stairs and entered the dining room.

Adelina walked in and immediately espied Michelle standing, staring out one of the large windows that lit the room. Henry was conversing with Billy and Thomas at the other end of the room. The door closed loudly behind Adelina, alerting everyone to her presence.

"Miss," Thomas greeted with a nod.

Adelina smiled and walked over to the three men and placed herself as far away from Henry as she could. She looked to Thomas and then up to Billy, still in awe over his height. "Good morning, boys."

Billy smiled and Thomas blushed. Henry glared at them and turned his attention to the floor before responding. "Good morning, Adelina"

Adelina kept her eyes leveled and her voice even. "Good morning, milord."

Henry cocked his eyebrow at the resentment that clearly filled her voice. *Are we back to that now?* "Shall we eat?"

Billy and Thomas walked past him and Henry moved to put his hand across Adelina's back to lead her to the table. For a fleeting moment, he thought he had felt her stiffen. Thomas reached the table first and claimed the second seat left from the head of table, respecting his position as a cabin boy while Billy, being the quartermaster, took the seat to Henry's right. Michelle hastened her pace so that she could have the seat on his left.

Henry noticed Michelle's intention. "Would you do me the honors of sharing the seat next to me, Adelina?" he asked just as Michelle touched the chair.

Adelina looked at Michelle, who stood there angry and dumbfounded. Her jaw was clenched and her lips were drawn into a long thin line. Her eyes narrowed and Adelina could not mistake the warning sparks directed to her.

"Are you sure? You preferred Michelle's company last night. Would you like to reconsider?" Adelina asked, trying to sound innocent. She looked up to see Henry's eyes turn an icy blue. Michelle gasped and either Billy or Thomas snort behind her. Henry didn't answer. "Well, then I accept," she said as she walked past Michelle and sat down between Thomas and Henry's empty seat.

Michelle slowly turned red and walked around the table to sit down next to Billy, who covered his mouth with his large hand. Thomas turned and gave Adelina a sympathetic smile.

Breakfast was slow and agonizing. Billy and Thomas lost what smiles they had and refused to look up from their food. Michelle remained the same shade of red and wouldn't make eye contact with Adelina or Henry. Henry stared directly ahead and ate without tasting his food. No one said a word throughout the meal as tension filled the air. Adelina realized that she had crossed the line and couldn't bring herself to eat. She moved the food around on her plate and wished that she could turn back the clock.

Why did I have to say that, anyway? Not like it really matters if he wants to have relations with Michelle. He can do whatever he wants. I'm just here until my ransom is paid, then I will never see him again, Adelina determined.

Henry broke the silence. "I would like to meet you in the library in a few minutes, Miss Ellingsworth," Henry growled without looking at her.

Adelina nodded and stood up, feeling her whole body tremble. She tried to catch Billy's eye, but he wouldn't look at her. Fear began to sink in as she turned away from Henry and made her way to the door. *Oh, why did I have to say that?*

As she opened the door, she heard Michelle push back her chair and stand up. "I guess I'll head home now," she said, dramatically. "I'm glad you're home, Henry."

Adelina ducked into the library before Michelle could catch up to her. She breathed a sigh of relief when she heard Michelle's footsteps pass by, then moaned inwardly when they approached again.

"I don't know what happened in there, wench, but I am sure that Henry will have your pretty little hide for it," Michelle hissed. "Trust me, peasant, you don't want to see him angry."

Adelina took in a slow deep breath. *What could I say? She's probably right*, she thought. Michelle saw the distress in Adelina's eyes and gave a satisfied smile. Without another word, Michelle left the room.

Adelina sat down on the feathery couch and tucked her knees under her chin. She stared at the heavy pendulum of the grandfather clock across the room. She began to rock from side to side in rhythm with the loud ticking in a feeble effort to keep her mind from wandering. Before long, she found herself counting the ticks. At exactly six hundred forty-seven ticks, she heard Henry's heavy footsteps approach the room.

Henry entered the library without a word. He pulled up a chair and placed it so that he was face to face with Adelina. He sat down and watched her turn her attention to the floor.

"Look at me," Henry commanded. Her attention still kept to the floor. He leaned forward so that his face was just inches from hers. "Look at me, Adelina."

Adelina looked up into his blue eyes, found them cold and icy. She could feel his angry emanating from him, filling the room. She licked her lips and took a deep breath as though she was preparing for battle.

More ticks from the clock sounded in the growing silence. His eyes burned heavily into hers without blinking. Determined, Adelina decided to play his game and stare back.

It wasn't long before Adelina found herself counting the ticks again. She reached three hundred twenty-two before her right leg fell asleep and began to tingle. She continued counting ticks, trying her hardest not to move, but it was too much. Soon, it felt like thousands of tiny needles shot painful sparks up and down her leg. Adelina stood up to relieve it.

"Sit down," Henry commanded without moving his glare.

"My leg is—" Adelina started.

"Sit down," Henry repeated. When she returned to her seat, Henry continued. "Don't embarrass me in front of my men like that again."

"I'm sorry, milord," Adelina whispered. "I didn't mean to."

Henry snorted. "Yes, you did," he said, standing up, nearly pushing over his chair. "What the hell would make you say something like that?"

Adelina stood up and moved across the room. She fingered the glass on the grandfather clock, carefully considering her answer. "You left awfully fast last night and I know you went to her. I thought I had done something wrong," she said, turning to face him. "I know I did—it was my fault—I'm betrothed—it's just that—"

"It's not your fault," Henry said, cutting her off. He took a step closer to her. He took a breath and kept his voice calm. "I got carried away and it won't happen again."

Adelina nodded, turning back to the clock. She heard Henry moving toward the door.

"And for what it's worth, I didn't go to Michelle," Henry said gently. His voice hardened again. "Just don't embarrass me again. Come to me first if something is bothering you."

Adelina heard Henry's footsteps leave the room and go across the foyer. *He lied. He totally lied to me. They were in the river together and he lied about it*, she thought. As though in a daze, Adelina slowly left the room and went through the kitchen to leave the house without anyone seeing her. She walked down to the river and carefully made her way into the jungle that bordered the sand. She wanted to be alone for a while.

The noon meal had long since been served and cleared by the time Adelina had returned to the manor. She went to the kitchen and helped herself to the various fruits and breads left out on the counter. She began eating a slice of bread when Henry walked in, banging the door open. Adelina looked up and saw raging anger in his icy eyes.

"Where were you?" he asked harshly.

Adelina shrugged. "I was taking a walk by the river," she answered, and took a bite of the thick slice she had cut herself.

"Please take me or one of my men with you next time. We're not the only pirates on this island, my dear," Henry said, trying not to sound as angry or worried as he felt. He was not ready to admit that he searched the house, stables, and the immediate surrounding land when she didn't show up for lunch. Nor was he going to admit that he was about to organize a massive manhunt in hopes of finding her. *She's too valuable to me.* He turned to leave.

"Milord—Henry—wait," Adelina called. Henry stopped and turned back to face her. *What to say? I want his affection again...or at least his kindness over his anger.* "Um, would you care for a walk after dinner?"

"I would like that very much." He smiled. He turned to leave with his blue eyes sparkling again.

Adelina leaned back against the table and smiled at herself. She forgot her hungry stomach and went up to her room to ready herself for dinner.

"Catherine!" Adelina almost screamed. She stood in the middle of her bedroom—what was her bedroom. It was now chaos. The bed was completely in shambles, with all the sheets pulled off in different directions, and the pillows torn and defeathered. Someone had taken a kitchen knife and carved long slits in the mattress so that feathers escaped in thin whispers. Each drawer from the dresser was pulled out and dumped carelessly on the floor, spilling their contents. The closet was open, and not a hanging garment was left in it. Gowns from the closet were hurled about the room. Many were torn and soiled from footprints. The porcelain trinkets and long candlesticks used to decorate the room were scattered about and broken, littering the floor with small pieces of glass.

Catherine stopped in the door frame. "Me word," she murmured.

"Who?" Adelina gasped as she picked up an empty pillowcase and turned to face the housekeeper.

Catherine slowly shook her head as she took a few, cautious steps into the room. She paused as she reached the bed and picked up a folded sheet of paper. "What? Mizz, I think this es for ye."

Adelina looked down and took the paper from the housekeeper. *Miss Ellingsworth* was printed neatly on the cover in fancy script without a wax seal to secure the fold. She opened it and carefully read it aloud. "Miss Ellingsworth," Adelina paused, "please feel free to help yourself to the rest of my wardrobe as you have done so already. Not to mention, you are welcome to my bath chamber and bed. Signed, Michelle Debnam."

"I shall go and get me masta," Catherine said.

"No," Adelina said as she crumbled the note. "It might make things worse. Besides, it's probably what she wants."

Catherine nodded and began to remake the bed while Adelina began picking things up from the floor. She tossed aside gowns and trinkets that were completely destroyed and ruined, wondering what she could do with them. Several gowns were placed in a corner so that Adelina could repair them, hoping that she could alter them so they looked different. It was shortly before suppertime when the room finally looked presentable.

"Thank you, Catherine," Adelina said. She grabbed the housekeeper's elbow as they left the room, laughing at Michelle's feeble attempt to hurt Adelina.

"Hello girls," Henry greeted as Adelina and Catherine entered the dining room.

"Even'n, Masta." Catherine curtsied. Henry nodded and she quickly slipped out of the room.

Adelina smiled. "Hello, mi—Henry."

Henry escorted her to a nearby chair and pulled it out for her. "I hope you didn't forget about our walk tonight."

Adelina shook her head. "Where are Thomas and Billy?"

"They are on ship duty tonight," Henry answered. He sat down and began to cut his food. "Did you hear about the ball that's coming up in next month? Mid May, I believe."

"A ball? No." Adelina said. She gave a half-hearted smile. "Oh, that's quite alright. There's really no need for me to go."

"Why not?" Henry asked as he straightened in his seat.

Adelina took a breath, unsure of what to say. "It's inappropriate. After all, I am your captive."

Henry shook his head. "Not good enough."

Adelina fought not to smile. "I don't have anything appropriate to wear."

Henry smiled. "We'll find you something."

"If you insist…" Adelina said with a soft smile.

"I do," Henry said, tossing his napkin onto the plate. He stood up. "Ready?"

"Sure," Adelina said. She smiled softly as they exited to the warm, dry air of the night.

"It should be fun. The ball, I mean. Dinner and dancing," Henry said as they reached the river.

"Who's hosting it?" Adelina asked.

"Mayor Ramsey and his family. He's sort of the authority figure around here." Henry bent down and picked up a handful of pebbles, three of which he tossed into the water. "Would you consider being my escort?"

Me? Adelina knew she shouldn't ask. Despite biting her tongue, it came out anyway. "Why not Michelle?"

Adelina heard Henry's quick intake of breath. *We just had this conversation.* "I'd much rather go with you, my dear," Henry said, forcing himself not to sound irritated.

Adelina nodded, swinging her arms and taking a childish skip. "Well then, I accept."

"Well then, good," Henry repeated, mimicking Adelina's tone. He laughed as he threw a small pebble at her and ran a few paces ahead.

Adelina shouted out in surprise. She began chasing after Henry, laughing as she dodged trees after him. All the while, Henry remained a few feet ahead of her tossing back rocks as he ran.

"Come on, Adelina. You can catch me," he shouted over his shoulder.

Adelina slowed down to pick up the hem of her skirt. She ran after Henry, following his dark figure and laughter. "Henry, wait! I can't breathe! Henry?"

There was no answer ahead of her. The man she was chasing had vanished. Adelina slowed down as found that she could no longer hear Henry running or his laughter.

"Henry?" Adelina repeated, a little louder. She stopped running and looked around. The night was dark and silent except for the soft buzz of insects and the distant gurgling of the river. She could feel her heart beating faster and faster as fear began to take over.

"Henry? Please, this isn't funny anymore," Adelina shouted. She carefully took a few steps forward, unsure of what to do. She took a few deep breaths, forcing herself to calm down and not let fear surpass rational thought.

Think Adelina, think, she told herself. *You've been in worse situations before. After all, you've been kidnapped by pirates and taken thousands of miles from home. You can handle getting lost in the woods.*

A twig snapped followed by a loud, snotty snort. Through the trees and in the dim moonlight, Adelina spied a dark silhouette of a man several yards ahead.

"Henry?" Adelina said, slightly above a whisper. The figure turned sharply in her direction. Although she couldn't see him clearly, she could feel his eyes on her and she suddenly felt cold. Deep inside of her, she felt the dread that told her that it wasn't Henry.

In that instant, Adelina could see that the man had a long face, scarred by the sun. His eyes were dark, bearing right through her. His nose was long and crooked, making him look surly. With a finger, he brushed his should length hair behind his ear and dragged his dirty knuckles across ragged beard. His clothes were tattered and dirty, indicating that he hasn't had a bath in several days, at least. He smiled, displaying a missing tooth with a gold one next to it. The way he smiled a half cocked grin sent shivers down Adelina's spine.

The man in front of her slowly reached to his side and pulled out something that gleamed brightly in the moonlight. The smile grew wider as he tilted the reflection away from her, showing that what he held was a knife. In a weak effort, Adelina dove behind a cluster of bushes.

Adelina gulped. Her heart was pounding so fast and so loudly that she thought it would either explode or lead the man right to her. Another twig snapped. Then another—this time, closer. Briefly, Adelina thought she could make it back to the house. But she had no idea how far it was nor if the man would catch up to her. She heard the snort again, telling her that the man was within feet of her now. Adelina's heart sped up further, sure to explode.

I'm not waiting around for it, Adelina thought. She took a deep breath and crawled as silently as she could in the black dirt until she reached the nearest tree. With a prayer in her heart, she peered around the other side of the tree and saw the dark figure of the man leaning against the same tree. He was inches away from her.

Chapter Five

From out of the corner of her eye Adelina saw a broken tree limb just out of her reach. She didn't think about possibilities or chances, she just lunged for it. Adelina scrambled back to her feet with the branch held over her shoulder, determined to put up a fight.

But before she could fully turn around, strong arms flew out of the dark and wrapped themselves around her torso. Adelina screamed with all the air in her lungs, startling the sleeping birds around her. Adelina turned, ready to strike her attacker.

She looked up to find Henry's smiling face. "I scared you."

Adelina grounded her teeth and spun around expecting to see the stranger smiling behind her. He wasn't.

He wasn't there at all.

"Are you alright?" Henry asked from behind.

Adelina ignored him and cautiously circled the tree. She spun around slowly, seeking desperately for the stranger. Nothing. The man was gone.

"Adelina?" Henry called after her.

Adelina waited a moment, unsure of what to say. "I thought I saw a man."

She heard Henry approach from behind. He lightly grazed her hand as he took a few steps past her. He reached into his pocket and pulled out the knife he always carried for protection. He slowly turned in a circle, concentrating heavily on the ground, pausing at every whisper of a noise. He stopped turning and faced the direction where Adelina had first seen the man. Henry cocked his head, as though he had heard something in that direction. Adelina couldn't hear anything except for the wind rustling the leaves.

Somebody was here. I can feel it. Henry returned to Adelina's side and put his hand against the small of her back. With a glance behind his shoulder, he whispered, "Let's go. Now."

Henry waited patiently outside Adelina's bedroom door for her to change into her nightclothes. She opened the door and stepped aside so he could enter.

"Thank you, milord," Adelina paused, "for keeping me company."

"Just until you fall asleep, my dear. Then I will go to my own bed," Henry said as he walked toward the balcony doors. He secured the locks and drew the curtain. Then he came to the bed, turning down the sheets and sat on a nearby chair.

"Thank you," Adelina said again as she climbed into the bed. She rolled onto her side, facing Henry. He turned the chair so that it was angled against the bed, better able him to prop up his feet.

Henry toyed with his knife, thinking about his men and how he had pulled them from their families to patrol the estate grounds. He knew he'd have to make it up to them, somehow. *Maybe I will buy them all a round or give them a longer rest or something.*

With a sigh, he looked up to see if Adelina had fallen asleep.

Adelina lay curled on her side with her knees tucked up to her chest in fetal position. One delicate hand was placed under the pillow while the other was sprawled across the top of the sheet. Her hair was tossed across the pillow in a large tumble of waves. He couldn't help but smile.

Henry turned in his seat to get a better view of the white face and pink lips, slightly open. Her mouth curved upward even so slightly as if she was smiling in her dreams. Henry found himself wanting to taste those sweet lips again.

He leaned forward and rested his head on his hands. He could feel his eyelids dropping. He tried to fight the oncoming sleep and make it to his own bed, but his body refused to move.

Adelina didn't expect to fall asleep so fast. She forgot all about the man in the forest with Henry so close. She yawned, stretched, and groaned before she reluctantly opened her eyes.

Henry still sat in the chair. He was slumped over in his sleep against the arm of the chair, with his hand dangling over the side. *He looks so peaceful*, she thought as she reached up and caressed his cheek.

Like a bolt of lightening, Henry jumped from the chair and reached for his knife.

"Who—" Henry started. He spun around quickly, ready to defend himself. He lowered the weapon when he discovered there was no one in the room that posed a threat. He faced Adelina who curled into a tight ball, with her knees tucked under her chin.

"I'm sorry, milord. I did not mean to frighten you," Adelina whispered.

Henry sat on the bed and massaged the back of his neck. He grunted when the knot twisted and pulled as he turned to face Adelina, reaching for the hand that rested on her knee.

"It's alright, my dear. I didn't mean to frighten you either." He smiled, heart still beating rapidly in his chest.

Adelina nodded and relaxed.

Henry patted her hand. "Well, it's morning. Why don't we have breakfast and go shopping for the ball?"

Adelina smiled. "If you're going to twist my arm about it."

Henry stood up and left the room so that Adelina could dress and ready herself. Catherine entered moments after Henry left and shut the door slowly behind her.

"Morn'n, Mizz," Catherine said as she pulled open the drapes to let in the sunlight. Adelina nodded as she stretched and yawned. "I already told the servants to bring up the hot water for ye bath. They should be here any—"

A knock sounded and Catherine opened the door. Four servants entered, carrying large buckets of hot, steaming water.

"Oh, good," Catherine said, ushering them in and quickly shooing them back out.

Adelina undressed and sank into the hot water. Catherine pulled out a banana colored gown, lightly trimmed with white lace.

"Thank you, Catherine," Adelina said as she reached for the lavender soap.

"Ye're welcome, Mizz," Catherine said, taking her leave.

Adelina lathered herself, first with her left leg, as she always done, and then her right. She went in little circles around her stomach and breasts before she rubbed the soap into her hair. She submerged herself under the water to remove all the soap and sat up, feeling thoroughly refreshed.

She lay in the cooling water until it began to wrinkle her skin. Adelina stood up and wrapped herself in a large towel. She dried herself, dressed, and brushed her hair.

Adelina opened the door to find Henry standing with an arm raised as though to knock.

"Are you ready, my dear?" Henry asked in surprise.

"Yes, milord." Adelina smiled as she sidestepped him to get by. Henry caught up with her and escorted her downstairs.

Catherine was waiting for them in the foyer. Her garment changed from the usual outfit of a high respected housekeeper to that of a middle class lady going out for a simple luncheon. The dress was the color of a dark, red wine that well accented the old woman's pear figure.

Henry turned to Adelina. "I hope you don't mind, but I asked Catherine to come with us. She has good taste for gowns."

Adelina shook her head. "No, milord, not at all."

Outside, Billy and Thomas were waiting by the carriage. A third man was with them. Adelina eyed him carefully as she stepped off the steps. The man was relatively short, maybe a few inches taller than her. He wore a dark blue suit that struggled to hold over his bulging figure. The dark blue color greatly contrasted the blonde hair that absolutely covered him everyone except his head, which reflected the sun.

"Morn'n, Cap'n, Miss," Billy greeted. Thomas smiled.

The bald man smiled beyond Adelina to Catherine.

"Hello," Henry greeted.

"Morn'n," Catherine said cheerfully. She moved around the men and proceeded to climb onto the carriage step. Billy and Thomas tipped their hats and moved behind the carriage where two horses were saddled and waiting. The other man wobbled to the carriage and climb aboard.

"Catherine, my sweet love, I said I was sorry. I swear I didn't mean it," he said, trying to give his wife a kiss.

Catherine turned the other way. "Ye'd be lucky if I don't ask the Masta to make ye sleep with thee dogs!"

"Aww, come on," the man begged. "Ye don't mean that."

"Norton, let her be." Henry laughed. He opened the coach door and offered his hand to Adelina. She accepted it and climbed inside.

The ride into Barbuda was short and quiet, except for the constant bickering of Catherine and Norton outside of the coach.

"How could ye say that about me?" Catherine asked.

"I was only jesting, me love," Norton begged.

"Ye said I was a big hen!" Catherine almost screamed.

From the inside, Henry began laughing. Adelina bit her lip to keep from giggling herself.

Minutes later, the carriage entered the busy port town of Barbuda. Outside the small window, Adelina watched the wide assortment of people. The first to catch her attention were the women standing outside the Madam's house. Again, they dressed in short, colorful skirts and bodices that clung too tightly to their bodies. They wore netted stockings and a lot of colorful makeup. Three of the women sat on the railing of the porch, calling to the men who passed by on the streets while lightly touching various parts of their bodies. Others leaned against the building, laughing as they hiked up their stockings, one of them being Annie.

Adelina forced herself to turn away from the house of ill repute and gaze elsewhere. She saw other women dressed comfortably in light, cotton gowns, which assured her that she wouldn't be the only lady on this island. She saw men walking on wooden sidewalks that were raised above the dusty street. Some were pirates, with teeth missing and tattoos printed on their bodies. Two of which, Adelina recognized as Henry's men. She saw sailors, merchants, wealthy estate owners, two beggars, and about four drunks wandering the streets.

The carriage came to an abrupt halt. Henry opened the door and stepped out before turning to help Adelina down.

"Catherine will assist you with the gown. I have some other business to attend to," Henry said. He glanced at Billy and Thomas who were tethering the horses to a post. "But I will be back shortly."

"That's alright. I'm sure we'll have fun," Adelina said.

Billy and Thomas approached them. Henry nodded to Billy. "Ready? Thomas, I think you'd be better if you stayed with Adelina and Catherine. Norton, if you don't mind, stay within eyesight of the horses," Henry instructed before he and Billy marched down the sidewalk.

Catherine clapped her hands together. "Come along, me dear. It es time to find ye a gown," she said with a huge smile. With a deep breath, she picked up the hem of her dress and crossed the street with great determination.

Adelina turned to Thomas. "I guess we ought to catch up," she said as she took into a brisk walk. Thomas followed.

From across the street, Norton called to Catherine and began to wave frantically. Adelina and Thomas returned the favor, but Catherine pointedly ignored him. Adelina watched as Norton's smile dropped and lifted his shoulders in a shrug.

The dressmaker shop smelt heavily of incense. To the right was a red loveseat and two wooden chairs surrounding an antique table. There was a lounge chair of the same material as the loveseat in the far corner, facing out the window. On the white walls were gown sketches and cloth samples. On the other side were four dress-making mannequins that wore gowns that were still in progress. She could see a narrow hallway off to the side, which Adelina took as access to changing rooms. Adelina waited in the center of the room while Thomas moved to sit in the lounge chair and put his feet up on the windowsill. Impatiently, Catherine went to search the back rooms for the tailor.

Catherine returned with a thin little man with a black mustache that made his face look oddly small. Adelina noticed that he had a black pencil tucked behind his right ear, making his face even smaller. He introduced himself as Mister Bakeoven in a high voice, wiggling his mustache as he talked. Catherine rolled her eyes, not caring about introductions and immediately began pointing to Adelina and explaining what she wanted as a gown. When the man stood next to Adelina, she could easily see over his head at Thomas.

"Catherine, please," Adelina begged, "I can—"

"Mizz, allow me to do this. Ye will look beautiful at the ball," Catherine answered.

Adelina stood rooted to the spot with her arms raised out to the side, while the dressmaker measured her and Catherine held up bolts of cloth and various lace designs against her. The designer held out a navy blue piece of cloth to her neck. "Do you like this color?" he asked Adelina in his high voice.

Before Adelina could answer yes, Catherine interrupted. "Oh no! She needs a much lighter color."

"What about this yellow?"

"Too light."

"Red or pink?"

"Too common and no."

"How about this green?"

"Looks too much like grass."

"This gold is pretty."

Catherine paused for a moment. She glanced from the gold to Adelina's eyes and back again. "No white lace or ribbon. It will take the attention away from her eyes."

"Of course," Mister Bakeoven said.

"Gold, Mizz? It es a little dark for spring, but light enough so that ye won't stick out." Catherine smiled.

"It's fine," Adelina shrugged desperately.

Catherine frowned at Adelina's lack of enthusiasm. "Good. We'll use the gold."

The man nodded. "Now for the design," he said as he left the room.

Adelina glanced at Thomas, who was beginning to doze in the corner. Catherine followed her gaze to the young man and stomped to his side.

"Wake up!" she growled and knocked him in the shin.

Thomas jumped up instantly.

"Ye are here to protect me and the mizz. Now, how would ye do that if ye were asleep?" Catherine asked, crossing her arms.

Thomas shrugged and mumbled lightly as he sat back down. "Adelina needs protection from you, you big hen."

Catherine glared at him before she turned to face the approaching designer. She grabbed the designs and immediately began commenting on each. "Too long. Too high. Too loose. Look at those bosoms…not high enough! This one's nice. Ooh, but this one's better."

Adelina gained Mister Bakeoven's attention and gave him a sympathetic smile.

"Which one?" Catherine asked Adelina.

The designs were so similar that Adelina couldn't depict any major difference between them, but rather than admitting so, Adelina nodded to the one on the left.

Catherine compared the two designs again and looked carefully at Mister Bakeoven. Without a word, she grabbed the pencil from his ear and began to draw on the parchment, indicating where she wanted the gown to be altered. She turned to the man with a stern look on her face. "I want this design. And when ye are done, I want the design destroyed. The mizz will be the only one with this dress…ever."

Mister Bakeoven nodded at her request. With a tilt of his head, he made a comment on how Adelina should wear her hair so that it would compliment the gown. Catherine shook her head and began toying with Adelina's curls, demonstrating how she believed it should be worn so that the gown would compliment her. Mister Bakeoven stood on Adelina's other side to show how what he thought would be best.

After another hour had passed, Henry walked in to find the room in chaos. Bolts of cloth were unraveled and sprawled across the floor. Different panels of designs and colored pencils were lined up against one wall. And ribbons and hair pins laid just about everywhere. Henry looked up and spied Adelina standing in the middle of it all, looking weary and out of place.

"Jesu, Catherine! What did you do?" Henry asked with a moan. He turned to find Thomas dressed in a dark blue gown, standing in the far corner. Henry's fists balled in anger. "What the hell did you do to my cabin boy?"

Thomas immediately blushed as Catherine stepped in his line of sight.

"Oh, hello, Masta. I didn't see ye come in."

Henry walked slowly up to his housekeeper and stood face to face with her. "What did you do to Thomas?"

Catherine crossed her arms to prove that she wasn't going to back down from his anger. "I wanted to show the Mizez what the back of the gown will look like. And Mister Bakeoven had one in Thomas' size," Catherine paused. "Besides, ye don't really know what the gown looks like until ye see it on someone. And ye can see, it doesn't go with his hair."

"And Thomas?" Henry growled, turning to his cabin boy.

"Called me a hen," Catherine said from behind.

Henry took his glare from Catherine and placed it on Thomas. He saw that what Catherine said was true: the gown really did fit Thomas' slim form but the dark blue clashed with his hair and made him look ghastly white. Thomas stared at the floor, feeling the tension that was slowly filling the room.

Henry began to laugh and everyone relaxed as the anxiety lifted. "That's your fault. I knew I should have come here instead."

"Yes, you should have," Adelina agreed. "I didn't get two words in on the gown."

"And ye'll thank me for it too," Catherine said, looking proud.

Henry took a couple of coins out of his pocket and placed them in Mister Bakeoven's palm. "For the mess…and Catherine."

"Thank you," he said, looking relieved.

"It's well past noon, ladies," Henry said, looking directly at Thomas. "How about some lunch?"

Adelina nodded. Thinking about food made her stomach growl. "Oh yes," she said as she brushed her hair back with her fingers.

The door swung open and Billy walked in. The shop suddenly looked half its size with Billy's large body in the middle of it. "Well, Cap'n, it's all taken…" Billy trailed off as he saw Mister Bakeoven unbuttoning the back of the dress on Thomas.

"Don't do it, Billy," Thomas begged, feeling his face grow red as he struggled to redress in his own clothes as fast as he possibly could.

His efforts were in vain, Billy was in hysterics.

"I'm hungry. I'm ready to eat when you are, Catherine," Henry said after Billy's laughter died.

"Actually, Masta Roark, I think I'll go eat with Norton," Catherine said with a devious smile. "He'll pay."

Henry smiled. "I don't doubt that. Get yourself something nice," he said as Catherine began walking to the door, dragging Thomas and Billy with her.

"I'd like to eat with the cap'n," Thomas argued.

"No, Thomas. The Masta and Mizz Ellingsworth need some—" the rest was cut off by the door closing behind her.

Henry smiled at Adelina and offered her his arm. She gladly accepted it and gave Mister Bakeoven a smile as he opened the door for them.

"What are you in the mood for?" Henry asked.

"I don't know," Adelina responded. Her stomach growled again, this time louder than before. Henry raised an eyebrow and Adelina blushed slightly. "Well, I am hungry."

"I can hear that," Henry said with a smile as they stepped from the wooden planks of the sidewalk to cross the dirt road to get to the other side. Henry led her to a small inn.

"Meghan," Adelina said reading the sign propped against the open door.

The inn was relatively noisy for people having a late lunch. There were sailors and pirates at the bar, men gambling at the tables in the back and numerous people with the only intention of eating. Henry led Adelina to a small table in the far corner near the window, and swiftly pulled out a chair.

"Miss," Henry said with a smile.

"Oh, thank you kind, sir," Adelina gushed as she stepped between the chair and the table. But before Adelina could sit, a tall man with a thin blonde mustache approached, extending his hand to Henry.

"Hello, Henry, my old friend. How was your trip?" he asked.

Henry readily shook his hand. "Just wonderful, Seth. I got everything I needed."

Seth turned to Adelina and bent for her hand. "And who is this gorgeous creature?" he asked as he brushed her knuckles with his lips.

Adelina blushed and tried to fight the oncoming smile. Henry saw the losing battle and his jaw tightened, but his tone did not change. "Seth, this is Miss Adelina Ellingsworth."

Seth straightened but did not drop her hand. "Miss Ellingsworth. Thankfully not Lady Roark. Am I safe to assume that you are available for courting?"

Adelina's smile dropped. *Brandon. It's been a long time since I thought about him. I can't believe I forgotten about him.* She shifted her gaze to Henry and gave him a cold glare. *I would have been happily married—at least married—if he had not intervened.* "I'm sorry. But I am to marry as soon as I return back to England," Adelina said without moving her gaze from Henry. Henry gave a smile and flexed his eyebrows upward for a moment. "I'm just here visiting cousins."

Seth dropped Adelina's hand. "Forever lost, I'm afraid." He patted Henry on the back and nodded to Adelina before he stepped away and strolled among the tables.

Adelina sat down, thoroughly relieved to be able to eat. Henry talked to a passing waiter for moment before he sat down across from Adelina.

"I hope you like pork," Henry started. "It's either that or fish and the fish has never been all that good."

"I really don't care. Just as long as it is edible," Adelina said with a hand to her stomach.

After several minutes the waiter returned with fresh pork and cold drinks. Adelina cut herself a sliver and just as it touched her lips, Henry gave a halfhearted smile.

"What?" Adelina asked, pulling the meat away from her lips.

Henry put down his fork and knife. "You'll see. And I'm very sorry."

Adelina shrugged and popped the piece of meat into her mouth anyway. No sooner did the juicy meat touch her tongue when a cold hand brushed lightly against her shoulder. Adelina sat up with a start, thinking that the very hand of Death was on her.

"Hello, Henry," Michelle greeted.

Henry stood up and smiled. "Good afternoon, Michelle."

Adelina turned in her seat to face the other woman. Michelle stood in a light astray gown with a handsome young man in a gray suit attached to her arm.

"Oh, Henry," Michelle began with a smile and roll of her shoulders. "This is Walter—excuse me—Sir Walter Cumberland."

The men shook hands as Adelina politely stood up.

"Hello," she greeted as she nervously flattened the curves of her gown.

Michelle cocked her head to face Adelina and gave a sly smile. Then she turned her attention back to Henry. "It looks like you could use some company for lunch."

"Well…" Henry started.

Michelle beamed as she moved to sit next to him, leaving Sir Cumberland to sit awkwardly between Michelle and Adelina. As everyone got situated, Adelina watched as Michelle moved as close to Henry as she could.

"Sir Cumberland, this is Adelina Ellingsworth," Henry introduced as he took a sip of ale.

Sir Cumberland turned in his seat to face Adelina. "Not Miss Ellingsworth, the daughter of Jonathon Ellingsworth of London, is it?"

Henry gulped and looked up with a start, glancing rapidly between Adelina and Sir Cumberland. Then a shadow fell over his face as he gave her a warning glare.

Adelina caught the darkening eyes from across the table and gulped. "Yes, Sir Cumberland."

Sir Cumberland beamed. "My, you're beautiful. I don't believe I've seen you since you were a little girl."

Henry's jaw clenched at Sir Cumberland's affection for Adelina. He noted how he looked at her from the corner of his eye and his fingertips would occasionally graze Adelina's wrist or hand.

No one said anything for a moment while the waiter returned with more pork and drinks. Michelle shook her head and pushed her plate away.

As Adelina cut herself another slice, Sir Cumberland placed a bold hand upon her wrist. "I used to work for your father when I was a young lad. Just sweeping his office and such."

Adelina pulled her hand away and continued cutting her meat. "Yes, I remember," she lied.

Sir Cumberland sprinkled a large amount of salt on his meat and took a greedy bite. Chewing loudly, he said, "Why are you here in Barbuda, Adelina?"

Henry started coughing on a piece of meat. "Sorry. It's a little salty."

Adelina took a bite and mauled over her thoughts. *If I tell Sir Cumberland the truth, I might be able to go home. But then I would be forced to marry*

*a man I do not love. If somehow Henry didn't let me go, he'd be angry with
me, and then what would I do? Henry has been a complete gentleman,
treating me like no one else has. If I lie, I'd be stuck here for a little while
longer. So far it hasn't been unbearable, except for missing my family. So,
in the end, what's the lesser evil?* Adelina swallowed. "Actually, Sir
Cumber—"

"Walter, please," he cut in.

"Walter. Henry is a...an old family friend," Adelina murmured.

Walter smiled. "Good then."

Henry nodded his approval.

"Well, that's nice," Michelle said distantly as she ran a delicate finger over
the length of Henry's thigh underneath the table.

The meal continued with a constant discussion of politics and the upcoming
ball. Adelina remained silent, thinking of her lie and the lost possibility of going
home to her family. Without warning and no way of stopping it, Adelina let out
a loud burp.

Adelina dropped her fork and knife and immediately covered her mouth as
her cheeks turned a deep shade of red. With her mouth agape, Michelle glared
directly at Adelina with all of Hell in her bright green orbs. Adelina couldn't tell
if they were condemning her or laughing at her.

She turned her gaze downward at her plate and felt her cheeks burn as she
reached for her glass of water. To her relief, Henry exploded with a much
louder and longer burp, relieving her embarrassment as he attracted attention
from surrounding tables. She looked up to see his face beaming before he
began to laugh. Adelina smiled when everyone at the other tables turned their
attention away from her and back to their meals.

Henry stood up. "Well, it's been a lovely time, but I would like to return
home before dusk. Adelina?"

Adelina nodded, eager to be out of the restaurant. Michelle and Sir
Cumberland stoop up and followed them out.

"Are you sure you must leave so soon? Can't you come by my home for
a little while? It's on the way," Michelle begged as she pulled Henry aside,
leaving Adelina and Sir Cumberland to walk together.

"I can't today, Michelle," Henry said. He put a hand across her back.
"Maybe some other time."

Despite Sir Cumberland's constant chatter about working for Lord
Ellingsworth, Adelina overheard Henry's last comment and frowned.

"Why the long face, my sweet?" Sir Cumberland asked.

"Oh, I'm a little homesick, that's all," Adelina said with a small smile.

Sir Cumberland nodded. "I can understand that. If you'd like, I am returning to England sometime in the next two weeks. I'll be happy to send a message to your family for you."

Adelina stopped walking and threw her arms around Sir Cumberland. "Oh, would you? I miss them ever so much. Thank you!"

"Good afternoon!" Henry said sternly from behind. Adelina released Sir Cumberland and looked up to see Norton and Catherine at the carriage. Billy and Thomas nodded when Henry saw them and galloped away on their horses.

"I guess I will see you later then, Henry," Michelle said with a pout as she wrapped her arms around Henry's neck. She turned slightly and planted a light kiss on the base of his neck.

"Goodbye, Michelle," Henry said as he stepped away.

Adelina waited for Michelle to step back away from the carriage. "Please don't forget, Walter. Please," Adelina whispered.

"No, no, my dear. I won't," Sir Cumberland said gently as he helped Adelina into the coach.

Henry brushed Sir Cumberland aside with a stiff nod and climbed inside the coach. He crawled past Adelina and sat in the far corner with his arms crossed.

"Are you alright?" Adelina asked slowly.

Henry took a deep breath and gave a single nod.

"You sure?"

Another nod.

Adelina stayed quiet for several minutes. "Henry?"

"Not now, Adelina."

Adelina was thankful for the soundless ride to be over when Roark Manor came into view. As soon as the door opened, Adelina descended from the coach, refusing Norton's helpful hand and marched to the library. She selected a folio of poems and climbed the stairs to her room. There, she changed into a pale chemise and settled on the bench left of her balcony door.

Meanwhile, Henry went to the parlor and pulled out a bottle of brandy and struggled to locate two small glasses. He stalked through the halls and stomped up the stairs and down the hall to his bedroom. He jerked opened the door and slammed it shut behind him.

Billy heard the slam from the downstairs study and decided he'd better go see if he could calm his captain down.

"Captain?" Billy called through Henry's door.

Henry opened the door and leaned against it. His shirt was off and he had a towel draped over his shoulders. He snorted and turned back into the bedchamber. "What the hell took you so long?"

Billy smiled as he stepped inside, closing the door behind him. With a sigh, he sat on the bed. "Alright, Cap'n. What happened?"

Henry poured a large amount of brandy into each of the glasses. He handed one to Billy before he gulped down his own, ignoring it as it burned his throat. Feeling thoroughly awake, he moved to the dresser to pour water into a porcelain basin sitting there. "Stupid wench."

"Who? Michelle or Adelina?"

Henry cocked his head for a moment before splashing water on his face. "Um—I don't know—both!"

"What did they do?"

"Well, Michelle is being…Michelle. One minute she is all over me. Next minute she's hanging all over *Sir* Cumberland," he mocked with sarcasm dripping all over the sir.

"And Adelina?" Billy inquired.

"I don't know. She's so fragile and doesn't know what to do," Henry sighed. "She lied for me today. She could have blown the whole damn thing open, but she didn't," Henry paused, shaking his head. "I knew I shouldn't have forced her into this mess."

Billy nodded. "I wonder why she didn't? You'd think Adelina would want to go home and get back to what's-his-name."

"I know. Sometimes I wonder if she isn't thankful that I came along," Henry said with a shrug. He walked over to the balcony doors and pulled one open, hoping it would catch any cool breezes in the air. He waited a moment, leaning against the door frame, letting a frittering breeze brush against his chest.

"Maybe," Billy said with a shrug.

"But then again, I saw her hugging Cumberland," Henry said, barely above a whisper. He could feel his hear almost ripping itself from his body for the second time today. "And I saw the way he looked at her."

"Does he want her for his own?" Billy asked moving away from the bed.

"Definitely."

"What about Adelina? Does she want him?"

"That's just it, I can't tell," Henry said, returning to the bed. "Why did she have to be so damn…her?"

Billy shrugged. He looked up at his friend and grinned. "I think you've been around the wench for a little too long."

Henry turned to face Billy. "Why the hell did I have to listen to you? You're the one who talked me into taking the girl in the first place!" He laughed, throwing a pillow at his friend.

Adelina leaned against a pillow with a light blanket over her legs. She patted herself on the back for getting out of the warm cotton gown and into the cool chemise. There was a light breeze in the early evening and it graced softly against her skin. She sighed quietly every time it brushed her skin, leaving goose bumps behind. Adelina pulled the blanket a little higher before opening up the book.

What dire offence from am'rous causes springs,
What mighty contests rise from trivial things,
I sing—this verse to C—Muse! is due;

She couldn't focus. The slight ruffle of the wind through the trees or the distant gurgling of the river would distract her. If it wasn't the sounds of the oncoming night distracting her, it was the sinking sun, filling the sky with its vibrant colors or the odd-shaped birds with bright, brilliant colors flying the pink and orange sky.

Adelina yawned and looked down at the first passage. With the sinking light, she knew she wouldn't have much longer to read before she would have to get up and fetch a candle. Through the walls she heard a door slam and knew Henry had returned to his room. Minutes later, she heard muffled voices.

She managed to continue reading until the word "wench" rang out, catching her attention. Adelina shook her head and begun rereading the first line again. A few minutes later, the balcony door to Henry's bedchamber opened. She looked up in surprise, never noticing the door a few feet away. Adelina froze remembering how she was dressed, but the man did not step out.

"I saw her…the way he looked," Adelina heard faintly. "Why did she…" he continued.

She shifted and returned to the book in her lap again. A few times there was laughter, but Adelina couldn't make out what was being said. Despite her attempts to ignore the noises inside, she still couldn't focus on the book. Her thoughts kept drifting back to Henry's conversation. *Who is the wench and what did she do? Is it me? What did I do?*

Adelina muttered an unladylike curse and brought her knees up to her chest. She leaned back against the armrest and took a deep breath. *It's getting far too dark to read the book now anyhow*, she thought as she shifted her attention to the reddening sunset.

Billy shut the door behind him. Henry could hear him laughing as he walked down the hallway into his own room. Unconsciously, Henry rubbed his upper arm where Billy had hit him, and laughed. *Yes, it was a jesting punch, but it still hurt.*

Henry lay on the bed with his wrists crossed under his head, letting his mind wonder about Michelle. He's known her for years. He met her almost six years ago when he first came to Barbuda. She was only fourteen and he eighteen.

"Pretty little thing," Henry mumbled. *Michelle was always pretty, but that was all she had going for her. She often used her beauty to her advantage, which was what had intrigued me. She was used to having men begging to court her.*

Henry's father, Lord Alfred Roark, came to Barbuda to help build the estate for Henry. He was going to use Barbuda as a temporary trading post until he could establish himself in the new colonies. Just after breaking ground, Michelle met Henry's father. After listening to the town's gossip, she assumed that he was going to retire his title to Henry when the building was complete.

That was the beginning of Henry's shadow. Michelle followed Henry everywhere and chased off any girl who came too close to "her man." Henry had enjoyed it when the most beautiful girl on the island paid attention only to him, and he quickly became enamored. He knew now that what he felt was nothing more than infatuation.

Shortly after Michelle's seventeenth birthday, when the estate was in the final stages of completion, Henry had asked Michelle's father for her hand in marriage. A year later, with the estate finished, they were wed at the local church and celebrated in the reception at the newly furnished Roark Manor.

Just hours after the vows, Michelle introduced herself as Lady Roark to some of Henry's friends who had journeyed from England for the celebration.

They snickered and Henry had laughed. Michelle stammered her confusion and blushed a shade of red.

"I won't become lord until the death of my father," Henry had explained. He watched as Michelle's color deepened and the smile fade from her face.

"Oh, I'm sorry," she responded.

Henry could still picture her face as she stepped away from him and walked through the crowd as though in a daze. He watched her pause and look at his father, a man approaching old age, who was laughing as he danced with a young brunette less than half of his age.

Guess there's no hope of him having a heart attack by morning, Michelle thought, feeling her heart sink.

Henry was dumbfounded when Michelle had requested a separate room from his on their marriage night. But he shrugged it off, thinking she was just nervous. The next morning, Michelle asked Henry for an annulment for reasons of deception, breaking his heart. After that, Michelle refused to talk to him.

About eight months later, Lord Roark died in a tragic accident, leaving everything to his only son. A few weeks afterward, Michelle began "coincidentally" running into him while he was in town. Once, she showed at up at Henry's home and courageously admitted that she was far too young when they got married, but she still has feelings for him. She said that now that she was older and therefore more mature, she wanted him to court her again.

Henry wanted to believe her, and he almost did, but couldn't quite put his finger on why he didn't completely. And since she did make a good companion at times, why cast her off altogether?

Henry rolled onto his side, in an effort to forget about Michelle. He glanced out toward the balcony and thought about how Adelina was just feet away on the other side of the wall. They even shared that balcony.

She shouldn't be here, Henry thought. He had met her father at the tavern and discussed methods of making money. They had agreed to meet again seven months later, this time with Lord Ellingsworth's associates. Everything had to be perfect: no names, no representation, and absolute secrecy.

Henry doesn't trust secrets.

First, he had to find out their identities—a much easier task than he anticipated. The next morning, unaware of Henry's return, the three men were very generous with their names and representatives to the wenches that worked at the tavern. Henry had followed them to London and asked several business associates if Lord Ellingsworth and William Wexford were reliable. They were, and Henry believed he had nothing to fear. But he knew he had everything to caution.

Six months later, Henry waited outside the London's town hall as they had agreed upon. He had brought enough gunpowder, ammunition, and pistols to destroy almost six blocks of London in exchange for fifty thousand quid, as their agreement. He got there at the exact meeting time, but didn't see Lord Ellingsworth or either of the Wexfords.

Henry knew something was wrong. He couldn't shake the feeling that he was led into a trap. He wanted to get the hell out of there and fast. But it began to rain and the horses became difficult. Two minutes later, the sheriff and half of England's finest military ambushed him, arresting him on the spot. As he was cuffed and dragged into the jail cart, he looked back over his shoulder and watched as Lord Ellingsworth, William Wexford and his son, all dressed in cavalry uniform, take his horses and all the equipment.

Henry knew he had been set up.

The sheriff condemned Henry as a pirate and stated that his plans were to blow up one of the city banks and ordered him sent to the gallows without trial. Henry accepted his fate with a bland smile. Just a few hundred yards from the daunting gallows, the rain began to harden and the carriage got stuck in the mud. After nearly a half hour of trying to pry the wheels from the deepening muck, the guards and attendants decided that they would lead Henry there by foot. Henry, with a kind smile on his face, offered to help free the carriage as his last act of righteousness.

Foolishly, the guards accepted his assistance. Once the vehicle was free from the deepening mud, the guards turned to direct Henry back into the coach. They looked around in vain, unable to locate him in the accumulating crowd. He had disappeared.

It took just over four weeks, but Henry returned to the *North Star*, still faithfully waiting just east of London. Of course, by the time he climbed aboard he was dirty, tired and half starved. But more than anything, he was angry. Other than sailing back to Barbuda in defeat, Henry decided to remain in Canterbury until he could devise a plan and seek revenge.

All Henry wanted was the supplies, or at least its worth, back in his possession. If he received any extra wealth in the process, or ruined Lord

Ellingsworth and the Wexfords, which was his full intention, then Henry would be pleased. And it would be a well appreciated bonus if one or the other's head was served on a silver platter, so to speak. *I don't tolerate mutineers, even when they're landlubbers.*

Mark, Henry's informant in London, announced that Lord Ellingsworth had a daughter of eight-and-ten. Upon the informant's next visit, he told his employer that the daughter was to marry none other than, Wexford's son, and a ball is to be given in their honor later that week. Smiling, Henry dressed in his finest suit and traveled to London to see about gaining entry to a certain ball.

Henry forced the thought of Adelina out of his mind. Groaning, he stood up and walked to the basin sitting on the dresser. He splashed some water onto his face, letting it drip down his body until it dampened his trousers. Feeling refreshed, Henry walked through the balcony door and leaned against the railing overlooking his land.

From above, Henry could hear Catherine scolding someone in the dark. Although he couldn't see her, a few words drifted up. From her tone, Henry could tell she was certainly livid. Henry chuckled to himself, thinking that it was a good chance that her victim was Norton. With a smile, he turned around.

On the wooden bench, bathed in soft moonlight and dressed in a thin piece of cloth, was Adelina. Henry took a step closer and discovered that she was asleep with a book in her lap.

Henry knelt beside her and gazed at her features. Her hair was loose and tumbled over the back of the armrest in a sea of waves and curls. Her lips were slightly parted and twitched ever so. His gaze drifted downward from her rosy lips and followed the sweet path displayed by the open neckline of the chemise. In moments, Henry caught himself boldly gazing at her bosom where one full breast already pushed itself over the low neckline of the chemise due to her sleeping position. The other pushed dangerously upward, threatening to spill at any given moment.

Henry couldn't stop himself from reaching out and stroking the bare nipple until it grew hard and dark underneath his thumb. He felt a tightening in his groin as he watched the other nipple rise under the pale chemise. Henry fought the sudden urge of taking one of those dark nipples into his mouth and sucking the sweet taste.

It'll be too cold for her to be out here, Henry decided, noting the growing chill in the air. He bit his lip and shifted Adelina's weight into his arms. He carefully lifted her. As he stood up, Adelina's head settled into the corner of his neck and she softly murmured something against his skin. He took her into her bedroom and laid her in the bed. He sat down on the edge and gently replaced the chemise over her breast.

"My dear, Adelina," Henry whispered as he traced her eyebrows with his fingertips. He leaned forward to place a soft kiss on cheek. But Adelina shifted and he found himself against her lips.

Henry was about to pull away when he felt Adelina's lips part ever so slightly under his own. His tongue lightly traced her lips and he felt her open her mouth farther to accept his tongue, bringing a sudden surge of heat in his groin.

Adelina moaned softly in response to the dancing tongue on her own. After several moments, the mouth parted from hers and began to suckle gently on her earlobe. Slowly, Adelina opened her eyes and watched Henry's hand move from his side to cup her left breast, soft and gentle. Through the thin chemise she felt his thumb lightly trace her nipple. She sighed dreamily, enjoying his touch.

Henry freed her ear and began a slow, tantalizing trail of kisses down her neck, and across the top of her breast. As he reached the neckline of the chemise, he pulled the cloth down so that her breasts were fully exposed. He paused, taking a deep breath, and then fully attacked the erect nipple that he had so tenderly toyed with.

Adelina gasped the instant his hot mouth took hold of her breast. The distinctive feeling of yearning exploded in her bosom as her breasts ached for more. A knot twisted in her stomach, and a growing sensation that she couldn't explain developed between her legs, suddenly making her feel as though her lower body was empty—missing something. It felt like a fire had erupted inside of her, waking every nerve in her body.

Almost instinctively, Adelina arched herself into the devouring mouth, giving it further access to her body. Her delicate hand flew to his muscular chest hovering above her and rubbed the small patch of hair in the middle. The other hand found its way to the top of Henry's trousers.

Henry made a path of kisses from one nipple to the other. She gasped again, nearly pushing all of her body against him. Achingly, he led Adelina back to the bed, his mouth never leaving her breast. His hands slowly pushed the hem of her chemise higher over her thighs, exposing all of her creamy legs. It was almost to her hips when he laid a bold hand tenderly on her inside of her thigh, barely an inch from her womanhood. Henry moaned when he realized that he was close enough to feel the heat and the wetness escaping from the inside of Adelina.

As Henry parted her thighs, he lifted himself from the bed and centered himself above her. Ever so carefully, Henry eased his weight on top of her, using his knee to further part her legs.

Adelina took a deep breath as she felt Henry's manhood press against her abdomen. She sighed softly when he returned his lips to hers again. Eagerly, Adelina began pulling the strings that held Henry's trousers together, freeing him.

Adelina pushed his pants past his buttocks and there he was—all of him— hard and ready. A thick rod of throbbing steel covered in a thin layer of satin. In a swift motion, Henry slipped his pants past his legs and feet and discarded them on the floor. Once he was liberated from the confinement of his trousers, he guided Adelina's hand to his manhood. She touched him, so light and so soft, that he nearly collapsed on top of her.

"Henry..." Adelina whispered.

Henry nodded briefly as he slowly pulled the chemise over Adelina's head and cast it aside. He paused for a moment so that he could look at her. She lay naked and beautiful beneath him. Her creamy skin glistened in the soft candlelight, causing her breasts to look erotic and inviting. The soft curls of the dark mound between her legs drew his attention and he moved his hand there.

Adelina gasped as his finger tenderly touched the opening to her womanhood. He played in the wetness, just outside, not wanting to sink in yet. He found a spot, a spot so sensitive that it made her cry out in pleasure. Adelina moaned as the fire burned hotter, making her want more.

"Henry, please!" she gasped.

"Not yet," Henry whispered, shaking his head. He slipped his finger inside, causing Adelina to cry out in pleasure. He could feel her beginning to tighten and grow wetter as the unyielding sense of urgency began to consume her. "Now you're ready."

Henry carefully positioned himself between Adelina's knees. Instinctively, she grabbed Henry's shoulders as he lifted her hips. She watched in wonder as he grabbed his massive staff and placed it at the opening of her core.

She was on fire, just knowing that he was right outside of her—on her edge—made her insides burn. Adelina didn't want him touching the edges of her core—she wanted him to be on the inside. She wanted him to touch the one spot that would bring her agony to an end and bring her the greatest pleasure she's ever known.

"Look at me!" Henry commanded. "I want to watch your eyes."

Adelina did as she was told and was amazed to find that his eyes had darkened by the passion that filled them. They were so deep and fervent that it distracted Adelina for a split moment. No one has ever looked at her with such tenderness.

Henry took a shallow breath as he tenderly guided his manhood just inside of her womanhood. He could feel Adelina's fingernails digging into his skin, but he couldn't feel the pain. Adelina's eyes widened as she gasped and tighten her grip on his shoulder. There was a growing pain, but Adelina could feel that there was pleasure behind it. She wanted him deeper.

Henry swallowed. He knew it would be best to surge himself inside of her, all at one time, and to break her virginity. He watched as she bit her lip, ready for him to do so. He adjusted his grip on her hips, and took a deep breath, preparing himself for what he was about to do.

Without warning there was a loud uproar and shouting outside the bedroom door. There was a single, quick rap on the bedroom door, then it flew open.

Chapter Six

Catherine raced through the open portal with Thomas on her heels. "Mizz Ellingsworth, we need to find the Masta and get ye to saf—oh."

Henry dropped Adelina and spun around on his knees in full nudity. Immediately Adelina grabbed the pillow from behind her and covered herself as Henry bellowed a roar, causing Catherine to jump and Thomas to move behind her for protection.

"What the hell are you doing in here, wench?" Henry shouted, clenching and re-clenching his fists. Passion rapidly drained from his body as complete rage replaced it.

"Um…well," Catherine stammered, trying to decide how to confront her master.

"Out with it, woman!" Henry commanded, fighting the oncoming urge to shake his housekeeper.

"Me'lord," Catherine started, thrusting her chin upward, "there es something in the forest. I went to yer room but…ye weren't there."

Henry didn't say anything for a long moment. He glanced longingly back over his shoulder at Adelina. With a curse and reached for his trousers. Henry turned his back as he shoved his foot through the pant leg. "Who?"

Catherine stepped forward. "I did. It was a man. Big, tall, but I couldn't see his face. I was quiet, so I don't think he saw me."

"You? Quiet?" Thomas muttered from behind. Catherine turned around and smacked the back of his head.

"Sure it wasn't one of my men?" Henry asked. "Thomas, go get my sword and wake up Billy."

"Aye, aye, Cap'n," Thomas said before he ran from the room.

"Positive," Catherine answered. Henry got the location just as Thomas returned.

"Catherine and Thomas, you two stay here. I'll send someone to bolt the downstairs doors, but I want you to do the bedroom one as well," Henry instructed as he left the room.

Catherine shooed Thomas outside the bedroom for a few minutes while Adelina dressed. It was a long, awkward silence while Catherine located Adelina's chemise and pulled a robe from the closet. Adelina refused to move from the limited protection that the pillow had to offer.

Catherine threw the clothes on the bed. "Get dressed," she demanded through clenched teeth.

Adelina bit her lip and grimaced at the thick taste of blood. She pressed her face into the pillow to soak away the threatening tears. Without looking, Adelina knew that Catherine was glaring at her, making her skin crawl and burn.

Catherine turned her back against Adelina. "Mizz, please get dressed so that Thomas may come in," she spat.

Ever so slowly, Adelina dressed. She did her best to ignore the aching sensation between her legs as she adjusted her chemise and secured her robe. She groaned as she sat back on the bed; her insides hurt so badly.

I deserve it, Adelina thought as she brushed away a tear. *I'm so very sorry, Brandon. It won't happen again.*

Once Adelina was fully dressed and hidden under the bed sheet, Catherine opened the door to permit Thomas into the room, quickly locking it behind him. He smiled briefly at Adelina and unloaded his sword, dagger, and a loaded pistol on the breakfast table. He sat down and began shuffling a deck of cards. Catherine pulled up the lounge chair and Thomas dealt her a hand.

Feeling neglected and ashamed, Adelina rolled onto her side, facing away from them. The agonizing pain of need was almost gone now, for which she was thankful. But it didn't keep her mind from roaming…or her heart from aching.

Henry shot out of the kitchen door like a bat out of hell. He was livid, and anger flowed heavily in the blood that was rapidly pumping through his veins. Every movement he made echoed and brought intense pain throughout his genitals. *I was almost inside of her. I was so close.*

"Too close," Henry mumbled as Billy caught up to him. He tried to push Adelina out of his head, but the thoughts of being right there, right outside her virginity, filled his mind. *I swear I will kill whoever interrupted me.*

Slowly and cautiously they made their way to the *North Star*. Through carefully made hand signals, Henry learned that no one on guard on the ship had seen anything suspicious. Without further ado, Henry and Billy started down the path where the trespasser was last seen.

About twenty feet into the forest, Billy knelt down and said in a hushed voice, "Someone was definitely out here. Just look at these footprints."

Henry knelt down next to Billy and saw that the ground was all stirred up. It was one, maybe two people who paced and waited in this particular location. From the corner of his eye, Henry could see where a set of footprints led into the forest, angling back to the mansion. Henry followed them and through the trees and was horrified to find that out he could make out the mansion—and the balcony that Adelina was on. Henry cursed and walked back to where Billy waited.

Billy pointed deeper into the forest. "He went that way. I think. It's such a mess out here, with all the mud and vegetation, it's nearly impossible to tell which way he went."

Henry followed the weak set of footprints and led Billy deeper into the forest. They tried to remain hidden amongst the shadows and the trees. Every time either of them heard a whisper of a noise, they would freeze and strain their ears to determine the cause and the direction of the sound. When nothing prevailed after several long minutes, they continued their search.

Henry and Billy followed the tracks for about half a mile before the footprints became lost amongst the thick vegetation. They continued for about another mile or so following unusually broken branches and the occasional discarded cigarette.

While standing in one of the shadows, Billy nudged Henry. "I think we're being watched."

"Me too," Henry whispered, placing a ready hand on the handle of his cutlass. "Shhh…"

Someone up ahead snorted.

Less than fifteen feet in front of them was a man hunched in the shadows of a low hanging branch. There was an awkward limbo between Henry and the intruder as they both realized they've been sighted. They stood still for a brief moment and at the same instant, they took off in a dead run with Henry a short distance behind the stranger.

Henry swore as branches whipped him in his face and chest. He could hear Billy cursing a few feet behind him. Apparently, the man up ahead was not in the mood for a run the woods either because Henry could hear him muttering the same few choice words.

"Stop!" Billy shouted from behind. Of course, the man continued to run.

"Does that ever work?" Henry shouted over his shoulder to Billy. He glanced back and saw that Billy was drifting back slightly. Looking ahead, the man up ahead was getting steadily closer.

The scenery around them was long since unfamiliar. He's never been this deep into the forest. He knew that the river was to his left and the mansion was some distance behind him, but it still didn't reassure him.

Henry was beginning to lose his breath. It was coming hard and fast, making his chest burn from the lack of oxygen. And he could hear his heart pumping loudly in his ears. He was thankful that the dull pain between his legs had left before he began the pursuit. In minutes, he noticed that he could no longer hear his quartermaster behind him. Henry urged his legs to pump faster.

The features of the man were slowly becoming distinctive in the pale moonlight as Henry closed the distance between them. The man had long hair secured in some kind of knot that bounced in the air with each step. He was slightly shorter than Henry and, when the man changed his course or glanced over his shoulder, Henry could see that he had a large, crooked nose, bushy eyebrows and a goatee.

Suddenly, the man up ahead stopped running and clutched his side as he bent into a ball. Henry saw him too late, as he ran into the man. The man toppled over and Henry did a flip in the air before landing hard on his back. There was a moment of stunned silence and rapid breathing on both parts.

Henry was the first to recover and get to his feet. He drew his sword and angled the cold metal so that the point was just inches above the man's back.

"And you are…" Henry breathed heavily.

"Jack," the man barked into the dirt. He rolled over and scrambled to his feet, pulling out his sword as he did so. With a half-cocked smile, he met blades with Henry.

"Burton," Henry spat. "Last time we met like this, I left you for dead."

"Bite me, Roark," Jack sneered. Slowly, the two men began to circle, crisscrossing their legs in preparation for the first move, never parting their weapons.

Henry couldn't help but feel an overwhelming hatred for man in front of him. "What the hell are you doing here?" Henry asked as he swung his sword in a wide arc toward Jack's stomach.

Jack blocked it. "Revenge, Henry. Why else would I be here in the dark?" he answered sarcastically. He took a step backward and swung hard at Henry's neck.

Henry ducked down, but still felt the cold metal comb through his hair. It sent shivers down his spine and filled him with even more anger.

They clashed swords again and Henry stepped forward. They pushed hard against each other so that their faces were just inches apart.

"The way I see it, Burton, I still owe you one," Henry said. He released some pressure from his sword and used the slight give to swing his free hand back and punched Jack in the stomach. Henry smiled as Jack lost his footing and fell onto his back with his sword lying by his side.

Henry took the step between him and Jack with ease. He tilted his cutlass so that the blade was against Jack's chest, directly above his heart. In déjà vu, Henry noticed that Jack lay almost exactly in the same position he had just over years ago when they had last seen each other. Except then, Jack's shirt was bloody and much dirtier. Henry believed that Jack deserved every cut under his shirt—even the one that *should* have killed him.

It had been a little bit over three years ago when Henry first crossed Captain Maraca's path. His marriage had been annulled the previous month and he had just found out that Michelle was engaged to some wealthy count. Like any other man, it was a severe blow to his heart. Every evening that past week, he went from tavern to tavern, searching for any means to escape his troubles. Twice, he nearly succumbed to the temptation that the women offered to him at the brothel. Both times he was too drunk to perform and give them anything.

One afternoon, Lord Roark, who remained in Barbuda because "Barbuda is the place to be" was asked to help repair a merchant ship that was damaged in a passing storm. Being the man that he was, Lord Roark complied and immediately left for the docks. Henry left a few hours later in the search of a quiet tavern.

Henry found what he was looking for overlooking the merchant ship his father was working on. He spied him working on the main mast and waved. He's blamed himself for waving ever since. Henry was shocked to see him raise his arm and return the favor. He smiled and turned to open the door.

Before the door swung shut behind him, he heard the unforgiving sound of wood splitting. He remembered pushing the door back open and step out in time to watch the mast split and fall into the water. He remembered hearing someone scream, but for all he knew, it could have been his own. He remembered distinctly being pulled out of the water and fighting those preventing him from going back in.

Henry was dragged into the tavern and given drink after drink until he passed out. That empty blackness surrounded him and comforted him. He swam in that darkness and danced in wide circles, forgetting about his father and how he had distracted him from his work. Had he not have waved, his father would have lived. It was such happiness and bliss.

But he was abruptly awakened from this bleak paradise. A man in a wide brim hat and a tattoo on his shoulder that read Emilee had touched his shoulder and placed a cold hand against his chest, feeling for a heartbeat.

"Son of a bitch—don't touch me!" Henry yelled, tumbling out of his chair. Still stupefied with drink and suffering from a pounding headache, Henry made a weak attempt to swing at the man.

Henry didn't remember what happened after that. Someone had returned him to the blackness he had made friends with earlier. Sometime later, he awoke and discovered that he was on a ship. The man in the wide brim hat was there…and he had a black eye.

Henry was announced as the newest seaman of the *North Star* and was forced to clean up everything any where at any time. At first, the crew was cruel and mean, seeing that they all had higher stations than he had, including the cabin boy. The quartermaster, Jack Burton, was the worst. Jack gave him disgusting and inhumane chores that didn't have to be done in the first place. In two weeks, all but Jack fell to Henry's humor and charm. After serving for Captain Maraca for two months, Henry was promoted to boatswain. When the second lieutenant fell ill and passed away, the crew unanimously gave Henry the position.

Captain Maraca was heavily involved in pirating. He sailed up and down the Atlantic Ocean from England and the Mediterranean to the Caribbean and the colonies. He targeted mostly merchant and trading vessels that didn't carry passengers. He especially enjoyed attacking pirates who bamboozled simply because he hated cowards.

Most importantly, he made sure that his men respected women whenever they made port. That was one rule that was *not* allowed to be broken. As Henry had witnessed to a powder monkey who had beaten and raped a prostitute, the consequence of assaulting a woman, physically or sexually, was receiving half of Moses Law, followed by keelhauling. Depending on the degree of the assault, if the man survived, he would then be marooned on the nearest island. Each man feared Captain Maraca's punishment, for they had agreed upon it when they signed the Articles as they were taken aboard. Henry assumed there was devotion to the name on Captain Maraca's arm.

Despite his cruel punishments, which were scarce, everyone loved Captain Maraca. He was taller than most men, with dark red hair and blazing green eyes. He was the kind of man who always supported the ordinary seaman and was there when anyone had a problem. Yet, he was the leader that everyone looked up to and admired.

That is why it was such a shock when he mysteriously vanished from the ship one day while they were at berth. Henry noticed that Jack was missing as well, but didn't think twice about it until he returned a few days later and demanded that they leave the island as soon as possible. Henry, the boatswain at the time, refused to forward the order. Instead, he organized a search. In his anger, Jack swore he'd hang everyone as mutineers, but his threat was ignored. It was obvious that Jack wanted to get off the island.

Nearly a week and a half after Captain Maraca's disappearance, his body washed up on the beach just a few hundred feet away from the ship. His ankles and wrists were bounded tightly to a small anchor with a large piece of rope. His nose was cut off, his eyes were gorged out, he had deep, random cuts throughout his body and his throat was slit from ear to ear. Small beach crabs and insects had made their way into his gaping wounds and mouth. He was beyond recognition except for the tattoo on his arm. With heavy hearts, they gave him a proper burial at sea burial before returning to shore.

It is custom for the quartermaster to be promoted to captain when the captain passed away, was sick, or otherwise indisposed. Although Jack was determined to uphold this tradition, the crew was not willing to commit. They mutinied against him and elected Henry as captain of the *North Star*.

Jack was not thrilled. In fact, he was quite angry and ready for a chance to seek revenge on any one of his crew—principally Henry. He stalked Henry into town the following night and made a harsh attempt on his life. Henry stood outside one of the closed shops that outlined the cobbled street of the town, admiring a piece of furniture on display. He looked up when something reflected in the moonlight on the pane of glass. Henry wasn't able to dodge the sword in time as it sliced across his back.

Henry bellowed a scream and moved aside, pulling out his own sword and barely managing to duck as Jack made a second attempt. With both hands on the grip, Jack raised the sword over his head. Henry used the advantage to sink his blade into Jack's stomach, surprised at the sickening give. Henry watched with tears welling up in his eyes as the first man he's killed collapsed onto his back, with the sword still protruding from his stomach.

Henry heard Jack mumble something about killing him the way he had Maraca. Overcome with white anger, Henry took his sword out of Jack's stomach and raised it above his chest. Henry ignored Jack's pleading eyes and plunged the blade deep inside as hard as he could and twisted the handle. Jack didn't stir, but a bloody gurgle escaped his lips.

A light in the house across the street blinked on and there was shouting inside. Henry pulled his sword out of Jack's chest and returned the bloody blade to its sheath. He ran down the street as fast as he could, begging his legs to go faster despite the piercing pain he felt throughout his back. When he got to the docks and urged his crew to make haste and depart from the island.

Henry's free hand felt along the white scar that was engraved across his back. Then Henry did something he knew he would regret—he hesitated and he didn't even know why. But in that split second, Jack opened his eyes as his arm shot out and grabbed Henry's ankle. Before Henry could react, Jack pulled Henry's leg out from under him, picked up his sword and stood up before Henry had even hit the ground.

Henry tried to scramble away, but Jack got behind his head and stepped on both his upper arms, pinning him to the ground with nothing to do but look up Jack's nose. Smiling, Jack put a hand on his hip and brought his sword in front of him, admiring how it reflected the moonlight.

"You know, Captain Roark, I dreamt of this moment for a long time. You see, Henry—may I call you Henry—it took me a long, long time to recover from those chest and stomach wounds you gave me. Not to mention that I had to spend nearly a year in prison for dueling.

"When I got out—stop wiggling—I bought a cheap ship. Beautiful ship. Then I hired my own band of begotten miscreants and became Captain Jack Burton of the *Blood Water*—ever heard of me—I plunder and steal whatever I want. But about a year ago, I decided it was time to search you out and get my revenge.

"I found you in England, which surprised me. I never thought I'd see you there, in that tavern one day. You were with three other men, do you remember? So, I followed your every move until I could find your weakness—

please stop moving, Henry. I'll kill you when I'm good and ready. Anyway, I thought I had you on the Atlantic. Did you see me? I was surprised to see you run. Nevertheless, I don't blame you. If I had a wench like that, I would do everything I could to keep her from someone like me too. In fact, I've determined that she is your weakness. Henry, stop moving. You're not going to throw me off balance.

"I decided that after I kill you and most of you men—I will have my crew sneak into their bedrooms at night—I will offer my services to that young woman. She'll be in such distress and relieved for an opportunity to return home that she will accept my offer. Except I won't," Jack snickered to himself. "But I do intend to think of you when I spread her legs around my hips and plunge myself—"

Billy charged out of the darkness and plowed into Jack, toppling him to the ground with Billy landing on top of Jack. Henry retrieved his weapon and got to his feet in time to hear a heart wrenching groan escape from his first mate. Henry looked down to discover a sliver of moonlight protruding from Billy's side. It lingered there for a moment before Jack slid his sword from Billy's body. Billy clutched his side and rolled over, sweating and already beginning to grow pale.

Shaking, Jack stood up. He looked from Billy to Henry and felt a vile taste rise in his throat. In the moonlight, Jack could make out Henry's eyes and saw that they were dark and narrow. He knew that Henry would kill him without a second thought. Fighting an enraged man is hopeless and, with that thought in mind, Jack turned on his heels and dashed into the forest.

There was loud, continuous banging on the door downstairs. Lord Ellingsworth flew out of bed and ran down the steps. Out of breath, he reached the door before anyone else in the household even appeared in the foyer. He peered out the window and ordered the gathering servants back to their rooms. When he spied his wife lingering at the side of the foyer, he instructed her to return to bed. Once everyone had left the room, he opened the door.

"William!" Lord Ellingsworth exclaimed, voice filled with irritation. "What the hell are you doing here at two o'clock in the morning?"

Wexford held a lad of about three-and-ten at his side. Sneering, he slammed the boy to the marble tile at his feet. Lord Ellingsworth looked down and saw that the boy's wrists were bound painfully behind him. "I got the son of a bitch."

Lord Ellingsworth smiled. "You mean—"

"Yes."

"Where's your son?" Lord Ellingsworth asked, with a quick glance behind his friend.

Wexford chuckled. "Last I heard, he was busy with Towson's daughter Julian, or something like that. You know, I always liked the way her hips moved when she walked."

"Good for him," Lord Ellingsworth said, forcing himself to smile.

"Well, can I come in?" Wexford asked, licking his lips.

"Not here—the family's home. Let's go down to my office and have this…discussion," Lord Ellingsworth said, grabbing his jacket. With a glance over his shoulder, he stepped out into the chilly night air.

Elizabeth didn't go back to bed as her husband had ordered her to. She and Mary hid in the dining room and watched from the window as her husband and Wexford grabbed the boy by his ankles and dragged him, face against the ground, down the steps and on the cobblestone path to Wexford's waiting carriage. Together, they tossed him onto the floor of the coach and kicked him aside as they climbed inside.

Elizabeth waited for the carriage to speed off before she reached for her shawl. "Something is going on. Let's go," she said, handing Mary one of Adelina's long forgotten shawls.

Without another word, Elizabeth and Mary left the house. They hid behind bushes and parked carriages to keep from being sighted. Elizabeth didn't think about the drunks or muggers or any other scoundrels that were out at this time of night. Her only thoughts and concerns were about her daughter. She knew in her heart that this boy could be the key to finding Adelina.

After nearly almost an hour Elizabeth and Mary had traveled the five blocks that distanced the house and Lord Ellingsworth's office building. The windows were dark and there was no sign of Wexford's carriage.

"Let's go around back," Elizabeth whispered. Cautiously, she moved around the back of the building, keeping a listening ear out for her husband. She came to a window and stood on her toes to peer in. In the darkness, Elizabeth could make out a vague shape of the boy on the floor. Elizabeth moved to the back door and turned the handle, not surprised when she found it locked. "We have to get in there."

Mary nodded. "Excuse me, mum."

Elizabeth stepped aside and stood uncomfortably amazed as Mary took a hairpin from her hair. With ease, Mary jiggled the lock open, feeling Elizabeth's heavy eyes on her as she walked past her to enter the building.

Mary stumbled blindly in the shadows for a moment before she found an oil lamp. She lit it and grimaced at the thick smell of blood. She heard a faint, wet groan come from the next room. They followed the sound to a naked, mangled body on the floor.

"Oh, my God," Mary mumbled. She knelt beside the body, feeling warm feeling of blood against her knees. Carefully, she removed the gag from his mouth. "Mum, he's still breath'n."

Elizabeth knelt down next to Mary in the same pool of blood. She took the lamp from Mary and held it close to the boy's feet and tried to wipe some of the blood with her shawl only to discover that he was missing two toes. In disgust, Elizabeth moved the lamp up his body, finding deep puncture wounds along his thighs and stomach from a fire poker that lay off to the side. There were long, shallow cuts from a knife on his torso that cut through his body from his naval to his neck. His left nipple was burnt and charred, black from the damage done. His right index finger and left earlobe were removed.

"Mary, I need you to run to Doctor Mason's house. Tell him to come here right away and bring some men to help. Now—go!" Elizabeth commanded. Mary nodded and left.

Elizabeth slipped her fingers into the boy's good hand. "You'll be alright. Do you hear me? You're going to be just fine," she whispered. She thought she saw the boy's lips move for a moment, but it was hard to tell in the candlelight.

Elizabeth didn't know how much time had passed since Mary left. Nor had she any idea where her husband went or even if he was coming back. The possibility of him walking in and discovering her over the boy…she didn't want to think about it the consequences.

She heard the door creak open in the other room and heavy footsteps entered. Elizabeth wet her fingertips and put them to candle wick, plunging the room into darkness. She held her breath, too afraid that even the slightest movement would give her away.

"Mum?" came a soft voice.

"Mary, thank God," Elizabeth said, breathing a sigh of relief. She could see faint movement in the darkness behind her servant. She felt her heart leap into her throat again when she heard whispering. A match was struck and a lantern was lit, warming the room with its soft glow. Elizabeth could see the doctor holding the lamp with three other men standing behind him.

"Lady Ellingsworth?" the doctor asked, stepping forward.

"Doctor Mason, I think he's still alive," Elizabeth whispered.

The doctor knelt beside the young man and held the lantern next to the body. In the light, Elizabeth could see the doctor's eyebrow twitch and his jaw clench as he looked over the wounds. He turned to the three men waiting beside Mary. "I want one of you to get the board from outside. The other two, help me dress these wounds quickly. We'll take him back to my office and finish there."

Elizabeth stood up and took Mary in her arms, pulling her aside so that the men could move more freely. She found herself smoothing Mary's hair as she had done to Adelina when something was bothering her.

One of Mason's men gave Elizabeth and Mary a ride home about a half an hour later. He offered to return in the morning with news, but Elizabeth denied his request, fearing it would make her husband suspicious. Instead, she made arrangements to stop by in the afternoon or the following morning. She thanked the man and quickly dismissed him.

Elizabeth and Mary raced up the stairs. She gave Mary her bloody shawl and began to remove her nightgown.

"Listen, Mary. I want you to take these and hide them in your room," Elizabeth ordered as she handed the blood-soaked gown to Mary. She poured water into a basin and began to wipe blood off her skin.

"Yes, mum," Mary said shifting her gaze to the floor.

"Good. Tomorrow, I don't care when, as long as no one sees you, burn them. And yours as well," Elizabeth instructed. "Do you understand—"

Downstairs, a door slammed shut. Rapid, heavy footsteps ascended the stairs.

"That's Jonathon. Mary, go!" Elizabeth ordered, nearly pushing Mary from the room. Elizabeth closed the door behind the maid and ran back to the basin. She quickly scrubbed the remaining stains off her skin and picked up the bowl. With little else to do, Elizabeth opened a window and dumped the red water outside.

Lord Ellingsworth had one hell of a night. The pirate's informant never said a single word and had received tremendous torture because of his dedicated silence. *In all honesty*, Lord Ellingsworth told himself as he dragged himself up the stairs, *it was William who held the instruments. I was just helpless to stop it.*

He made Wexford stop after he took the finger off. Lord Ellingsworth thought for sure that the kid was dead. *There was so much blood. No one could have lived through it.*

He couldn't be in there, with that disgusting smell of blood. He asked Wexford if they could go to the tavern down the road for a while before they decided what else to do and clean up the mess. When they got back four hours later, the body was gone—it just disappeared.

Lord Ellingsworth reached the top of the stairs and saw Mary cross the landing. Apparently she had come from the room he shared with his wife. *What would Elizabeth be doing up at this hour?*

Lord Ellingsworth fists tightened at his sides as he took long strides to the door. He turned the handle and pushed open the door. He discovered his wife dressed only in moonlight, standing by the window. She put the basin she was holding on the windowsill and faced him. *She looks beautiful*, Lord Ellingsworth decided. *Maybe my night might not be so bad after all.*

Thousands of miles across the ocean, another door slammed shut. Someone downstairs was screaming for help, disturbing the entire household. Adelina sat up and watched Catherine and Thomas pick up their weapons and run from the room.

Adelina tried to swing her legs over the bed, but her feet got tangled in the covers. It took her a few brief moments, but she managed to kick them off and stand up. She scurried to the door and threw it open. As soon as Adelina took a step from the room and into the hallway, Henry and Thomas turned the corner. They struggled to carry Billy's large, unconscious body between them. Adelina fought from gagging when she saw that his right side was covered in blood.

"Move, wench!" Henry grunted. Adelina didn't move. She stood there dumbfounded, rooted to the spot. "Damn it, Adelina, get the door!"

Adelina blinked twice before she flew into action. She skirted down the hallway and flung open the first door she came to. It was the upstairs study. She went to the next door and threw it open: a bedroom. She stepped aside so that Henry and Thomas could pass her. They carefully placed Billy on the bed and propped him up with pillows. Fresh blood trickled from under his shirt, turning the white sheets a dark red.

Catherine ran into the room moments later, juggling an armful of bandages and bottles of medicine. "Masta—here!" she said, thrusting everything into his arms.

"Can I help?" Adelina offered, stepping into the room. She caught sight of Catherine removing Billy's shirt, displaying the gaping wound beneath it. "Oh, God—" Adelina groaned and turned to expel her stomach contents in the nearest corner.

"Attractive," Henry muttered over Catherine's head. "Go wait in the hall, my dear."

Red-faced, Adelina wiped her lips. "I think you might be right."

"Oh, and, Adelina…send up a maid or two," Henry said after her.

It was midmorning before Henry emerged from Billy's room. He took a deep breath as he closed the door behind him. Taking a step, he nearly tripped over Adelina, sleeping against the doorframe. Henry sat down next to her and reached for her hand, causing Adelina to stir.

"How is he?" Adelina mumbled.

Henry sighed. "I don't know. He's weak now, but he should make it. But if infection sets in…he saved my life."

Henry and Adelina sat in silence and listened to Catherine's movement through the walls. Slowly, Henry lifted his arm and slid it over Adelina's shoulders. She leaned into him and rested her head against the crick of his neck.

"He'll be alright. Just wait and see," Adelina whispered.

"I hope so," Henry mumbled as he laid his head heavily on hers. His eyelids dropped and his breathing slowed as he drifted off to sleep.

Adelina sighed and breathed in his scent of sweat and blood. She lay against him, enjoying his closeness. *I've never felt this before.* Adelina smiled to herself, nestling closer to Henry.

Light quick footsteps sounded, disrupting her thoughts. Adelina looked up to find Michelle, red-faced and thin-lipped, stampeding down the hall. Her fists were in tight little balls at her sides and swung like heavy pendulums.

Adelina got to her feet, causing Henry to awaken. "Hello, Miss Debnam. Pardon me, but I think that I will go and look in on Billy," she said, ducking into the bedroom. She felt like a coward, hiding from Michelle, but she was in no mood to put up with someone she didn't have to.

Inside, Adelina looked around. The room was slightly smaller than her own and much darker. There was a deerskin rug on the floor and a select assortment of weaponry displayed on the wall. The bed was in the center of the room, with the iron headboard against the right wall. The curtains were drawn tightly to prevent to morning sun from filtering into the bedroom. The only source of light came from a few low burning candles by the bedside. Catherine sat on the corner of the bed, lightly wiping the perspiration from Billy's forehead. Adelina looked into the housekeeper's lap, where the bodice of her cream-colored nightgown was caked with dried blood. Thomas knelt on the floor, holding onto Billy's hand.

"How is he?" Adelina asked.

"He's sleeping. At least he made it through the night, that's a good sign," Catherine said without looking up from Billy.

"I'll sit with him—er—that is, if you like," Adelina offered.

Catherine nodded and stood up. She gave Adelina the washcloth and nodded to Thomas, hinting that he could use the time to rest as well. "I'll be back in an hour to change his dressings."

Adelina sat down and reached for Billy's hand. It was cold and clammy, but she could still feel a hint of warmth. She turned and watched Catherine straighten her skirt and open the door for Thomas.

"Henry, I really don't—" Michelle hissed in the hallway.

"Drop it, Michelle," Henry answered her.

Adelina watched him walk past Michelle and heard his bedroom door close down the hall. Catherine nodded her greetings to Michelle and closed the door behind her, plunging the room back into his silence and gloom.

The tranquility only lasted for a brief second for the moment the latched clicked shut, the door reopened. Michelle stepped in, slowly closing the door behind her. Adelina watched as Michelle walked around the bed and approached her, swinging her hips in a purposeful way with her arms clenched behind her. Adelina turned away from her and forced herself to focus wiping the sweat that had accumulated on Billy's brow.

Adelina felt Michelle lean over her shoulder. She could smell her heavy perfume and choked back a cough. The silence and tension in the air grew so quickly that Adelina felt like she would suffocate. She coughed lightly to clear her throat, hoping that Michelle would take the hint and move back a few paces.

Michelle didn't move. She was so close to her ear that Adelina could hear her swallow. No one spoke and the deadly silence made her ears ring. Finally, Adelina could stand it no longer. "Can I help you?" whispered Adelina, cutting through the stillness. It felt as though she had screamed the words.

"No."

Adelina nodded. "Then…can you move? I hate it when people look over my shoulder."

"I'm fine, thank you."

Abruptly, Adelina stood up, knocking Michelle's chin with her shoulder. Adelina walked around the bed and sat back down. Calmly and softly, she began to stroke Billy's cheek, praying that he'd wake up and save her from Michelle.

Adelina felt Michelle's eyes bore down on her. It made her skin burn and sent cold shivers down her back. To distract her mind from Michelle, Adelina focused on Billy by caressing his check. Adelina adjusted in her seat and pulled Billy's hand in her lap. *What is Michelle's problem, anyway?*

The uptight wench sitting on the bed is my problem, Michelle thought. *Ever since Henry brought her to Barbuda, he's been a little distracted. Whenever Adelina is around, Henry always focuses on her. I finally got close enough to Henry that he might ask for my hand in marriage again, or at least start inviting me to his bed. It's this little bitch thinks that she can stay here and put everything to hell. It makes my blood boil just thinking that Adelina is betrothed to another man and here she is with mine. At least she's a pawn in Henry's plan, meaning nothing to Henry. Or she had better be.*

Michelle crossed her arms over her breasts and grounded her teeth. *The way Adelina is touching Billy is almost caring, not once had I seen Adelina touch Henry in that way. Maybe Henry should be aware of this attraction. After all, Billy is rather handsome, strong and probably perfectly capable in bed. Not to mention that when Henry retires, Billy is entitled to be promoted to captain. Adelina deserves to have Billy if she is unable to return to her betrothed*, Michelle decided. *I'll rid of her one way or another.*

Adelina turned to Michelle. "What do you want?"

"Nothing," Michelle smiled. *Adelina isn't competition*, Michelle determined as she eyed her up and down. Michelle swung on her heels and strolled out of the room, carefully shutting the door behind her.

Adelina sat in the silence again, listening to Billy's shallow breathing. She reached for the washcloth and began patting Billy's brow with it. Carefully, with her free hand, Adelina lifted up the covers. Billy lacked a shirt and there was a large amount of dried blood on his chest and the sheet. But the bandages around his stomach remained clean—that's a good sign.

"It's too damn quiet in here," Adelina said softly. "So, I'm going to talk and you're just going to listen."

Henry stepped from his room, barely managing not to be clabbered over by Catherine. He felt exhausted from the night before and his narrow escape from Michelle. He tried to sleep, but all he could do was toss and turn and think about Billy.

Henry turned and followed Catherine down the hallway toward Billy's bedroom. She juggled an armload of fresh bandages and struggled to free a hand to open the door. Henry went around her and reached for the door handle.

"Do you hear that?" Henry asked as he cracked open the door.

Catherine nudged Henry aside. "He's awake!" she exclaimed pushing the door open with her large body.

Adelina immediately stopped talking and looked up to find Catherine and Henry rushing to Billy's bedside.

"Is he awake?" Henry asked kneeling down next to Adelina.

"No, not yet."

"I heard voices," Henry said, growing irritated.

"It was me," Adelina muttered. "I was just talking."

Catherine shook her head. "He needs his rest, dear."

Adelina stood up. "I'm sorry. It was just so quiet in here that I took the opportunity to get some things off my chest. You know, talk to someone who'll listen."

Henry chuckled, standing up. "And an unconscious man is just about the only person who'll listen to you."

Adelina glared at him. "I'm sorry. Being kidnapped right before getting married is just a tad bit stressful," she said sarcastically.

Henry laughed. "Imagine being the kidnapper. I almost didn't think I'd make it in time. And then I had to find something to wear..."

Adelina awoke the next morning to loud disturbance downstairs. She donned her robe and slippers and cautiously tiptoed down the grand staircase to see what was happening. She found Henry and Sir Cumberland in the foyer, nearly screaming at each other.

"No! I won't let you see her!" Henry yelled, his fists in tight balls at his side.

Sir Cumberland stood a few feet in front of Henry, hands clenched to the umbrella he carried. His voice remained calm and even. "I promised Adelina."

"I really don't care. Get off my property before I—" Henry said raising one fist. He was not about to let this man seduce Adelina in his own home.

Adelina stepped off the staircase and marched between the two men. Facing Henry, she asked calmly, "Is that any way to treat a guest, milord?"

"Adelina, get up to your room," Henry said through gritted teeth. Despite the robe, he could still faintly see the curves of her body. He wanted to reach out and caress her breasts until her nipples rose in little peaks as he had done the night before. *It can't be like this*.

"My dear," Sir Cumberland said from behind. "I'm here to receive that letter you wanted to send to your family."

Adelina turned to Sir Cumberland with a large smile. "Oh, that's right! I had forgotten about it with all that commotion yesterday. Let me write them a note. You can wait in the parlor. It won't take but a moment."

Adelina quickly left the foyer, feeling Henry glaring at her back. She entered the study and found Henry's box of stationary sitting on the corner of his desk. She removed the folded notes on top and took out a few sheets of paper from the box. Adelina grabbed the quill and ink next to it and brought it closer. She dipped the quill into the ink and paused, feeling along the raised H and R and smiled.

Several minutes later, Adelina returned to the parlor. She found Sir Cumberland waiting patiently by the window overlooking the garden. Henry remained seated, arms crossed, glaring hard at the wall across from him.

"Here it is," she said, handing the sealed envelope to Sir Cumberland.

He took it graciously and smiled. "Thank you, miss. I'll be sure to keep it safe until I reach England." He leaned forward to plant a light kiss on Adelina's cheek. Henry stood up behind him. "I'll see myself out. Thank you, Mister Roark."

The moment the door clicked shut Henry stepped in front of Adelina, preventing her from leaving the room. "What did it say?"

"I told my mother that I missed her. And I told Christopher a happy late birthday and that I will try to get him some real pirate booty. I also told them that I was alright and that I love and miss them. Is that permitted?" Adelina asked, crossing her arms and leveling her gaze.

Henry took a breath and his dark blue eyes softened. "Yes, I suppose it's fine. I'm sure you miss them greatly."

"Why, thank you, milord," Adelina said sarcastically.

Henry moved to the door. "Oh, and, Adelina...we don't greet our guests in nightclothes," Henry said, leaving the parlor.

There was a good thirty to forty more men at the manor than what Adelina had grown used to. Most, she recognized from Henry's recent voyage from England, in which she had traveled. Several were there to give Billy their wishes, but the majority acted as though they were guarding the estate. Four of these men seem to follow her. Disturbed, Adelina asked Catherine about them.

"They're here to protect ye," she had said. "No one can leave here without me or the Masta's permission."

Adelina laughed when Catherine had told her how Michelle came to the house one afternoon while Henry was on the ship. Catherine had denied her entry, infuriating Michelle. Michelle had ranted and raged for hours, threatening to have Catherine sent back to Europe. But the housekeeper simply crossed her arms and said that no one is permitted without consent, and Michelle did not have her consent. Only when Henry saw Michelle was she given clearance.

For two and a half weeks, Adelina noticed that Henry was particularly concerned with patrolling the estate. He often spent most of the day on the *North Star* or patrolling the grounds on Buttercup, searching for Jack.

Michelle had arrived and convinced Henry to spend the morning with her, forcing Adelina to excuse herself to the veranda. She didn't mind being outside in the late June afternoon with a book in her lap. As long as she wasn't around Michelle, Adelina wouldn't have cared if it rained.

Adelina laughed at a comical retort that the wife of Bath said in Chaucer's *The Canterbury's Tales* in a weak effort to ignore the ever watching eyes all around her.

One set of eyes belonged to Henry. He had crept from the porch and silently made his way down to the veranda. He saw Adelina there, with a sly smile on her face and was half tempted to turn around and return to the house.

"Henry," Adelina called from the chair. "Good afternoon."

"Hello, Adelina. How are you this afternoon?" Henry greeted as he walked to the chair across from her. With a smile, he sat down.

"I'm fine," Adelina said as she closed the book. "Henry, can I ask you something?"

"Anything, my sweet," Henry said. He put a heavy boot on the table between them. He knew where this was going.

"Are you avoiding me?"

"No," Henry lied. He was avoiding her like he would the Black Death. He found it quite difficult since they lived in the same house and he so badly wanted to be near her. *That's the problem. Even after these past two weeks, I could still see her in the chemise and still feel the soft touch of her skin*, he thought. "I thought you were avoiding me and I figured that you could use the space."

Adelina shifted under his gentle gaze. She was avoiding him and had found it pretty easy. She spent her time with sitting with Billy or helping Catherine around the house. Whenever Michelle came to visit, Adelina would escape and sit by the water to read. She wanted to be with Henry, to feel his touch again. Late at night she would felt wetness between her thighs when she thought about what had almost happened. "No, not at all."

Henry nodded, finding nothing more to say.

Adelina found herself in the same predicament and offered him a quick smile before she averted her eyes away from him. She was thankful when Thomas came around outside.

"Cap'n! He's awake! Billy's awake!" Thomas cried. He spun back around and ran inside.

Adelina and Henry sprang from their seats. Without thinking, he reached for Adelina's hand and was caught off guard when she took it. With her free hand, Adelina lifted her skirts and together they ran inside.

Henry barged into the room first, with Adelina on his heels. Catherine stood next to the bed with a wide smile on her face. Billy was sitting up against propped pillows, inspecting the wound beneath the bandages.

"Billy, my friend!" Henry called, approaching the bed.

"Hey, Cap'n." Billy smiled from the bed. He grimaced as he adjusted himself to face Adelina. "Miss."

"Hello, Billy," Adelina said softly as she patted Billy's feet through the bed sheets.

Henry looked up and saw the gentleness in her eyes. Fighting to keep his smile, he pulled up a chair. "'Tis nice to see that you're going to live. Did you have a nice nap?"

Billy nodded.

"How's your side?" Henry asked.

"Hurts like a bitch."

Catherine smacked him lightly in the head with the washcloth.

"Sorry. It hurts really bad," Billy mumbled, with a smile. He yawned as he rubbed his eye.

"Alright, everyone," Catherine said. "We're all glad Billy's awake, but he needs his sleep. Now, ye all get out and Thomas and me will change his bandages and ye all can come back in the morn'n."

Henry stood up. "Come on, my dear."

"Yes, milord," Adelina said to Henry. She turned back to Billy with a smile. "Goodnight, Billy. You'll be up and about in no time."

Henry placed a hand softly on Adelina's lower back as they left the room. "Care for dinner?"

Adelina nodded, putting a hand to her stomach. "I'm starving."

They agreed to have meat and bread on the dock where they could see the ship. Henry brought a blanket and smoothed it along the edge of the dock while Adelina lit the lantern. She removed her slippers and dangled her toes in the water. Henry sat down next to her and handed Adelina her plate of meat. She thanked him and took a bite.

"Why aren't you eating?" Adelina asked, using a slender hand to cover her mouth.

"Not hungry," Henry said, roughly. He tore a piece of bread from its loaf and dropped it into the water. It floated for a moment before it casually slipped below the surface.

"Is something wrong? You seem like you're lost in thought," Adelina asked after swallowing.

"No," Henry lied. His thoughts were elsewhere. *Michelle was right. Adelina does care for Billy.* "I was just thinking about Billy."

"Me too. I'm glad he's going to be alright," Adelina said, finishing off her dinner.

"I'm glad you two are getting along so well," Henry muttered. He stood up and tossed his plate of meat into the river. Without another word he began marching back to the house.

Adelina turned and watched Henry stop to talk to one of his men. They exchanged a few words and Henry pointed at her. Then he continued on his way as the other man walked in Adelina's direction.

The man never approached her, nor attempted to make conversation. He simply stood there where the dock meets the sand with his hands clamped to his sides and a blank, open stare on his face.

Adelina shuddered and turned her attention back to the river. The ship loomed in front of her and looked ominous against the black sky. It was hard to believe that filthy, murderous pirates sailed in the vessel.

Pirates like Henry, Adelina remembered. *I keep forgetting that. Why did he storm off in the way that he did? What did I say?* Adelina knew it wasn't like her to sit around and wait for an answer. She didn't have that kind of patience. She needed to find Henry and figure out what is going on.

Adelina stood up and folded the blanket. She picked up the lantern and followed Henry's path back to the house. She left the blanket and lantern on the kitchen table and headed for the parlor. Henry wasn't in there. Nor was he in the library. Determined, Adelina headed for the stairs. But a carriage parked outside the window caught her. She recognized it as Michelle's carriage.

Adelina quickened her pace as she climbed the staircase. She peeked into the study and found it empty. *He must be in Billy's room*, Adelina thought. She passed by her bedroom and was about to knock on Billy's door when she heard faint voices from where she had just come.

Moving toward the voices, Adelina noticed that Henry's bedroom door was slightly ajar. She was about to knock on his when she heard Michelle's voice. "Henry, believe me, I'm right about Adelina."

Adelina froze. *What is Michelle's doing in his room? What is Michelle right about? Hmm, I've never noticed this painting before*, Adelina thought as she moved in front of a large oil painting of a man on horseback, hanging on the short wall that divided Adelina and Henry's bedroom doors.

"I know, Michelle. I saw it. You were right," Henry said softly. He mumbled something that Adelina didn't hear.

"At least they'll be happy," Michelle said. "We will too…just you wait." Adelina didn't have to be in the room to know that Michelle was tossing her hair back and pushing her small breasts outward. She always did that when Henry was around. "I'll make the arrangements. You won't have to worry about a thing, my love,"

My love? Adelina's head screamed. She heard footsteps approaching the bedroom door and she barely managed to duck into her room, nearly knocking over a table as she did so. She thought about running back to the door and closing it, but she feared it would attract their attention. Shaking, Adelina stood by the table and held her breath. Henry and Michelle stopped in front of her doorway.

"Forgive me, Michelle, for not seeing you home. I'm rather tired tonight," Henry said, plainly.

"That's alright. Goodnight, my sweet," Michelle said. She stood on her toes to plant a kiss on Henry's lips, but he tilted his head and her lips landed on his cheek. Michelle stuck out her bottom lip in a pout for a second but he didn't look at her. She forced a smile, and turned to leave. Adelina could hear her footsteps down the hall and stairs.

Henry didn't move. He strained to hear the sound of the front door closing. After the informative sound that assured Michelle had left the house, Henry took a deep breath and turned to go back to his room. Adelina relaxed, but a split second later, Henry filled her doorway.

Adelina felt her heart lurch into her throat. Her room was dark and she hid in the shadows. She couldn't see his face to read his expression. *Could he see me? Did he know I was here?*

"Adelina?" Henry called into the room.

She didn't answer. He stood in the doorway for another minute before returning to his room. As soon as Adelina heard his door close, she skirted from the shadows and softly closed the bedroom door. With a sigh, she leaned back against the door. In front of her stood the table she was standing next to, silhouetted by the pale moonlight that came through the balcony doors.

After a curse, Adelina slowly undressed and changed into her chemise, letting her thoughts wander in the dark.

Henry is Michelle's now, Adelina thought as she climbed into bed and pulled the covers over her legs. *It's just as well. I'm still betrothed to Brandon.*

Adelina shuddered and rolled onto her side. *It's no use trying to sleep*, she thought as the first tear fell.

It was the following Friday that Adelina wandered down from her room to find Michelle walking through the foyer with a young servant boy following behind her, writing frantically what was being said.

"Oh, hello," Michelle said curtly as she passed Adelina up the staircase.

"Can I help you?" Adelina asked.

She acts like she owns the place. Michelle smiled. "Oh, I'm just getting a list together of things to do."

"Oh, alright," Adelina shrugged. She felt her stomach growl with hunger and decided to forget about Michelle as she climbed down the staircase.

"Let's do downstairs, first," Michelle said to the lad behind her. She pointed to a corner near a window. "I want a plant there—in that corner—ferns or something. And I want all those guns taken down from the foyer. I want a new chandelier brought in, and I want the candles lit every Sunday night. I want the ballroom completely refurnished and cleaned in, oh let's say, three weeks. That's where we'll have the reception."

Adelina rolled her eyes as she stepped off the landing and made her way to the kitchen. Michelle followed her, repeating her demands.

"And I want this kitchen painted pink. And a French cook. A good one. Not one of those British cooks who think they're French. And he just has to have a mustache," Michelle said. She looked over the shoulder of the boy as he wrote down what she said. "I want pasta every Tuesday night for dinner and a cup of tea every morning for breakfast. No coffee. There will be no coffee in this household the minute I come."

Adelina reached across the counter and pulled a banana from its bunch. Adelina rolled her eyes. "But Henry drinks coffee in the morning."

Michelle's eyes narrowed. "Or bananas. They're disgusting. Even the smell of them."

Adelina's curiosity was peaked. "What's going on?"

"Oh, Henry and I are to be married! Didn't he tell you? I'm just planning what I want done now so that way he can get started on it for our wedding day," Michelle said in a light tone.

"How wonderful. Let me know if there is anything I can do to help," Adelina said sarcastically as she peeled a banana. She took a step closer to Michelle and took a big bite of the fruit, humming softly as she enjoyed it.

Michelle made a revolting face as she watched Adelina chew the banana. She rolled her eyes and left the kitchen. Through the door, Adelina could hear her bark more orders as she moved about the next room.

Smiling, Adelina walked outside and spat the fruit out behind the bushes. "Blah," she said. *I hate bananas.*

Michelle remained in the house until dinner. She made sure that she was seated next to Henry and across from Billy before Adelina entered the room. Adelina walked in and saw Michelle sitting next to Henry, caressing his fingertips and felt the urge to walk back out. Instead, she held her head up high and sat next to Thomas.

"And I'm going to have new carpets and new curtains and new bed sheets and that cute little desk in the shop of Sarah's store. And that library will be my sewing room and...let's see what else?" Michelle paused. She glanced at Adelina. "Oh, I can't wait, Henry. It'll be lovely. This time. I promise."

Adelina watched in disgust as Michelle blew a kiss to Henry. He didn't say a word throughout dinner as Michelle talked on and on about how she wanted to change the house. He simply stared ahead.

Michelle turned to Adelina. "Will you be here for the wedding, Adelina?"

Henry shifted his gaze to Adelina, his eyes softening with apologies.

Adelina fought a sudden urge to reach across the table and strangle the woman in front of her. Instead, she shrugged. *Not unless Hell freezes over— and we* are *in the Caribbean.*

"Henry, are you feeling alright?" Michelle asked, turning her attention back to man next to her.

He nodded, distantly. He looked over at Adelina, making contact with her honey brown orbs. She smiled, softly and he immediately felt his heart ache for a moment. "Excuse me, I think I shall lie down."

Adelina watched him push back his chair and leave the room. *He's been acting strange lately. I guess he's nervous about getting married.* She waited a few minutes as the dishes were being cleared before she excused herself and made her way to her room.

She walked to the balcony and leaned against the railing. With a long sigh, she turned and supported her weight on the railing using her elbows. The curtains to Henry's room were open and she could see inside. He was standing next to the wall they shared, with one palm against it, head down.

Adelina looked at him carefully, studying his stance in the candlelight. He looked as though he was hurting tremendously on the inside, as though he had lost something dear to him. It pained Adelina to look at him in such a state. She fought the urge to enter his room, take him into her arms and caress him.

Instead, she turned from Henry's room and entered hers. She walked along the wall to about the spot where she saw Henry standing. With a sad smile, she lightly touched it with her fingertips, picturing his hand on the other side of the wall touching hers.

A pain grew in her chest, as though her heart had given up and swallowed itself. She could feel herself longing for the man who had kidnapped her some months ago and wished for more than anything that the wall before her was gone. Then she thought of Michelle.

Adelina shook her head and stepped back. *It's no use anymore.*

Chapter Seven

Adelina sat sideways in the little dinghy boat that was always left tied to the dock, leaving her feet to dangle in the cool water. She wore a light peach dress that was bundled at her hips, not caring that she wore no undergarments to cover herself. The weather in Barbuda, even on this early May morning was much hotter than what she was used to back at home.

She heard footsteps echoing on the wooden dock and looked up to find Henry staring down at her.

"Hello, beautiful," Henry greeted as he tried not to notice Adelina's creamy thighs.

"Good morning, Henry," Adelina said, moving the hem of her dress back over her knees.

Henry smiled. "Would you like to go into town and put the final touches on your ball gown?"

"Oh, that's right!" Adelina exclaimed as she attempted to stand up, careful to keep herself balanced. "The ball is in two weeks!"

Henry reached a hand out for Adelina. "I can't believe you forgot. I have never known a woman to forget about a ball."

Adelina made a face at him as she reached up to accept his hand. With a grunt, she put a foot against the side of the dock as she had seen the men do. "Is Billy going to go?"

Henry looked away for a second at Billy's name, but he forced himself to return his attention to her and smile. "Not if I can help it. He's still complaining about his side."

Adelina nodded and lifted her other foot from the boat. Henry wasn't ready for the extra weight and lost his footing, dropping her back into the dinghy as he fell head first into the craft. His weight caused the boat to flip over, spilling Adelina and himself into the water.

Adelina stood up from the murky water gasping for air. Henry was standing next to her, laughing and rubbing his shoulder. The boat floated on its side, steadily sinking into the water. While he watched Adelina wipe the water from her face, he moved to the boat and corrected its position.

"Are you alright?" he asked.

Adelina smiled. "Yes, I'm fine," she lied. She could feel her wet hair lay heavily against her back and her feet slowly sinking into the thick sludge. She sidestepped Henry to get to the shore, but slipped in the mud.

Henry caught her by her waist just before she went back under the water. He slipped his arms around her and pulled her against his body. "Are you sure?"

"I hope so," Adelina said with a small chuckle. She felt herself slide in the mud again and flung her arms around Henry to steady herself.

"I'm sure," Henry said with a smile.

Adelina's smile died when it dawned on her how close she stood next to Henry. She could feel his heart beating in his chest almost as wildly as her own. She became aware of his strong muscles against her body, causing her nipples to rise under the thin fabric of her dress. His arms had encircled her, pulling her close to him. Adelina looked up, hoping Henry didn't know that she wanted him to feel her too.

But he could feel her. Henry could feel the silky touch of her skin, the brief, soft give of her breasts when she inhaled, and those tiny nipples pressing against him. And more than anything, he could feel her warmth. Suddenly, he felt the urge to be inside of that womanly heat.

"Henry?" Adelina muttered.

He looked down and saw Adelina's upturned face. Her eyes were half closed and her lips were slightly puckered. Those lips, those soft, cherry lips just begged to be kissed. "Yes, my love?"

"Um, Cap'n?" came a voice from the dock. Over Henry's shoulder, Adelina could see Thomas, turned away from them, but obvious as to what was going on.

Henry cursed loudly as he released Adelina. "What do you want, Thomas?"

"Uh, you told me to find you when the carriage is ready," Thomas reminded him, feeling rather awkward.

Henry groaned inward. "See that there is hot water for two baths and tell Norton to wait an hour."

"Yes, Cap'n," Thomas muttered before he ran back to the house to relay the message, leaving Henry and Adelina alone.

"Do you still want to go into town?" Henry asked. He struggled slightly as he pulled the boat farther onto the beach so that the incoming tide would not take the boat into the river.

"Yes, if we can," Adelina answered. She picked up the hem of her dress as she stepped from the water onto the sand. She avoided Henry's eyes and didn't speak to him as they made their way back to the house and upstairs to their separate rooms.

Adelina waited nearly ten minutes on the cold marble tile for the water to heat up. She ditched her wet gown in a corner and slipped into the hot bath the moment the hot steam grew in the air. She poured scented oils into the sweltering water and picked up the bar of soap. Adelina vigorously began rubbing the soap over her body and in her hair.

When her skin was red and raw, Adelina stepped from the tub. She dried herself with the towel and dressed again, this time in a light lavender dress with loose sleeves that draped over her shoulder. She quickly brushed the knots from her hair and pinned it high on her head so that her neck could remain cool in the afternoon heat. With a smile, she left her room and descended down the stairs.

Henry was waiting by the door. Catherine was with him, holding a picnic basket. He looked up and smiled, his blue eyes beaming with delight, as Adelina stepped off the bottom step.

"Are you ready, Adelina?" Henry asked, just barely above a whisper.

"Yes, milord," Adelina answered as she wrapped a light shawl around her shoulders.

Adelina, followed by Henry and Catherine, walked out to the waiting carriage. Norton and Thomas were finishing re-securing the horses and gave them a warm smile. Henry lifted a hand to help Adelina into the coach before climbing in himself.

Through the small window, Adelina watched Thomas enter the house. She saw Norton kiss Catherine on the fingertips and kneel down before the carriage's high step. Catherine laughed and stepped on his knee before climbing upon the bench.

Adelina smiled. "How sweet."

Henry gave her a questioning look, then turned to gaze out the other window. The carriage jolted into motion with the quick turn around the drive, causing Adelina to fall into his lap.

"I'm sorry," she mumbled as she lifted herself up and returned to her seat.

"It's alright," Henry whispered. But the damage had already been done. He felt her against him, even for that split moment. His arm had brushed against her breast, and her hair had fallen softly over his elbow. Her perfume—jasmine and a hint of lavender—still lingered around him. Oddly, he found that he wished that the carriage would jolt again.

Henry didn't trust himself to speak, afraid that his words might betray him. He closed his eyes and pretended to nap, unable to stop himself as he thought of Adelina as she lay naked beneath him. He was thankful when carriage halted again in front of the garment shop.

Mister Bakeoven was conversing with a young woman outside his shop when he spotted Adelina and Henry climbing out of the coach. He shouted something inside and strolled over to greet them.

"Mister Roark, Henry, I see you finally arrived to retrieve the ball gown and the other garments you ordered for the misses," the thin, little man said as he shook Henry's hand.

"Other garments?" Adelina repeated in confusion. "I just have the one dress."

"Uh…yeah…I ordered you a few extra outfits so you'd have something new to wear," Henry mumbled as they stepped into the shop.

"Thank you." Adelina smiled, not knowing what else to say.

Catherine followed them in. "Now, Mister Bakeoven, where es the ball gown?"

"Susan! Bring me Roark's wardrobe!" Mister Bakeoven called toward the back. Minutes later, three petite girls, barely over the age of four and ten, carried twenty-two white boxes into the room. They giggled and whispered to each other when they laid the boxes at Henry's feet. They stood up and huddled together as they continued to whisper and snicker with each other. Mister Bakeoven cleared his throat and the girls immediately stopped dallying. With a brief curtsy, they departed.

Mister Bakeoven peeked into the top box and shook his head. He moved it aside and opened the second. "A-ha. Here it is!" he announced, pulling out the gown.

Adelina had to smother a laugh when the short man needed to raise his arms over his head to keep the hem from dragging on the floor. She forced her attention to the gown so that she could suppress her giggles.

Henry saw her distress and smiled. "Does the gown meet your liking, my dear?"

She turned to face him, her eyes shining with happiness. "Oh, Henry, it's beautiful. May I go try it on?"

Mister Bakeoven nodded and called for one of his assistants to tend to Adelina while she dressed. He smiled as Adelina followed the assistant to the back rooms, proud that he could bring such happiness to the girl. He turned back to Henry and Catherine and suggested that they sit on the couch while they waited. He presented them with coffee and tea on a silver serving tray and set it on the table. After they each took a cup, Mister Bakeoven sat down in the chair across from them.

The door opened and Mister Bakeoven stood up to welcome his guest. He stopped in his tracks and expelled a heavy sigh. "Good afternoon, Miss Debnam."

"Hello," Michelle said as she closed the door behind her. She crossed her arms and stared down at the little man. "Look, I'm tired of your excuses. I don't care how difficult the design was or how hard the material was to get. I want my gown and I want it—Henry, hello."

"Michelle." Henry smiled, putting his cup of coffee on the table and standing up.

Mister Bakeoven left the room and quickly returned with a white box. "I have your gown right here, Miss Debnam. I apologize for the—"

"Oh, yes. It's quite alright," Michelle said, taking the box without shifting her gaze from Henry. "Would you like to see it? It'll be the talk of the town."

Henry shrugged. "Sure."

Michelle beamed and rushed to one of the back rooms.

Henry gulped down his coffee and stared out the window. Mister Bakeoven refilled Henry's cup, feeling the growing tension. He tried to talk about the current gossip in the town, but Henry would simply nod or shake his head, not listening to a word being said. Catherine had turned on the couch to face the dressing room. She began tapping her foot with impatience as she sipped her tea.

Catherine put her cup of tea on the tray with a start, spilling some of the hot liquid over the rim. "Well, just look at ye! Mizz Adelina, I must say, ye are a pretty little thing."

Henry looked up when he saw Adelina take another step further into the room. The gown she wore was a pale yellow gold, the color the sun gives off just before a sunset. The neckline was wide and followed the curves of the top of her breasts before it gave into broad sleeves that draped over her shoulders. The materials of the sleeves were free and extended down just beyond her elbows making her look like an angel. The bodice held her tightly, accenting her womanly curves before it gently spread to the floor. At the moment, Adelina's hair, a sea of tumbling waves, flowed down her back with a few strands framing her face. Henry couldn't take his eyes off her—she was just too beautiful.

"What do you think?" Adelina asked a second time, bringing Henry's attention back to reality.

"Huh? Oh, it's nice," Henry said, bending over to pick up his coffee.

Adelina gave an uncertain nod as her smile faded. "I'm going to change back now," she said, trying to keep her voice normal in an effort to disguise her disappointment. She spun around to return to the dressing room.

After Adelina was out of earshot, Catherine turned to face Henry with her hands on her hips. "If ye were any younga, Masta Roark, I'd have ye ova my knee 'til ye apologized to Mizz Ellingsworth," she said, barely over a whisper.

Adelina turned the corner, spying Michelle in an olive green ball gown leaving the dressing room next to her own. She stopped as she waited for the woman to pass her.

"Hello, Miss Ellingsworth," she said curtly as she walked past Adelina.

Adelina was rooted to the spot, unable to tear herself away from the conversation that was being held in the other room.

"What do you think, Henry?" Michelle asked. Adelina was sure that, once again, Michelle was pushing her breasts outward again.

"You look wonderful," he answered.

"Then I'll see you…" Adelina didn't wait to hear the rest. She entered the dressing room and rapidly changed her clothes. She listened for Michelle to return to the dressing room before she stepped out.

Adelina found Henry pulling his change purse out of his coat pocket to pay Mister Bakeoven. Gratefully, Mister Bakeoven ordered the gowns to be brought outside to the carriage.

Henry looked up to find Adelina openly staring at him. With a smile, he extended his arm to escort her. She approached him, but didn't accept his offer.

"Thank you for the gowns, milord. I will pay you back in full upon my return to England," Adelina said through her clenched jaw.

Henry opened his mouth to say something, but she brushed past him and marched determinedly to the carriage where Norton was waiting.

"Are you hungry, Miss Adelina?" Norton asked as he helped her into the coach.

"No, Norton. I just want to go home," Adelina murmured as she climbed inside.

"Then to Roark Manor it is," he said with a nod as he walked away.

"No...England," Adelina whispered. But no one heard her.

Adelina passed Billy on the stairs. "I got my gown for the ball today."

Billy paused on the step. "Good, I'd like to see it."

Adelina nodded and quickened her pace up the stairs. She skipped to her room and closed the door behind her. Humming to herself, Adelina undressed and stepped into the ball gown. Catherine knocked once and entered in time to help Adelina button the tiny buttons along her spine.

"Try'n to show the Masta again, sweetie?" Catherine asked as she fastened the last button.

Adelina shook her head. "No, he doesn't care. But Billy asked to see it."

"Oh, Mizz Ellingsworth, he does care. He just doesn't know how to show it," Catherine said.

Adelina shrugged. "I don't think he does at all," she said as she opened the door. Catherine opened her mouth to say something, but Adelina quickly shut the door behind her, cutting the housekeeper off.

Adelina lifted the hem as she slowly tread down the steps so that she wouldn't trip and damage the gown. After a few minutes of searching, she found Billy sitting in the library reading a book.

"What do you think?" Adelina asked. She spun in a circle and curtsied.

Billy gripped his side as he stood up. "My, my, Miss Ellingsworth. You do look absolutely lovely. Any man would be lucky to take you to the ball."

"Why, thank you, Billy," Adelina blushed. She made an effort to turn and leave, but she spied Henry sprawled out on the couch against the wall. "I'm happy somebody thinks so."

Billy waited until Adelina left and began her ascent on the stairs. "Listen, Henry—"

Henry grunted as he stood up. "William, I've never seen her look more beautiful and more delighted," he said as he walked to the door. He paused in the doorway and rubbed the frame as though he was inspecting it. "You'll be very happy."

Billy watched his captain sulk away. He sighed and sat down to return to his book, curious as to what just passed between them.

Adelina sat alone at the dining table. Billy took his meal in his room as he often did when he was in pain. She figured that Thomas was with him. She noticed that the young lad looked up to Billy, spending much of his time with him, keeping him company and doing things for him.

Almost like a father, Adelina thought. *I wonder where Henry is tonight? Probably out with Michelle. Oh, I don't care where he is. He can do as he pleases.*

By the end of the meal, Adelina had numerous questions as to why she ate alone. But instead of wandering around the estate like she usually did in search of answers, she simply retired to her room. She prepared a hot bath, hoping it would raise her spirits, but she found that she couldn't relax in it. Instead, she crawled between the cool sheets of her bed for a restless night's sleep.

The next morning, Elizabeth received word from Doctor Mason. He had sent a young messenger boy while Lord Ellingsworth was away on business to tell the lady of the house that the lad was awake. The child also stated that she needed to come right away.

Elizabeth took a few coins from her purse and placed them gently in the boy's eager palm. "Thank you, young man."

The moment that the boy left, Elizabeth called for Mary. Immediately, Elizabeth arranged for her carriage and they left the house.

No one said a word during the twenty minute ride that ended in front of the doctor's home and office. Elizabeth stepped out and ran to the door with Mary on her heels. Doctor Mason opened the door the moment the women reached the stoop.

"Hurry, Lady Ellingsworth," he said, ushering them inside.

"We came as soon as we could, doctor," Elizabeth said.

Doctor Mason closed the door behind them. He pointed to a doorway off to the right. "This way."

"How is he, sir?" Elizabeth asked as she lifted her skirts to follow.

The doctor sighed. "Not good. An infection set in, causing him to swell and hallucinate. There's nothing much more I can do. He's been in and out of consciousness for the past two nights. And he's been mumbling something about Adelina. That's why I called for you…I thought you would want to see him," he said, stopping in front of the second white door.

"Will he make…" Elizabeth trailed off. She couldn't finish.

Doctor Mason shook his head. "He'll be lucky if he makes it until tonight."

Elizabeth took a deep breath as the doctor opened the door. She stepped into the room. It smelled thickly of stale blood, almost making her gag. There was a constant dripping sound, which she took as bad blood. She glanced around, noting that everything was white: white walls, white sheets, white marble, white curtains, white everything.

Slowly, Elizabeth walked to the bed. The young lad whose face had haunted her dreams for the past three weeks laid in the bed sleeping. He had bloody bandages wrapped around his head and ear. Slowly, as not to alarm him, Elizabeth slipped her fingers inside of his. He immediately opened his eyes and attempted to sit up. He struggled for a brief moment before giving up and returning his head to the pillow. Weakly, he opened his mouth to say something.

"I…I didn't hear you, Sweetheart," Elizabeth whispered as she leaned closer. Her ear barely touched his lips before she could make out what he had said.

"Ad—e—ena…" the boy moaned.

"Yes, son. I am her mother," Elizabeth murmured.

"Mot—er," the boy said, almost relieved. "Hen—reeee Ro—ck… Bar—boo…" he turned his head away from Elizabeth and began coughing, spraying blood on the white pillow and sheet.

"Shh, it's okay," Elizabeth coaxed, waiting for the boy to breathe in and return his attention to her. He didn't. She cocked her head and placed her ear against his chest.

There was no sound echoing back at her.

Fighting a wave of oncoming tears, Elizabeth stood up. Mary came to her side and slipped an arm around her mistress' waist. The doctor went around to the other side of the bed and slowly pulled the sheet over the boy's head. Elizabeth bit her lip and led Mary from the room.

"Should I get the Masta?" Mary mumbled as they stepped back outside.

"No, that's the last thing we should do. He doesn't care at all about getting Adelina back," Elizabeth said, biting back a tear.

"Then, what do we do now, Mum?" Mary asked as they stepped back to the carriage.

Without hesitation, Elizabeth responded. "We are going to find Brandon. He'll help us rescue my daughter!"

It wasn't long before Adelina found herself on the veranda finishing Chaucer for the third time. There weren't as many eyes watching her as there were a week ago. Henry had his men do a thorough search of the surrounding land for days to find any hint of Jack Burton. Meanwhile, other men sat in the taverns and bars in town listening for anything suspicious. When nothing prevailed after a week, Henry returned half his men back to their regular duties.

Adelina couldn't tell if it made her feel better or worse. Henry tried to assure her, claiming that Burton had probably left the island for a few months to gather confidence or to cowardly plunder unsuspecting ships. But it still left a rather uneasy feeling inside. She was sure she'd feel better—safer—if Henry spent more time with her.

The only time she'd seen him was when they took their meals together. Throughout the day he would go into town on business or oversee the repair to the ship. At night, if he returned, Henry would barricade himself in his bedroom without with an explanation. Adelina knew he was on the other side of the wall they shared because she could hear him pacing and slamming things in his bedroom, often keeping her up at night. Twice, she went to knock on his door to ask him to calm down so she could get some sleep, but he wouldn't answer her.

She knew that something was tormenting him. *He never seems to want to be around me anymore. Every time I see him, he'll excuse himself from the room. I don't understand it. I've often seen him stare at me with this…look in his eyes.*

Billy came around the corner, causing Adelina to lose her thought. He stopped for a moment near one of the bushes and gently broke a blooming bud off a vine before he walked to Adelina.

"Hello, milady," Billy greeted as he pulled out a chair and sat down.

"Good morning, Billy." Adelina smiled as she laid the open book in her lap. Billy awkwardly handed her the flower and she smiled. She took in its exotic scent and gave Billy a smile before placing it between the pages of her book and closed the novel.

For several minutes, nobody spoke. "Um, can I ask you something?" Billy asked, breaking the silence.

"Sure," Adelina nodded.

Billy nodded and nervously wiped the corner of his lips with his thumb and forefinger. "Well, I was athink'n about the ball next week. And I know that you and the cap'n have been having some problems…"

Adelina nodded, shocked that her problems with Henry were so apparent. "It comes with the situation, I guess."

Billy smiled uneasily. "Well, um, would it be easier if you went with me?"

Adelina raised her eyebrow, speechless.

"Henry asked me to," Billy stammered out. He quickly made a fist and released it.

Adelina bit her lip. *He really doesn't like me anymore.* "I can't believe…"

"Hmm?" Billy asked, not hearing her.

"Then I'd be honored," Adelina said, forcing herself to smile.

Billy blushed. "Thank you," he said, getting up to leave.

Adelina stared after him. *Why would Henry change his mind about me? It boils my blood that Henry would so easily dismiss me.* She cursed and stood up, throwing the book back in her seat.

Adelina balled her hands into tight fists as she marched back to the house. She reached the side entrance and threw open the door. Shocked by her own aggressiveness, Adelina took a deep breath and counted to ten. When she felt herself relax, she stepped inside.

On the far corner of the kitchen, she saw Catherine and Norton sipping a cup of tea.

"One of her servants told me," Catherine said with a sigh.

"I just can't believe it," Norton moaned. "What will we do?"

"I don't understand why the Masta would even want to marry that awful wench anyway," Catherine mumbled. "Maybe I should speak to him. After all, I've been with his family before he was even born."

Norton shrugged. "He won't listen. I guess we can always go back to—"

Adelina continued her march through the kitchen, holding her head up high. She paused on the staircase, recognizing Henry and Billy's voices coming from the parlor.

"Well, I asked her, Cap'n," said Billy.

"Yeah, and…" Henry inquired.

"She said yes," Billy mumbled, barely audible.

"Good," Henry said roughly.

Adelina heard approaching footsteps and turned in its direction to find Henry leaving the parlor. He stopped when he spied her on the steps and ran his fingers through his hair. He looked away for a moment, not certain if he was ready to confront Adelina. He took a deep breath and marched past her.

"Adelina," Henry greeted as he mounted the steps.

"Henry—wait," Adelina called after him.

He stopped in his tracks and turned around. "Yes?"

Adelina licked her lips. "Nothing."

And there was nothing for a week.

Chapter Eight

Adelina stretched and smothered a yawn with the back of her hand. The clock on the far side of the room softly chimed 10:30. The room had grown steadily warmer since the sun rose in the east. Since then, she had kicked off the covers in response to the heat. With great effort, Adelina rolled onto her side and watched the curtains flutter in the morning breeze. She stood up, stretched again and walked toward the coolness that the draft had to offer.

A light knock sounded on the door a few minutes later. Catherine opened the door slowly and stepped inside.

"Oh good, ye're awake." Catherine smiled as she began to remake the bed. "I was hoping ye wouldn't sleep through the ball."

Adelina waved her hand to fan the air around her. "It's much too hot to sleep."

Catherine nodded as she finished making the bed. She straightened her skirt and proceeded to the closet. "That it es, me dear."

Adelina watched Catherine pull out four white boxes secured with pink ribbons and laid them on the bed. She pulled fresh white undergarments from the first box and softly spread them over the sheets.

"Do you think I could have breakfast before I begin to get ready?" Adelina asked.

Catherine nodded. "We really don't need to start until about noon."

"Good. I'll be back around then," Adelina said. She rummaged through the closet and pulled a dress from the back of the closet and held it at arm's length. It was simple, lacking lace and embroidery. Adelina put the dress on over her nightgown and secured her hair back with a ribbon. "I'm glad I saw this awful thing."

Adelina skipped from her bedroom to the kitchen. She cut herself a slice of fresh bread and pulled a mango from the bowl of fruit. She ate her meager breakfast while she walked to the dock where she could watch the men sand the ship and climb the ropes like talented monkeys. After finishing her breakfast, Adelina laid down with her arms crossed under her head, watching the clouds above her. Her mind drifted with the clouds, leading her thoughts back home.

I wonder if Brandon had forgotten about me and married someone else? It wouldn't surprise me the least. I've caught him eyeing other ladies as they walked by numerous times. But I do miss Mother and little Christopher. I wonder how his birthday went? How would I look at Father again? Does he regret what he had done, even if I wasn't involved? How stupid he must have been to cheat a pirate—I can't believe that Father was really that dishonest. But how can I call him Father? I do still love him, I mean, he is my father, Adelina thought with a sigh. *Pirate— ha. Henry. Life here hasn't been at all what I had expected…with him. I'm actually quite content here.* Adelina smiled. *Not content. Happy—here— with him.*

It felt like only a few minutes had passed in the warm sun when Adelina heard heavy footsteps behind her. She sat up with a start and relaxed when she saw that it was Henry.

"Sleep well?" he asked, sitting down next to her.

"Yes, actually," Adelina said with a smile.

"Good, because Catherine has been hollering for you for the past hour." Henry smiled.

"Oh, what time is it?" Adelina asked, standing up.

"A bit after one."

Adelina cursed and ran back to the house, leaving Henry's laughter behind her. She found Catherine upstairs in the bedroom, arms crossed and tapping her foot.

"Ye're late," Catherine said sternly.

Adelina removed her dress and chemise. "I know. I'm sorry."

Catherine led Adelina into the bath chamber and helped her into the scented water. Without a word, Catherine began scrubbing Adelina's hair and skin. The moment that the rose scent became overpowering, never mind that her skin had turned beet red, Catherine whisked Adelina out of the water to dress.

It was nearly five hours later before it was time to depart for the Ramsey ball. Henry, dressed in all black, was the first to descend the stairs. He patiently waited in the foyer. Billy entered a few minutes later, dressed in dark gray trousers and a white shirt. He greeted his captain with a smile and a handshake. Nearly ten minutes later, Michelle pulled up to the house in Henry's carriage, annoyed that Henry had sent Norton to pick her up instead of going himself. Henry met her at the door and eyed her as she stepped down from the coach. He scowled when he saw the low neckline of the gown that barely covered her nipples. He wondered how he had missed her indecency when she wore the dress at Mister Bakeoven's shop.

Henry didn't lose his frown as he led Michelle inside and saw that Billy was aware of the same thing. Henry rolled his eyes, noticing Catherine waiting on the upper landing with a large smile on her face.

"Yes, Catherine?" Henry called up to her.

Catherine gave a slight grimace toward Michelle before she made her announcement. "I would like to present…Mizz Adelina Ellingsworth!"

With Catherine's introduction, Adelina stepped from behind the corner. Henry smiled as Adelina gracefully descended the stairs. She was far more beautiful than the first time she wore the gown. The pale gold made her brown eyes stand out and seize your attention. The sunlight from earlier that morning gave her cheeks a radiant pink glow that shone even brighter when she smiled. Her hair was loosely pulled at the base of her neck with a pearl comb, leaving a river of tumbling waves down her back. The wide neckline elegantly hinted at the bosom beneath it. The bodice moved gracefully with her as she walked. As she stepped off the stair, Henry noticed how the waistline ended with a soft dip as the gown fell to the floor, gracefully echoing her footsteps.

"You look…breathtaking," Henry sighed as she approached.

Michelle clenched her jaw.

Adelina blushed. *He finally noticed.* "Thank you, milord."

"He's right, you do look wonderful," Billy muttered.

"Thank you, Billy," Adelina said with a modest smile. "You look lovely, Michelle."

Michelle rolled her eyes and looked away. "I think we should leave soon," she said as she entwined her arm with Henry's. "We don't want to be late."

"Ready?" Billy asked, presenting his arm to Adelina. She took it and gave Henry a soft smile.

Billy escorted Adelina outside to Henry's waiting carriage. "Jesu. Look at those rain clouds. Looks like we'll be in for a big one tonight," he said to Adelina. He looked back to Henry, who nodded in response.

With a shrug, Billy helped her inside the coach. Michelle entered and sat across from Adelina. Henry climbed in and sat next to Michelle. Billy followed him, shifting his weight uncomfortably in the small coach as he took the seat next to Adelina. He hunched forward, protecting his head from being bumped against the ceiling. When the carriage jolted into motion, Michelle threw her arm across Henry's torso and laid a bold hand on his inner thigh where it met the rest of his body.

"Oh, I'm sorry," she lied, not bothering to move her hand.

Adelina shook her head and turned her gaze to the scenery outside the window, ignoring the flirtations of Michelle to Henry. She briefly glanced at Billy, with hands folded in his lap, staring heavily at the floor. No one said a word during the short ride to Mayor Ramsey's estate.

When Norton turned onto the street, he came to an abrupt halt. Adelina peered out the window to find the entire street lined with carriages waiting to disperse their occupants. She turned in her seat to give Billy a quick smile and a pat on his elbow. Minutes later, the carriage pulled up to the manor and Billy escorted her out of the coach.

"They have a nice home," Adelina said to Billy as she stepped from the carriage. The brick house stood two stories high with extravagant columns along the entryway and tall windows. There were well maintained shrubs that led up the drive and two small statues on either side of the door. As Adelina approached, she noted that the statues were of a lion and a unicorn.

"Hello, Mayor Ramsey," Henry greeted the elderly gentleman at the door. "You know Billy and Michelle, but this jewel," Henry gestured behind him, "is Miss Adelina Ellingsworth."

"Oh, hello, my dear. It is good to meet you," the gentleman said in a deep voice. He tenderly took Adelina's hand and kissed her fingertips.

"It's good to meet you too, milord." Adelina smiled. She greeted Ramsey's wife and two young grandsons with a curtsy before she followed the other guests into the ballroom.

Billy remained at her side. "Don't worry—they'll forget you in about five minutes. I'm sure you'll have to repeat your name to them several times before the night's over."

Adelina gave Billy a polite laugh. Looking around the ballroom, she saw merry couples dancing in the center while others waited on the side for an opening. A few chairs and tables were placed strategically about the room where tired dancers could rest while they socialized.

Billy continued to escort Adelina about the festivities. Adjoining the ballroom was the dining room, where numerous amounts of refreshment dishes and beverages were being served. Adelina recognized a few of the meat trays, but many of the dishes looked foreign and enticing. She noticed that there were more chairs and tables available in this particular room for the tired and parched guests.

Billy led Adelina out into the hallway where the ballroom was to her right and a glow of light came from a room down the hall. She heard men laughing and a slight, spicy smell of cigar smoke traveled down the hallway.

"That's the parlor," he explained. "You could probably find me...or Henry...in there sometime later in the night—if you need us."

Billy led Adelina back to the ballroom and guided her through the thickening assembly. Eventually he broke through the crowd and stepped onto the dance floor. She looked up at him and was still amazed that he was at least a foot and a half taller than her, putting her even with his rib cage. He put a hand high on her back and pulled her to about her arm's length away from him. He extended his arm and barely kept from touching her fingers.

"Shall we?" Billy asked with a nervous smile.

Adelina laughed. "I think we should. We'd look awfully silly out here just standing."

Billy spun Adelina in a full circle before he stepped back and began to lead her about the dance floor. He stared continuously downward at his feet while the waltz played in the background. He glanced up for a moment and smiled, but quickly returned his attention to the floor. She saw his lips moving and his head nodding every few moments, but made no attempt to converse.

"What?" Adelina inquired.

"Nothing," Billy mumbled with an out of place nod.

"Billy?"

"Shh—I'm concentrating," Billy whispered. Just then, he bumped into the back of another dancing couple. "I'm sorry."

Adelina gave Billy a curious look, but shrugged it off. The dance picked up speed and Adelina quickened her pace. Billy tried, but ended up stepping on her feet twice in a matter of seconds.

"I'm sorry," he mumbled as he did it again.

"It's alright." Adelina smiled. *Billy doesn't know how to dance!* It dawned on her that he was watching his feet and counting the steps.

He was relieved when the song ended and he could lead her back to the sidelines. "Thank you for the dance, milady."

"May I dance with the fair lady?" a man asked from behind. Adelina turned around. The man was tall, almost the same height as Henry, with fine, yellow hair that lightly grazed his shoulders. He had hazel eyes that constantly searched about the room. Below his high arched eyebrows, his nose extended from his face like a long board, ending with a slight curve toward his mouth. On his fair face, his cheeks were smooth, as though he had never shaved in his entire life.

Oh my goodness, it's the Pardoner! Adelina smiled.

Billy looked him up and down in a long stare. After almost a minute, Billy gave him a stiff nod. "Yes, if she wishes."

"I would like that very much." Adelina smiled. She glanced over her shoulder at Billy as the man led her onto the dance floor. She was relieved to see him cross his arms and wink at her, letting her know that he would remain where he could watch over her.

The man held her hand and stretched out his arm. His other hand moved boldly around her hips to her lower back, far lower than what Adelina had expected. The song began and the man pulled her roughly to his chest, where he could feel her soft breasts against him. Without a moment's notice, he took a step to the side, nearly dragging Adelina with him.

"You are very beautiful, milady," the man whispered near her ear.

Adelina nodded. With a turn, she glimpsed where Billy was still watching. "Thank you."

"How long are you going to remain in Barbuda?" the man asked, as he dipped her to his side.

"I don't know yet," Adelina mumbled. From the corner of her eye Adelina spied Michelle on the far side of the room. Adelina noticed that she was pressing her body up against someone who was *not* Henry. As Adelina moved to the side with the other dancers, she watched as the man's hand moved from Michelle's back to her buttocks. Another dancer crossed her line of vision and in that instant they were gone.

"Was that giant of a man your betrothed?" the man asked. He lightly brushed his fingertips against her posterior, returning Adelina's attention back to him.

"No, he's not. My betrothed is…elsewhere," Adelina said through clenched teeth.

"Well, if he's not able to, remember me and I will surely take you…home tonight. I do pay quite handsomely." The man smiled. "My name is Robert, by the way."

Adelina fought a shudder. "My feet hurt, Robert. I would like to sit down now," Adelina said, freeing herself from the man's grip. She crossed the dance floor to Billy, carefully avoiding being clobbered by passing dancing couples.

"Wait, I didn't catch your name," Robert called as he tried to follow her. A dancing couple wove between them, causing him to stop in his place.

Adelina looked back over her shoulder. "That's because I didn't throw it!"

"Are you alright? You look angry." Billy said, greeting her on the dance floor.

"Yes, Billy. I'm fine," Adelina sighed. "That man was…just a scoundrel."

"Would you like to finish the dance with me?" Billy asked, trying to win a smile from her.

Adelina laughed. *He is trying so hard.* "I would like that very much."

Billy gently took her hand and escorted her onto the floor just as a passing couple bumped into him. He dropped her hand and reached for his injured side with a curse.

"Billy! Are you alright?" Adelina asked as she put a caring hand to his elbow.

He nodded, grinding his teeth. "I'm going to sit down in the parlor for a while," he said as he began to make his way through the crowd.

Adelina walked with him. "Anything to keep from dancing."

Billy laughed. "You bet." He left her at the refreshment table and continued into the hallway.

Adelina accepted a glass of wine from a passing servant and moved away from the crowd to the open balcony doors, where a cool breeze fluttered in. She sat down on one of the benches and leaned forward to loosen her slippers. Adelina looked up and noticed that the sky was darker than what it should be, even at night. There was no moon, not even a single star. With a snort, Adelina swallowed a mouthful of the bright red wine.

"We have to stop meeting like this," a deep voice came from behind her.

"Hello, Henry," Adelina asked without looking up.

"Howdya know it was me?" he asked, trying to sound disappointed as he sat down next to her.

Adelina shrugged. "Who else would show up on a balcony at night?"

"Yeah…" Henry smiled. "Would you care to dance?"

Adelina shifted in her seat to face him. "What about your date?"

"She's otherwise preoccupied," Henry said with a grunt.

Adelina nodded, understanding, but smothered a laugh. "I think I can do one more waltz."

Henry smiled and reached for her hand. He held it gently against his side as he led her through the dining room and into the ballroom. When she reached the floor, he raised his arm and spun her in a circle before bringing her against his chest with a light hand against the small of her back. He stared deeply into her eyes while the band lifted their instruments. The waltz began and Henry slowly adjusted her fingertips in his grip.

He took a step back and Adelina followed. Through the music they danced, eyes never parting. He gazed down at her with deep blue eyes that bored through to her very soul. She tried to look away, look for familiar faces amongst the spectators, but she couldn't tear herself from those blue pools. They had captivated her. Suddenly, Henry smiled, causing Adelina to lose her step.

"Are you alright?" Henry asked, flashing a grin.

Adelina laughed and glanced around for a moment. "I'm fine, milord."

Henry stepped back, spun Adelina and caught her in a dip as the other male dancers did with their partners. Then he lifted her and pulled her closer so that her breasts grazed against his chest.

"Know what this reminds me of?" Henry asked.

"No…what?" Adelina said with a shuffle of her feet.

"Our first dance together," he said as he switched hands.

Adelina laughed. "Yes. How ironic is that?"

They switched hands as the dance step indicated. Henry used the opportunity to pull Adelina closer to him, forcing her breasts to push against his chest.

Adelina found that she couldn't breathe. The comfort and excitement she found in his arms came rushing back to her. *It's been a long time since he held me like this.*

The waltz ended a few moments later. Everyone began shuffling on and off the dance floor, but Henry and Adelina remained. He dropped her hand and slid both his hands to the sides of her waist. His eyes softened and darkened to a deeper blue than Adelina ever thought possible.

"Adelina…" Henry whispered, leaning forward, drawn by those honey-brown eyes that peered up at him ready to kiss the lips below them.

"Henry!" someone screamed from beyond the dance floor.

Henry awakened from his dreamy state and stepped back from Adelina. He looked up to find Michelle, red-faced and with clenched fists at her sides, stampeding toward them. Her hair was tangled and partially pulled from its careful arrangement. He glanced downward and noticed that the neckline was tilted and loose, as though her bodice had come undone. Off to one side, Henry saw Billy parting through the crowd, surprised and flabbergasted. Everyone in the crowd, including the band, stopped what they were doing and turned to watch.

"Michelle," Henry cautioned, as he stepped between her and Adelina.

Michelle marched up to Henry and pushed him aside, causing him to fly backward in surprise. She faced Adelina. "You little bitch!"

Adelina's jaw dropped. "Pardon?"

"You heard me. Henry is mine, you little whore. How dare you even try—"

Adelina threw her hands up in defense. "Whoa—I wasn't trying anything!"

"You're supposed to be here with Billy. And besides, you're already betrothed," Michelle hissed. The crowd that had accumulated around them gasped.

Henry returned to Michelle's side and grabbed her elbow. "Michelle, I think it's time to quit."

Michelle brushed Henry off. "Hell, no," she said as she took a step forward and pushed Adelina. "Slutty bitch."

Adelina caught herself on the first step back. She took the step between her and Michelle. Sucking in her bottom lip, she made a fist and brought it back past her. In a fast motion, she swung her fist in front of her and landed it hard on Michelle's cheekbone. Michelle lost her balance and fell into the stranger's arms behind her. Everyone went silent for a moment and stared at Adelina. Henry sidestepped Adelina and knelt by Michelle, inspecting her injury. Someone from the back of the crowd clapped a few times and shouted, "Thank you," bringing weak laughter from the audience.

Henry stood up, his eyes changed to an icy blue, indicating how angry he was. "Adelina…"

She didn't wait to hear the rest. Adelina glanced from Henry to Michelle, then turned and quickly disappeared in the crowd. She heard Henry calling after her, but she didn't care. Like a coward she flew, and she hated it, but she would rather run than face his wrath.

Adelina found her way out of the ballroom and into the foyer. She pulled open the heavy door and escaped into the night. A flash of lightening and an explosion of thunder sounded above her just seconds before the skies opened up and fat, heavy raindrops fell. She ran through the rain, not caring that the water and mud ruined her dress, to the long line of waiting coaches. It took her a few minutes, but she found Norton under the shelter of an umbrella, calming the horses.

"Good evening, Miss Ellingsworth, what are ye doing out here in this weather?" he called over the rainfall. He reached over, giving Adelina the protection of the umbrella. Another crash of thunder sounded, causing them both to jump.

"We have to go, Norton. I have to get away from here," Adelina cried, wiping the wetness from her face.

"Oh—what about the others?" Norton asked as he opened the coach door.

"I don't care about them. I'm afraid I've done something terrible," Adelina muttered as she left the shelter of Norton's umbrella and climbed inside. Norton gave her a sympathetic smile as he closed the door. He climbed onto the base of the carriage and lifted the reins.

"Norton! Stop! Damn it, Norton, stop!" someone shouted through the rain.

Norton glanced over his shoulder and saw Henry running alongside the carriage. "Whoa! Masta Roark! What are you doing out here?"

Henry didn't answer. Instead, he threw open the coach door and climbed inside. The moment the door slammed shut, Norton jolted the carriage into motion again, wondering to himself about what was going on.

It was dark inside, but it was at least dry. It took Henry's eyes a moment to adjust, but Henry could make out Adelina's small form in the darkness. She was curled up into a tight ball, with her knees against her chest.

"Adelina?" Henry called, trying to sound calmer than he was.

No answer.

"Do you want to tell me what went on tonight?" Henry asked, anger beginning to show in his voice.

Still no answer, but he thought he heard a sniffle over the rainfall.

"Damn it, Adelina!" Henry cursed as he slammed a boot on the cushioned seat opposite of him. He glared at her with all the fury of the world until they reached Roark Manor. When the carriage slowed, Henry moved to block the door. *She's not going to leave until I get an explanation.*

Adelina saw him move to trap her. She turned and reached for the handle on the door nearest her and threw it open. She stepped out, skirted around the carriage and ran up the steps before Henry knew what had happened.

Catherine heard the front door bang open and ran to see what the cause was. She made it in time to find Adelina flying up the last few steps of the grand staircase to the second landing. She moved to close the door, but Henry's wide frame passed through it. She could see in his icy blue eyes the anger that flowed through him. Catherine muttered a silent prayer as Norton took her in his arms.

Adelina made it to her room and locked the door behind her. She saw the open balcony doors and quickly skirted across the room to lock those as well, never minding how hot it would get when the rain stopped and the sun rose in the morning.

Minutes later, Adelina heard heavy footsteps approaching on the other side of the door. They stopped in front of her bedroom door and remained there for a minute. Adelina closed her eyes and held her breath. Then the footsteps continued into Henry's room. Adelina breathed a sigh of relief and closed the curtains over the glass doors before she sat down at the edge of her bed.

Just as she removed her slippers, Adelina heard footsteps on the balcony. She looked up and watched in horror as a dark figure of a man was silhouetted by a flash of lightening, standing in front of her doors. A hand reached out and jiggled the handle, only to discover that it was locked. Adelina stared helplessly as the shadow removed its shirt and stepped back. A loud crash of thunder sounded just as the man punched through the glass, using his shirt to protect his hand. He reached in and dropped the shirt. The intruder rotated his hand and unlocked the door.

Adelina swallowed a scream and ran to her bedroom door. She fumbled the lock and managed to get the door open a crack before a hand slammed it shut from behind her. She spun around and pressed her back against the door and turned around. He was close enough to her that when she inhaled, her breasts pressed against his chest. Taking a deep breath, she looked up at the culprit. "Henry, please—I need to be alone right now."

"What the hell happened tonight?" Henry asked through clenched teeth. He gripped her shoulders, fighting the urge to shake her.

Adelina swallowed. "I don't know. She made me so mad and…"

Henry released her arms and moved away from the door, standing in the middle of the room. He held his arms akimbo at his sides. "That's still no excuse for hitting her. Why didn't you just let me handle her?"

"She wasn't attacking you!" Adelina yelled. Her hands balled into tiny fists, held fast at her sides.

"Yes, she was," Henry shouted back. As he admitted so, he felt the anger beginning to drain from his body.

Adelina took a few steps forward, rage pulsing through her veins. She marched in front of Henry and stood inches away from him. Putting her hands on her hips she sneered. "I'm sorry. Are you the slutty bitch she was referring to? Because it sure as hell looked like she was looking at me."

"Well—maybe she was right!" Henry nearly screamed. He felt his breathing quicken as he began to fill with anger again.

Adelina cocked her eyebrow. "What?"

Henry took a few strides backward until he reached the open balcony doors. One hand rubbed the back of his neck and he pondered his words. He took a deep breath and spoke carefully, keeping his voice even. "Adelina, there's a man waiting for your return in England—or have you forgotten about him? Hell, I took you right before the damn vows! Now you're over here prancing around with Billy! Jesu girl, have you no shame?"

Adelina's jaw dropped as she watched Henry pick up his shirt and leave the room through the balcony doors. Her hands clenched into fists as she stormed after him, mindful of the broken glass under her bare feet. She stopped a few feet into his bedroom. "What the hell do you mean 'prancing around with Billy?'"

Henry threw his shirt across the room and turned around. "I've seen the way you look at him. You care about him."

Adelina tilted her head. *Is that what has been bothering him?* "I care about him, yes, but not in the way you're thinking," she mumbled as she turned to leave.

Henry chased after her, carefully stepping over the glass as he entered her room. "Don't try to play innocent with me. Michelle saw—"

"Michelle saw nothing!" Adelina shouted, cutting him off. "She likes to think we're all her little puppets. Hell, now I'm glad I punched her!"

Henry threw his arms into the air. "I am *not* her puppet?"

Adelina put a hand on her hip. "Then why have you decided to marry her all of a sudden?"

Henry didn't say anything for a moment. He was captivated by the way she jumped when the lightening would flash behind him, bringing loud thunder after it. The few candles in her room gave her skin a radiant glow and he could almost see the fire burning in her eyes. He found that it was hard to be angry at someone so beautiful. He was shocked to find that he wasn't angry anymore. "I don't know where you got that idea, my dear, but that will never happen. I can't even stand her half the time—why would I *want* to marry her?"

"Fine. You don't want to marry her. So, then why did you go to the ball with her?" Adelina asked, sarcastically.

"Because I thought you'd rather go with Billy over me," Henry mumbled as he walked to the bedroom door that led to the hallway. He opened it and stepped out.

"Henry, milord, I never wanted to go with Billy. I wanted to go with you," Adelina said as she followed him into his room. She could feel the anger draining from her body.

Henry reached behind Adelina and pushed the door closed. "You shouldn't want to go with anyone. You're getting married, remember?"

Adelina felt herself becoming annoyed again. *Why did I follow him in here?* "Don't try to make me feel guilty, Henry," she said as she moved toward the balcony doors.

Henry waited until she had walked past him. "But you should."

Adelina stopped and pivoted on her heels. She drew her right hand back, palm open, and swung it toward Henry's cheek. He caught her by the wrist, barely an inch from his face.

"I hate Brandon," Adelina said through clenched teeth.

"Good," Henry whispered. He pulled Adelina's wrist behind him, forcing Adelina to step forward. With her body pressed against his, Henry opened his mouth to devour Adelina's sweet kiss. Fully prepared for a slap with her other hand, he was surprised when Adelina opened her mouth to accept his tongue.

Adelina didn't expect Henry to pull her against him. All at once she could feel his muscular chest against her breasts, his stubble against her cheek, the strength of his arms around her, and more than anything she could feel his rapidly growing manhood. Her anger against him melted the instant his lips touched hers, and a fire erupted in her loins. She found that she wanted more.

She slipped her hand out of Henry's grasp and moved it to the base of his trousers. Her other hand rose upward to briefly toy with his nipple before she ran her fingertips through his thick chest hair. Henry moaned against her mouth and slid his hands to her hips.

Adelina sighed as Henry left her lips and began teasing the soft, sensitive spot where her neck met her shoulder with warm, wet kisses. She slipped her hand from his chest to the back of his neck to hold him there for a bit longer. He did, tantalizing every nerve in her body and sending shivers down her spine.

She felt Henry's hands slide around to her lower back. They lingered there for a minute, as if debating, before they reached around to her posterior and pulled her harder against his manhood. She gasped and, in response, Henry straightened and lifted her onto her toes so that she may feel his need while he sucked her earlobe.

"Adelina," Henry whispered against her ear as he began a trail of suckling kisses down the column of her throat to the neckline of her gown.

The tingling burning sensation returned to her breasts as they longed to be touched. The feeling distracted her enough that Adelina didn't hear Henry until he said her name a second time. "Hmmm?" she breathed, barely audible.

Henry took a step back and peered deep into Adelina's brown eyes. "I don't want to force you into anything you don't want to do."

Adelina didn't even glance away as Henry had expected. She nodded and returned her lips to his.

Henry groaned deep within his throat as he wrapped his arms around her. Adelina felt him reach for the tiny buttons along the back of her gown. He fumbled with the buttons for a minute before he cursed and ripped the seam apart, spraying buttons in every direction. In one quick motion, much to Adelina's surprise, Henry pulled the gown to her feet and lifted her out of it. She wrapped her legs around his waist and straddled him as he carried her to his bed.

He laid her down gently on the side of the bed closest to him. Adelina watched as he stood up and turned away from her, where he proceeded to remove his trousers. He turned back to Adelina, with his manhood extending outward.

There was a brief flutter in her stomach as Adelina's eyes slowly traveled from Henry's dark blue eyes, down past his tan, muscular chest, and over his hard stomach to his throbbing manhood. Adelina bit her lip when she saw that darkening color, which declared how ready he was for her. He reached for her hand and gently guided it to him.

He groaned and glanced up at the ceiling when she grasped him. She held him for a moment, exploring his member with her fingertips. As she fondled him, she felt a warm wetness develop between her thighs and the empty feeling returned. She yearned to be filled by this hard shaft.

Her touch was light, almost nothing at all. He had to envelope her hand to show her how to grip him, hard and strong. Slowly, she slid her hand up and down his member, eliciting short gasps from Henry. Not able to stand any longer, Henry sat down on the edge of the bed. He leaned forward, straightening his body as he lay down next to her, and took Adelina's mouth to his own.

His fingers danced along her skin. Adelina vaguely felt Henry loosening her undergarments and lifting her hips to remove them. She exhaled deeply, body shaking uncontrollably as his finger traced ever so lightly over her nipple.

Henry freed her lips so that he could watch his large hand overtake her left breast. It was full and ripe under his grip and he couldn't help but tenderly squeeze it. He slid his hand to the side so that his thumb and forefinger could gently massage the rigid nipple. Without removing his hand, he led a trail of kisses to the other. He danced his tongue over her nipple, receiving intense gasps and moans from Adelina.

The aching in her breasts increased, even with the pleasure that Henry was giving to her. She could feel the fingers from his free hand gradually move downward toward her loins. He stopped at the curls concealing her womanhood and made small slow circles with his palm. Adelina moaned, feeling the need grow beyond all possibility. She needed his touch—she needed his touch all over her body.

"Kiss me," Adelina begged. Henry obeyed her plea. The moment his tongue touched hers, Adelina arched her back against him.

He knew she was growing more and more ready for him. He slowly sank a finger into Adelina's wet crevice, pressing against the softest part of her body, bringing her closer to that ecstasy she's never known. She broke free from his kiss and gasped for breath. She cried out in a whimper and rotated her hips slightly, giving herself more intensive pleasure.

Smiling, Henry moved his body downward and made a circle of kisses around her naval. He slid his free hand under Adelina and lifted her hips. He removed his finger and quickly replaced it with his tongue. He made a slow circle around the opening, bringing moans and shudders from Adelina. He licked the sensitive spot that hid deep in her curls and felt himself arouse even further as Adelina gripped the bed sheet to keep from crying out in pure ecstasy. Carefully, he dipped his head fully between her thighs and entered her with his tongue.

Adelina gasped as his tongue grazed over her womanhood. She instinctively spread her legs, opening herself to him. She wanted him to go deeper, to caress her everywhere he could with his tongue. She grabbed a handful of hair and pushed him harder against her pelvis. The fire, the need, the agony wasn't where he was—it was deeper inside. She needed to tell him that but the words would not come.

Henry groaned heavily against her. Her reaction to his caressing excited him and his hands tightened around her waist as an effort to keep his senses. His manhood throbbed in anticipation to envelope himself inside of her. Unable to stand the waiting any longer, his hips naturally began moving against the silky bed sheets, causing more agony than pleasure.

She couldn't wait any longer. Adelina sat up and pulled Henry on top of her, bearing all of his weight on her small body. He immediately took her lips again, letting Adelina taste her own sweet self in his kisses. He lifted his body slightly and parted her thighs with his knees. Using one hand, he lifted Adelina's hips up. His other hand had guided his massive shaft to the opening of Adelina's hot haven.

"Adelina, look at me," Henry whispered. She looked into Henry's eyes, finding them the darkest shade of blue she's ever seen.

Adelina watched Henry take a deep breath just before he pushed himself into her. He expanded and filled her insides as slowly as he possibly could. He stopped for a moment and licked his lips before he slid himself another inch. A bursting pain shot through her abdomen, causing her to cry out and dig her nails into his shoulder.

Henry stopped again, afraid of going any further. He started moving in and out of her, as slow as he could, causing the pain to quickly melt into erotic ecstasy. When her breathing slowed, he knew that the pain of her maidenhood had ceased and he could now bring her to the moment she's been longing for.

He pushed himself deep inside of her in one smooth, quick motion, filling her completely. She could feel him at the very end of her, at the very core of her body. It was there where she longed to be touched. He slowly began to slide himself outward and Adelina cried out, tightening her grip on his shoulder. She slid one hand to his hip and weakly tried to push him back inside.

Henry moaned at her response to him, increasing his desire to please her. She felt the muscles of her insides suddenly grow tight around Henry, almost excruciatingly painful. He pushed himself inside of her for a second and began to pull himself out again. With a moan, he thrust himself into her, feeling her tighten around him as he quickened his pace with every stroke.

She could feel beads of sweat that had accumulated on his back, chest and brow, showing that he was determined to please her. Her heart was pounding in her chest and her breath came in short gasps as he pulsated against her body. She could feel him driving himself into her faster and faster.

Henry pulled himself out of her, nearly completely. Slower than he had before, he pushed his manhood inside of her, releasing the tension of her muscles so that she could feel the rapture of her ecstasy.

With a gasp, she cried out Henry's name as he pushed himself into her one last and final time. She dug her nails into his shoulder as her body shook and shuddered uncontrollably around him. A sudden wave of relief enveloped her as she felt her muscles relax around him.

Henry felt the inside of her body contract rapidly and grow wet with even greater heat. His body went rigid for a second before he gasped for air and cried out, exploding his seed. Then he collapsed on top of her, but his hips still continued to pulsate in her for another minute before he stilled.

They laid there for several minutes, both gasping for air, neither wanting to move from the dampness of her thighs. Between breaths, Henry stretched and placed a light kiss on Adelina's nose. Adelina sighed weakly and Henry kissed her, opening her lips with his tongue

"Adelina." Henry smiled, lifting his head slightly. He tenderly caressed her cheek with the back of his fingers. "My Adelina."

Chapter Nine

Henry skipped downstairs into the kitchen to fetch breakfast. He rummaged around the kitchen for several minutes, opening cabinets and removing lids from jars in search of something to eat. He found an open bag of oats in the pantry and decided to make porridge over the fire. He was in the process of stirring the meal when Catherine entered.

"Masta Roark?" Catherine said in surprise as she yawned. She looked him up and down, wondering why he up was earlier than usual. It's been years since she had seen him in the kitchen cooking something. "What are ye doing up at this hour? It's barely even sunrise."

Henry nodded. "I know. I wanted to make Adelina breakfast, then take her horseback riding today. I think she'll enjoy that."

Catherine smiled, thankful to see that her master and the misses had finally accepted one another. "I'll have a picnic lunch made for ye two in about an hour or so."

"Thanks, Catherine," Henry said as he spooned the porridge into a bowl. He put the bowl and two spoons on a serving platter. "Oh, and have Thomas prepare a hot bath in Adelina's chamber before he goes into town. With candles. The good ones."

Catherine nodded.

"Oh, and one more thing—Adelina won't need any aid this morning," Henry said as he left the kitchen.

Adelina awoke to find Henry sitting the breakfast tray on the corner of the bed. She sat up, using the covers to hide her nakedness. "Good morning."

"Hello, my love." Henry smiled as sat down and pulled the porridge off the platter so that it would sit between them. "I made breakfast for you."

"Thank you." Adelina smiled. She brought a spoonful to her mouth and fought every urge to spit it back out. Not only was the porridge lumpy, which

Adelina could tolerate, it was dry and salted. She managed to swallow what was in her mouth and display a smile as she reached for a second bite. "It's good. Why aren't you eating?"

"I'm not hungry after all," Henry said, smiling that Adelina enjoyed his breakfast.

Adelina managed to swallow a few more bites before giving up and claiming that she was full. A few minutes later, a knock sounded. It was Thomas informing Henry that the bath chamber was just about ready.

While Henry was turned, Adelina escaped from the bed and donnede of Henry's discarded shirts. Henry turned and found Adelina securing the strings of one his large shirts around her neck, struggling in the long sleeves that over took her hands by a good eight inches. The hem of the shirt almost reached her knees, exposing her creamy legs beneath it.

"Your bath is ready," Henry whispered as he stared at the luscious legs that couldn't hide under the protection of his shirt.

Adelina thanked him and hurried into her bath chamber. She looked around as she removed the shirt and stepped into the steaming water, noting the dozen lit candles about the room, giving a romantic glow in its golden light. Adelina leaned backward, submerging her hair into the water and closed her eyes, thinking of the past two days she had spent in Henry's bedchamber. She smiled when she thought how Henry had ordered their meals to be brought up to their room just because he couldn't bear the thought of her leaving his presence so she could dress.

"I've wanted to hold you like this since I first saw you," he had said to her last night, holding her close after he passionately made love to her again. "I've wanted to feel your heart beating against mine for a long time now."

Adelina opened her eyes and spied the scented oils across the room.

"Come to me," Adelina jestfully ordered, with no intention of getting out to retrieve them.

Footsteps approached the tub and Adelina looked up to find Henry standing over her, naked. "As you wish, my dear."

"I wasn't talking to you." Adelina laughed as she bent her knees to her chest.

He stepped into the tub across from Adelina, and sat down, spilling water onto the floor. "I guess it's alright now to bathe naked."

Adelina laughed and waved her hand. "By all means."

Henry leaned forward and gently pulled Adelina over his long, hard body. She gasped when her stomach slid over his erect member. "By *all* means."

Nearly three hours later, Henry and Adelina ventured from her room. Henry, again dressed in all black, smiled down at Adelina as he paused for a moment so that she could descend the stairs first. He remained a few steps behind her so that he could gaze at the ample view of her hips swinging naturally from side to side in her sea-foam color dress.

Henry led her to the kitchen where Catherine waited with a picnic sack. He informed her of his plans to take Adelina to see the native Arawak statues, took the sack from Catherine and escorted Adelina to the stables.

"There's only one horse ready," Adelina stated, seeing only Buttercup standing by the stables.

"Yes. I am having the others brushed and shoed today," Henry lied.

Smiling, Henry helped Adelina mount the horse. He secured the lunch to the saddle and mounted the beast behind her. He slipped his arms around her slim waist and reached for the reins. With a quick kick and click of his tongue, the stallion entered into a brisk trot.

They followed the pebbled drive off the estate and to the dirt trail, still caked with mud from the night before last. Other than turning left, as was the direction to Barbuda, Henry turned the horse to the right. With another kick, the horse quickened his pace into a gallop.

Adelina watched the passing scenery. They followed the dirt path along the edges of a tobacco plantation where Adelina watched the dark-skinned laborers. They entered the extremity of a dense forest and crossed a shallow stream. In minutes they were out of the forest, following along its border as it grew thicker with vegetation.

Henry pulled hard on the reins, causing Buttercup to slow down and turn back into the forest. Henry hunched forward and lifted a hand to press Adelina against his chest to protect her from any low hanging tree branches.

Adelina could hear his heart beating rapidly in his chest. She brought her hand to her breasts and felt her own heart pumping just as fast. A dreamy smile formed on her lips as she thought about how his heart might be beating just for her, as hers was for him. She snuggled deeper into his chest and breathed in his sweaty scent.

The hand on her shoulder had wrapped a curl around its finger. He released it, never knowing he had captured it in the first place, and cupped her brow.

Henry leaned down and planted a kiss on the crown of her head before he informed her that she could sit up now.

"How do you know where we are going?" Adelina asked.

Henry pointed to a tree several yards to his left. "See those stones? The ones that look out of place? The first explorers who came to this island set those up so that they could find their way back to their ship."

"Then why don't more people follow them?" Adelina asked.

"Well, I don't know really. Most people come and go and don't really stay long enough to find out about them. Others who live here are too busy, I guess," Henry explained.

"Then...how did you find out?"

"My father," Henry paused. "He helped one of the old hermits who lives out here get supplies or something. I really don't remember. The hermit told him about it and he told me."

Adelina glanced up at Henry. He slouched slightly and stared ahead with a sad, distracted look in his eyes that said he was thinking about his father. Instead of pressing the subject, Adelina turned her attention to the scenery around them.

The base of the trees were the first to capture her attention. They differed greatly from the trees that surrounded Henry's estate, and even more so than the trees at home. She noticed that the roots of the trees closest to her stuck out of the ground in a giant fan with long limbs taller than her. The deeper they traveled into the forest, the taller the trees got.

High in the treetops, Adelina saw a colorful bird perched on a branch. It had a rather small body that seemed outweighed by its large, vibrant bill. On another limb, far below the colorful bird, loomed a yellow and red snake on a thick branch.

There were numerous exquisite flowers decorating the thick vegetation of the ground and along the vines that entangled the trees. Hovering just above these extravagant flowers were tiny hummingbirds, rapidly beating the air with their wings.

Suddenly, Henry jumped from the horse, disrupting Adelina's thinking. He gripped the reins tightly with his left hand as he pulled his cutlass from its sheath with his right.

"What are you doing?" Adelina asked, barely able to keep from screaming. Fear struck through her—*Father had waited too long to pay the ransom and now that he had his way with me, he is going to*—Henry raised his sword, but turned his back to her. In one swift motion he cut through several thick vines that had blocked the path.

"Cutting the weeds," Henry said as he stepped forward. He raised his arm and continued using the weapon as a machete.

Step by step, they made their way though the thick forest. Henry stopped once or twice to remove his shirt and wipe the sweat from his back. After nearly an hour, they finally reached a large grassy clearing divided by a large stream.

"Almost there, my dear," Henry said as he climbed back on the horse.

"Good," Adelina mumbled. She looked up into the sky, shielding her eyes from the blaring sun. There was not a cloud in the sky, leaving the sun alone above them.

They followed the stream for about a quarter of a mile until it came to a sharp bend. They turned with the path and Adelina was shocked to find large cut stones along the sand, protected by tall trees.

"We're here," Henry announced as he dismounted. He reached up and helped Adelina dismount off the horse.

While Henry tethered the horse to a nearby tree, Adelina explored among the ominous statues. They were slightly taller then her, designed of geometrical shapes, with large bulging eyes that stared accusingly at her as she moved about them.

"They're kind of scary," Adelina stated.

Henry pulled a blanket from the picnic sack and smooth out it over the ground. "Yeah, I thought that too. But now I think of them as some reminder of the past—a piece of history," he said as he pulled various fruits from the bag. "Just forget about them and come eat."

Adelina nodded and sat down next to Henry. She grabbed a ripe papaya and slouched against Henry's chest. Smiling, Henry slipped his arm around her waist and fell backward, pulling Adelina on top of him.

"Oh, hello." Henry laughed. He kissed Adelina, tasting the sweet fruit from her lips and tongue.

Adelina slid her hands from his shoulders to his stomach. She broke the kiss as she took another bite of papaya and threw the fruit over her shoulder. Seductively, she pulled the hem of her gown over her hips as she straddled him.

"Now that's what I'm talking about," Henry growled as he pulled his shirt over his head.

Thomas barged through the front door just as the grandfather clock struck one. He leaned forward, bracing himself on his knees in an effort to catch his breath. "Cap'n! Hey, Cap'n!"

Catherine came to the upstairs landing a moment later. "Stop that screamin'. What do ye want?"

Thomas staggered as quickly as he could toward the steps. He gripped the railing as he struggled to pull himself up the stairs. "Catherine, where's the cap'n?"

"He's out with Mizz Ellingsworth. I think they went to the statues. Why?" Catherine asked when Thomas climbed midway up the staircase.

"Damn it," Thomas cursed as he stopped on the staircase. "Where's Billy?"

"He's downstairs in the kitchen. Why? What's going on, Thomas?" Catherine asked as she chased after Thomas down the stairs.

"Burton," Thomas called back to her as he entered the kitchen.

"I'll ready the horses and get the men off the ship," Catherine said as she passed through the kitchen to exit through the back door.

"Good afternoon, Thomas," Billy greeted as he took a bite of his lunch. "Would you like some?"

"Billy, Burton is still on the island," Thomas said, leaning against the table for support.

Billy gulped, nearly choking on the food in his mouth. Without a word, he bolted from his chair for his room. "How do you know this?"

Thomas staggered after him as fast as he could. He followed Billy into his room and leaned against the doorframe, gulping for air. "I was in Barbuda and I heard two men talking about the *Blood Water* being on the other side of the island. Billy...they're at the statues."

Billy stopped in his tracks and cursed. "Alright, Catherine knows what to do in an emergency. Here, take this pistol and sword."

"What are we going to do?" Thomas asked, securing the sheath around his slim waist.

"Hopefully, find the cap'n and get him home," Billy said as he left the room. He flew down the steps with Tomas on his heels. Together, they ran out the door to the stables.

The attendants had just finished readying the horses as Billy and Thomas entered the stable. They mounted the horses and kicked them into breakneck speed without as much as a goodbye.

"And if we don't find him?" Thomas asked when they got off the property.

Billy turned and gave Thomas a worried look. "I don't want to think about that."

Adelina awoke to an insect buzzing near her ear. In her sleepy daze she attempted to swat at it, but found that she couldn't lift her arm. Peering down, Adelina found Henry's strong arms cradling her into him. His chest and stomach pressed against her back and his mouth nuzzled in the crick of her neck.

"Henry?" Adelina murmured, shifting slightly.

Henry released her and rolled onto his back, supporting his head with his wrists. "Hmmm?"

"I think we need to start heading back soon," Adelina said as she sat up. She grunted and stood up, clutching the gown to her breasts. She turned her back to him and began securing the buttons along her back.

Henry studied the length of a nearby shadow and stood up, pulling on his pants. "Yeah, I guess you're right. Hey, um, I was thinking…"

"About what?"

"About maybe going back to England in a few months," Henry mumbled. *I'll take the chance of being arrested and hanged for her.*

Adelina spun on her heels, about to throw her arms around Henry when the tall grass behind him unnaturally shifted. A burly man with a tangled mane of hair and dark tattoos on his chest stepped from the grass. One corner of his mouth turned upward in a snarl as he began bouncing a large stick against his palm, illustrating what he planned to do with it.

Everything happened so fast after that moment. Intense fear struck through Adelina as she took in a deep breath to cry out and warn Henry, but a large hand flew out in front of her and muffled her scream. Another hand overtook her arm and pulled her into her assailant.

Henry realized what was happening too late. He lunged for his cutlass and stood up with his weapon in hand, ready to defend Adelina. From the corner of his eye, Henry saw a shadow rise above his head. He turned, ready to sink the blade into the stomach of the man behind him, when a bursting pain shot through his head.

Adelina cringed at the splintering sound of wood against bone and watched in horror as Henry slumped to the ground with a sickening thud. The man nudged him with his toe. Henry rolled slightly, but didn't respond. The man winked at her and began to laugh. The man behind her snickered.

Despite what her brain was telling her, Adelina gave into her heart. She bit down hard on the hand that held her mouth until she could taste blood. The man cursed and instantly freed her.

With tears in her eyes, Adelina ran to Henry's side and knelt down, pulling him into her arms. He was still breathing—light and shallow—but at least he was still breathing. It took courage, but she managed to rotate Henry's head and look at his wound.

It's not that bad, Adelina lied to herself. The cut was about as long as her index finger, but it was deep and bleeding rather badly. He would certainly need a doctor to remove the embedded splinters and give him a dozen or so stitches.

While the two men continued laughing, Adelina retrieved Henry's shirt and tied it around his head in a makeshift bandage, securing the knot as tight as she could. She grimaced when she saw the black color of the shirt darken even further as it soaked up Henry's blood.

Fighting tears, Adelina leaned forward and placed a soft kiss on Henry's lips. The man with the tattoos stopped laughing and grabbed her elbow, forcing her to her feet.

"Let's go," he growled.

"No!" Adelina hissed through clenched teeth. Although her vision was blurred from the tears in her eyes, she pulled her arm back and swung it at the man, landing it on the side of his nostril. He released her as he stepped backward, holding his bloody nose in his hands. In that instant, she bent over for Henry's sword, but the other man had stepped forward to step on the blade.

"Vixen," he cursed. While keeping one foot on the blade, he lifted his other and kicked Adelina squarely in the chest, causing her to fall backward.

Adelina sat on the warm sand, pressing a hand against her chest where she was certain to get a bruise. Rage rapidly replaced her fear as she stood up and made fists so tight that her knuckles turned white.

"You sons of—"Adelina didn't finish. She ran her shoulder into the man who had kicked her. He staggered backward a few steps and rubbed his chest where Adelina had plowed into him. She turned and saw the man with blood gushing from his nose take a step toward her with his hands open, waiting for the right moment when he could capture her.

Adelina wasn't going to give him that chance. She picked up Henry's cutlass and stood near his head, where she could protect him and watch the two men. She adjusted her grip on the handle and held the sword erect from her stomach.

"Back off!" Adelina ordered. *I don't know how long I can defend Henry, but I'm going to as long as I possibly can.*

"My, my, aren't we a feisty one?" a third man said from behind her.

Adelina jumped and glanced over her shoulder. While turning back and forth between the two men on her left and the newcomer on her right, Adelina stepped carefully over Henry's unconscious body so she could keep all three men in view. There was something familiar about this new man with long hair and a crooked nose. She knew she had seen him before. "What do you want?"

The man stepped forward and displayed an open palm for a handshake. He smiled, showing a missing tooth next to a gold one. "I'm sorry. Let me introduce myself. My name is Captain Jack Burton."

Adelina gasped as recognition dawned on her. "You're the man from the forest—the one that they are looking for!"

Jack nodded and moved his neglected hand to cup his chin. "Yes, that's right. I tried a goatee for a while, but with all the heat I decided to give it up. Now, come along," he said, turning to walk down the sandy beach.

"No!"

Jack stopped and looked back at her. "No? Oh, my dear, yes, you will." He continued walking. "Someone please persuade her."

"Aye, aye, sir," the man with the tattoos said. He moved toward Adelina with a smile.

"What about that one?" the other one asked, pointing to Henry.

Jack stopped walking and turned to face him. He cocked his head, thinking. "He's no longer any importance. Leave him for the insects to chew on."

Adelina shrieked. "What! No!"

"It's just too bad we're in such a rush," Jack sighed, pretending to be sad. He turned to his two men. "Are you going to bring her or not?"

"Aye, aye," the tattooed man said. He made a playful grab for her and Adelina turned the blade toward him. The other man, with blood still streaming from his nose, circled around her in the other direction.

Adelina screamed as the two men lunged for her at the same time.

It only took them a moment to seize the sword from Adelina's grasp and cast it aside. The tattooed man wrapped his large arms around her, pinning her arms to her chest. The other man moved in front of her. Adelina turned her head and bit the forearm of the tattooed man, causing him to cry out and lift her off the ground. She used the brief opportunity to kick the other man in the nose, knocking off her slipper as she did so.

To Jack's amusement, it took the two men another couple of minutes to wrestle Adelina to the ground and gag her with a torn sleeve. He was amazed that she still continued fighting back, punching and kicking whenever possible. With a sigh, he offered them the idea of using the rope of their belts to tie her feet and wrists together.

With a grunt, the two men picked her up; one by her arms and the other by her legs. Struggling, they carried her, squirming for her life, down the beach to the waiting coxswain. One of the men had to almost sit on her to keep her from jumping overboard and swimming to the beach. By the time they boarded the *Blood Water*, she was physically and emotionally exhausted, but had managed to work the gag free and continued to curse and threaten them.

"Where should we put her, sir?" the tattooed man asked with a sigh, as Adelina wiggled in his arms.

Jack strolled to Adelina's suspended body and cupped her chin. "My quarters, perhaps?"

Adelina spat on his wrists and glared up at him. "Go to Hell."

Jack wiped the spit on his trousers. "Now where are our manners today? You haven't been ladylike at all since we met." He turned to the tattooed man. "Put her in the forepeak."

Adelina watched as someone opened a wooden hatch near the bow of the ship. The two men carried her to the opening, ignoring her meager squirming. A third man waited there with a knife, where he removed the ropes from Adelina's ankles and wrists. But before Adelina could retaliate and make an attempt to escape, the tattooed man pushed her into the hatch.

She fell the twenty feet without screaming, landing on a pile of discarded sails and soft bundles. She bit her tongue when she landed and spat the blood to the side.

Adelina looked up in time to watch Jack close the hatch above her. She heard him laughing while he shouted out orders to set sail. She looked around in the dimly lit corners for any means to escape before they were too far from shore. Nothing. Besides the sails in the center, there were a few discarded ropes and a couple of empty cargo crates against one wall. About a dozen buckets, four barrels and couple of planks of wood lined up against the other wall. The only source of light came from above, illuminating only a few square feet.

Adelina moved slowly about her prison, letting her eyes adjust to the darkness. She peeked inside each barrel, only to find three empty and one full of stagnant water. She returned to the mound of sails and made herself a makeshift cushion. After killing a few spiders and other uncanny insects, she kicked off her worn slippers and lay down.

There was nothing she could do to escape. There was no one who could save her. Not even Henry could come to her rescue a second time, for he was dead. Adelina buried her face into the rough cloth and cried harder than she ever remembered. "Henry..." she mumbled over and over again between sobs.

Chapter Ten

Catherine stepped from Henry's bedroom, fully exhausted and ready for a full night's sleep. But her heart went out to Billy and Thomas, who've waited nervously in the hallway all night long. Catherine sighed heavily. "Ye may come in now."

The doctor, dressed in his nightclothes, looked up and gave a sympathetic smile as he finished putting his various instruments into the black canvas bag. He stood about average height, but looked taller because of his slim frame.

Henry lay on the bed beneath him, void of all clothing but covered with a bed sheet. Thick bandages wrapped his head and a waxy ointment covered parts of his skin. Even in the dim candlelight and the first morning rays of sun that penetrated the room Thomas could see that his captain was pale and covered in a thin layer of sweat.

"How is he, sir?" Thomas asked as he approached the bed.

"I don't know, son," the doctor said softly. "There is no sign of infection as of right now. But if anything develops, call for me right away."

Thomas nodded and rubbed Henry's forearm. "When will he wake up?"

The doctor secured the clasp to his bag and gave Henry one last look. "I don't know that either. He's unconscious and isn't responding. It could be tomorrow, next week, or…" He trailed off, not wanting to finish. He picked up his bag and moved to the door. "Catherine, I'm leaving a few bottles of laudanum with you. If he begins to cry out in his sleep, give him a tablespoon."

"Thank ye, sir," Catherine mumbled, forcing herself to smile.

The doctor slowly moved to the open door, feeling guilty for leaving everyone in such despair. "Make sure that his bandages are changed three or four times a day, and check for infections and fever. And give him nothing but water and chicken soup broth 'til he wakes up. He'll be in a lot of pain between his head and the insect bites, just to forewarn you."

Catherine nodded. "I'll see to it meself."

"One more thing, if you don't mind me asking," the doctor paused.

"Yes?" Billy encouraged.

"Who bandaged his head with the shirt?" the doctor inquired.

"We think it was…his lady friend. Why do you ask?" Billy asked, crossing his arms, as if daring the doctor to say something offensive.

"She probably saved his life," he said, hoping to spread some hope on the situation. "I'll see myself out."

Catherine waited for the door to close before she looked at Billy. "I wish Mizz Ellingsworth was here. What do ye think happened?"

"I say Burton did it," Billy shrugged.

"Yeah, but he would have made sure Masta Roark was dead," Catherine stated. "It had to have been someone else, someone after the mizz and not the Masta."

Thomas nodded. "I saw a lot of footprints in the sand. And there was a trail of blood that leads away from the cap'n. So, someone else was out there, and *they* took Adelina."

"Her father or betrothed, perhaps?" Thomas asked with a shrug.

"No, Mark would have warned us by now if anything changed," Billy said. "We know that Burton was in the area and could damn well have ambushed the cap'n."

"So, let's say that it was Burton—what do we do now?" Catherine asked. The room stayed quiet.

Adelina awoke to whistling and obscene suggestions coming from the pirates who peaked in on her through the open sections of the hatch above. Stubbornly, and without looking up, Adelina moved to a corner protected by a dark shadow.

She used a discarded nail to scratch a line next to the other seven that marked how many days it had been since she was pulled from Henry's side. Adelina rubbed her dry eyes, not being able to cry over his death for two days now.

"Over a week," Adelina mumbled. She was sure that by now Billy or Thomas had made their way to the statues and found Henry's dead body, half eaten by insects and rodents. They were sure to blame her. If she somehow managed to get back to Barbuda, she would certainly die a murderess death.

But what would it matter? I'm already dead, she thought. *Not because of the uncertain fate I will surely suffer at Jack's hands, but inside. My heart was torn from my body and crushed before my eyes. Oh, Henry.*

"Food's acommin!" someone shouted down, disrupting Adelina's thoughts. The hatch lifted and a basket descended on a length of rope.

"Thank you," Adelina called up, deciding that it was better not to bite the hand that's feeding her. She emptied the basket containing mildly spoiled fruit, a small water canteen, a piece of meat and half a loaf of stale bread into a small crate before the rope was pulled back up.

Adelina sat down in the morning light with the crate on her lap and picked up the piece of meat. She took a small bite and suddenly felt a wave of nausea sweep through her body. She dropped the meat into the box and put it on the floor. With a hand to her stomach, Adelina raced to the corner on her right and expelled what little food she had in her stomach into a bucket.

After an hour, the feeling finally passed over. She called up to one of the men posted by the hatch and the rope descended again. Adelina attached the dirty bucket to the rope and looked away as it was being pulled up.

"I'm fine. Just a little nervous and scared, that's all," Adelina told herself. Then she thought of yesterday and the day before. "Again."

A few minutes later, a fresh bucket filled with water was returned to her. Adelina took the heavy bucket to the opposite corner from which it came, where she strung up a small sail three days ago to provide her some privacy.

Once hidden from anyone who could view her from the hatch, Adelina lifted her skirts, bunching the fabric around her hips. She picked up the slimy bar of soap someone had dropped to her and began to wash her legs using a tattered rag. Without removing her dress, Adelina proceeded to wash her arms, shoulders, face and hair. After feeling as refreshed as she could possibly get, Adelina pushed the bucket into the corner and stood up to fetch her breakfast.

As she stepped around the sail, a small, almost a clicking, noise sounded from the crate. It grew louder as she moved toward it. Cautiously, Adelina approached the crate. Standing on tiptoe and arching her neck, she peered into the box. A large black rat with glowing red eyes stared back at her.

Adelina screamed, startling the rat and herself. She reached for the nearest plank of wood, cutting a splinter deep into her thumb. The rat flipped the crate over, spilling its contents. With a screech, it scampered from the box into the shadows, carrying the piece of meat in its teeth. She chased after it, but to no avail—it had disappeared into a small hole in the wood.

Admitting to her defeat, Adelina returned to the patch of light and pulled out the splinter with her fingernails. With a sigh, she picked up the remaining part of her breakfast and returned it to the crate. While keeping an eye in the direction in which the rat disappeared, she placed a wide piece of wood on top of the crate containing her food and pushed it aside, not wanting to think about that disgusting creature touching her food.

The day had grown hotter, indicating that it was about noon and that the room will slowly continue to cook until dusk, making it difficult to breathe. Reluctantly, she moved to the shade, where it wasn't much cooler. Adelina sat in the shadows on a barrel, listening to her stomach growl.

"Hello?" she called up. No answer. With a groan as she returned to her breakfast. She picked up the bread and grimaced as she took a bite. It disgusted her to finish her breakfast, but it satisfied her hunger.

Jack appeared at the hatch. "Would you care for some fresh air?" he asked as he tossed down a rope ladder.

"No...thank you," Adelina nearly spat. She didn't want to be around those filthy, disgusting men any more than she had to.

"That's fine, suit yourself," Jack said as he moved to where she couldn't see him.

Adelina sighed in the smoldering hot room. *I don't want to go up there, but it will give me an opportunity to search for a means of escape.* Regretting every step she took, Adelina climbed the ladder.

Jack waited for her by the hatch and offered her a helping hand. Adelina refused it and struggled to shield her eyes from the sudden brightness of the sun as she awkwardly slid her body off the ladder and onto the boards of the deck. She stood up and arched her back until she felt the relief of a crack.

"Better?" Jack smiled. He gestured with his hands that she needed to accompany him as he moved about the ship.

Adelina followed, but she remained a few steps behind him. She looked out onto the horizon, praying for some hint of land. Nothing. Only the wide Atlantic Ocean stared back at her. A ship lingered in the distance, too far that she could signal for help, but close enough that she could vaguely make out the men moving up and down the masts.

She turned away and looked to the other side of the ship. What she found there was worse than the blank sea and the false hope. Nearly three dozen men had stopped what they were doing to turned and gawk at her. Some licked their lips and simply winked. Others were more provocative and grabbed their manhood, calling out offensive names. Looking at them, she was suddenly concerned for her safety, knowing what they could do to her. She knew that the captain wouldn't threaten keelhauling as Henry had done.

Jack saw the fearful look on her face as she eyes his crew. "Don't worry. They won't do anything to you."

Adelina cocked her eyebrow, almost certain of his lie. "Thank you."

Jack grinned. "I always get first share."

Adelina shuddered. "Sir, now that Henry is…" she couldn't say it. "What do you want with me?"

Jack stopped walking and turned to face her. "I can think of quite a few things," he said, reaching out with a dirty hand to caress her cheek.

Adelina swatted his hand away without moving her steady gaze, receiving cheers from the men watching her. "I'm serious."

"Me too," Jack whispered, ignoring them. He leaned back against the railing, using his elbows to support him. "But I have enough dignity not to rape an unwilling wench. I'd get much more satisfaction if you were to come to me."

"That would never happen," Adelina spat.

Jack laughed. "You will if you care about your life…or that babe in your belly."

Adelina's eyes widen. "Pardon?"

"I've been with enough women to know when one is heavy with child," Jack said matter-of-factly.

"Child? Oh, no. I'm not pregnant," Adelina defended herself. But as she spoke, she could feel herself go lightheaded and a tasteless vile rise in her throat. Adelina grabbed the ship's railing to steady herself. "I'm not."

Jack threw his hands up in the air. "If you say so."

Adelina rolled her eyes. "So, where are we going?"

"I still haven't decided yet. I'm thinking the colonies," Jack pondered. "I know of a man who'd give me a pretty penny for a pretty lady."

"What?" Adelina's jaw dropped. *I would never be bought or traded as a slave.*

"Prostitution, of course," Jack continued. "I think you'd make a lot of men *very* happy. Me first, though. But before we get there, we have to make port and get some supplies."

"I'd like to go back to my dungeon now, thank you," Adelina said quickly. She didn't wait for an answer. She spun on her heels and made her way to the bow of the ship, ignoring the catcalls that followed her.

Once in the safety of her dark haven, Adelina forced herself to take several deep breaths and relax. Feeling the heat of her prison, Adelina hid behind the sail and lifted her skirts. She used the soapy water to wash and cool her legs. When she finished, she leaned against the wall and curled her knees to her chin. "Henry…"

She was surprised to feel a tear dampen her cheek.

There was nothing now—simply darkness. At least the darkness was better than the screaming he often heard echoing inside of his head. It was worse when he caught a glimpse of Adelina fighting her for her life—no—his life. He was helpless to save her. Then, in an instant, she was gone and the darkness would return again.

Something wet and cold touched him. He shifted, but he felt it again. Slowly, as though waking up from a deep dream, he became conscious of the sounds around him. There was a light splashing of water and someone breathing on his right. A bird was calling outside and the flutter of wings near his window. There were voices in the distance.

With great effort, Henry opened his eyes.

Catherine gasped when she saw those sky blue eyes open and focus on her. She dropped the washcloth into the water and set the porcelain bowl on the night stand. Smiling, she grabbed Henry's hand and squeezed it. "Oh, Masta. Ye're awake."

Henry groaned when she spoke and brought his free hand to the back of his head. His fingertips grazed over the bandage, causing a piercing pain to shoot through the steady throbbing he already felt. Gritting his teeth against his pounding headache, Henry forced himself to sit up.

Catherine patted his hand and reached for a bottle on the night stand. "Here, this should help," she said, handing him the medicine. She stood up and quickly left the room.

Henry looked at the bottle and recognized the frosty liquid as laudanum. He dropped it into his lap, not wanting to give into its addictive power. Slowly, Henry reached up and unraveled the bandage from his head. He carefully examined the clean dressing, indicating that he was no longer bleeding. The door opened a moment later and he looked up to find Catherine leading Billy and Thomas into the room.

"Cap'n, how do you feel?" Thomas asked as he gave his captain a pat on the back. Henry yelped in pain. "Sorry."

"My head hurts. A lot," Henry said, rubbing his temples.

"Well, we're glad you're back with us." Billy smiled.

"How long was I out for?" Henry asked.

Catherine sat down on the bed. "Jest over a fortnight. Sixteen days."

Henry cursed. He looked about the room. Disappointment filled his voice. "Where is Adelina?"

Billy took a deep breath. "We don't know. We were kind of hoping you did."

Henry covered his face with his hands, waiting for his memory to come back. He didn't speak for a long time. "Burton."

"Are you positive?" Billy asked.

Henry nodded. "Except I don't know where they took her."

Thomas coughed. "The ship is man'd and supplied for you…when you're ready."

Billy glared at Thomas. "When you're feeling better, Cap'n."

Henry kicked off the sheet before he realized his own nakedness. Ignoring the growing pain in his head, he climbed out of bed and donned a pair of trousers. "I'm feeling better."

"Wait, Masta," Catherine stopped him as he approached the door. "Norton said something a week ago about two sailors talking about a ship. They said it came from the back of the island and they wouldn't have noticed it except it had a woman on board."

"Good. I'll have Norton go into town with me and see if I can find those men. Hopefully, they're still here," Henry said as he pulled on a shirt.

"Yes, Masta." Catherine smiled, running out of the room in search of her husband.

"Cap'n—" Billy cautioned.

"Billy, you're not talking me out of this," Henry grunted as he secured his cutlass and sheath around his waist.

"You have a head injury—"

"Stop it, Billy. I have to find Adelina," Henry said, growing agitated.

"But you could—"

"Damn it, William, I don't care!" Henry yelled, sending rivets of pain through his head. He closed his eyes and took a breath. "All I care about is getting my Adelina back." Without another word he left the room, catching up with Norton as he descended the staircase.

"The horses are ready, sir." Norton smiled. "Glad to see you up and moving."

"Let's go," Henry ordered with a stiff nod. He opened the door and stepped out. For a moment, he struggled to mount Buttercup as he tried to keep his vision from spinning.

Henry didn't wait for Norton to climb his horse. The second he was in the saddle, he grabbed the reins and kicked the powerful beast into a full breakneck run.

The scenery flew past him faster than ever before. The constant motion made his head pound harder, but Henry didn't care. He wanted to find those sailors, get the coordinates, and set sail on the *North Star* by nightfall. He wanted to find Adelina as soon as possible, knowing that she didn't have much time. He suddenly felt a heavy pressure on his shoulders, feeling that he wouldn't be fast enough.

He was so concentrating on formulating a plan of how to get Adelina back that he didn't even realize that he was in town until the horse began to kick up the white sand on the beach. He looked up in surprise and saw a ship in the process of dispersing its passengers and crew in the shallow lagoon. With an agitated sigh, Henry turned his horse around and led him to the first tavern.

Henry swung his leg over the saddle and landed on his feet with a grunt. His legs and back ached, causing him to hunch over. He felt dizzy as the sights before him began to spin around. He knew he needed to sit down for a few minutes. *Adelina needs me*, Henry thought and he immediately stood up and marched to the first tavern.

It was grim inside, full of dark, lifeless colors. A couple of hanging lanterns and chandeliers were lit here and there over the tables where several men sat and gambled, but nothing to accumulate to any significant source of light. Not even the windows were clean enough to permit the afternoon sunlight in. The stale stench of smoke, sweat, and blood lingered heavily in the air. *I still couldn't believe I had spent so much time in this awful place.*

"Gentlemen!" Henry shouted over the noise of the room. Several of the men glanced up while others grunted and purposely ignored him. "Did anyone come to this island a week ago and pass a ship called the *Blood Water*?"

"What's it to you?" a man with a gray beard asked from one of the gambling tables, not bothering to take his eyes off the cards he was holding.

"I'm looking for someone," Henry stated.

"Who?" the man asked, laying his cards down on the table with a grin. He collected his winnings while the other men at the tabled frowned.

Henry walked over to him and sat down in an empty chair next to him. He took a deep breath and forced himself to talk slow and evenly. "I'm looking for a woman. I heard that the ship that came in last week saw her. She was on the *Blood Water*."

The man nodded. "And?"

"I'd like to know where the ship is heading so I could get her back," Henry said, grinding his teeth. He felt himself growing angry and suddenly pressed for time. He eyed the man in front of him, determining if a flash of his sword would acquire the information he sought for. The other men around the table saw Henry's fingers brush the handle of his cutlass and shifted in their seats.

"Why?" the man asked as he gathered the cards together to shuffle.

"Because I love her, damn it!" Henry yelled, standing up, causing the chair to flip over. He took a deep breath and lowered his voice, shocked at his own words. "I love her."

The man looked up at Henry and smiled. "The ship was a barquentine."

Henry nodded, knowing that barquentines were the slowest ships in the Caribbean and often preyed on by pirates.

"Yes. I was tempted to plunder it, but I changed my mind when I saw that he had a woman on board. They're bad luck, you know," the man said, shrugging his shoulders. "But, anyway, they were heading northwest, toward Savannah or Charleston," he said before giving him the coordinates of the sighting.

"Thank you," Henry whispered.

"Wait…the wind was dying down when we came to port. Hell—I'm surprised that the ship out front made it, so they probably didn't get far, unless the captain's experienced and good at what he does," the man snorted as he shuffled the cards.

Henry shook his head. "He's not."

"And that means there's probably a good storm brewing to the south. So, use it for what it's worth," the man advised as he began dealing.

"I'll keep it in mind. Thank you," Henry said, leaving the tavern. He found Norton tethering his horse next to his. "I found the men already. I'm sorry to make you ride all the way out here for no reason."

"That's alright, sir. I rather enjoyed the ride, anyway," Norton said with a small smile.

Henry smiled and reached into his pocket and pulled out some loose change. "Here, why don't you stay for a while and have yourself a drink?"

"Thank you, sir." Norton smiled. As he opened the door to the tavern, he turned back. "Good luck."

"Bye, Norton," Henry called after him as the door swung shut. He turned to walk back to his horse, nearly tripping over Michelle.

"Henry, oh thank God, you're alright!" she cried as she threw her hands around his neck. "I've been worried sick about you. I've been up there almost every day checking on you."

Henry reached up and released her hands. "Thank you for your concerns, Michelle. But I have to go now."

"Well, gee, wait a second. You don't even want to talk to me?" Michelle pouted. She looked around, linking her hands behind her back. "Where's Adelina? I haven't seen her lately."

"That's because she hasn't been here," Henry said as he sidestepped her.

Michelle followed him, smiling. "You mean to tell me that you sent her away after she…after what she did?"

Henry shook his head. "Why would I do that?"

Michelle gasped. "You didn't?"

"Michelle, I don't have time for this. I have to set sail as soon as possible," Henry said as he reached his horse.

"Fine," Michelle huffed, balling her fists. She turned on her heels and stormed away, nearly bumping into the family who were approaching behind her. She gave the gentleman with red-brown hair a soft smile over her shoulder, swinging her hips as she walked past him.

"Pardon me, sir," came a soft voice from behind Henry.

Henry turned and found a tall, slim woman with graying hair and big brown eyes standing behind him. A small blonde-haired boy of about six hid behind his mother's legs, and a young woman of about five-and-ten, holding two pieces of luggage, almost did the same. Off to the side stood the young man in an outrageous yellow jacket that hurt Henry's eyes, carrying in a bag under his arm. Henry rolled his eyes when he noticed that the man's head was bent in a way that he could watch Michelle's swinging hips as she continued down the road. When a carriage pulled in his line of sight, the man turned back to face Henry with dark green eyes. Henry took a double take. There was something oddly familiar about him. "Yes, ma'am. What can I do for you?"

"We just arrived here and we were wondering if there was a nice place to stay for a few nights?" the woman asked.

Henry nodded and gestured across the street at Meghan's. "Over there is pretty much the only half way decent inn on this island. Tell 'em Henry Roark sent you."

"Thank you, sir," the woman said as she moved toward the inn.

The young man dropped the luggage onto the dirt and stepped forward. "Captain of the *North Star*?"

Henry swallowed as he made eye contact with the man. His right hand moved instinctively to the handle of his sword. "How may I help you?"

The man pulled out his sword and raised it. The woman gasped and pulled the child against her as she took several steps backward. "My name is Brandon Wexford."

Henry extended his sword and met it against Brandon's. "Wexford."

Brandon began to circle around Henry. "Where is Adelina?"

"Not here," Henry hissed.

Brandon arched his sword back and swung it at Henry. Henry tilted his wrist and blocked the oncoming weapon above his head. The clash sent vibrations throughout his body, making blood rush to his head in hot pulsations. He closed his eyes and shook his head to clear it. He opened his eyes a second later to see Brandon taking a step backward. In a single step, he lunged at Henry's abdomen. Henry stepped out of range, spun in a circle and made an attempt at Brandon's side.

Brandon barely managed to bring his sword down in time over Henry's to block it, forcing him to step closer. "Take me to her," Brandon ordered as he gasped for breath.

Henry lifted his foot off the ground and planted it in Brandon's chest, causing him to fall over onto his back. Henry kicked away Brandon's sword and stood above him, blade resting at his side. He wiped the sweat off his brow and sighed. "I can't. And killing me won't help the situation any."

"Why not?" Brandon hissed.

"Because someone took her from me," Henry admitted. Overwhelmed with pity for Brandon, he offered a helping hand.

Brandon felt himself become filled with rage. He kicked Henry in the shin, causing him to drop his sword and stumble back a few paces, using the tavern wall to brace himself and stop his fall. Brandon grabbed Henry's sword as he got to his feet. He put both hands on the sword and brought it over his head. Almost screaming, Brandon charged at Henry.

With ease, Henry stepped to the side, leaving Brandon to charge into the tavern wall. Behind him, Henry heard the boy snort and giggle.

Brandon stood still for a moment. Then the sword fell from Brandon's hands, hitting the ground with a soft thud. He staggered backward, holding his nose as it began to bleed. "Air es A-del-eena?"

Henry sighed and picked up his sword. After guiding it into its sheath, he turned back to Brandon. "You're her fiancé," Henry paused. "I can get her back for you. Actually, I was on my way of getting her back when you interrupted me."

"E'm gong wit yu," Brandon said, still holding his nose. He pulled a handkerchief out of his pocket and shoved the corners inside of his nostrils.

"Whatever," Henry mumbled. He turned to the woman and her son. "Am I to presume that you're Adelina's family?"

The woman nodded. "I am her mother, Lady Elizabeth Ellingsworth. This little boy is Christopher, her brother. And back here is Mary, her lady's maid."

Henry knelt down in front of Christopher. "Little boy? You look more like a young man to me. My name is Captain Henry Roark," he said, extending a hand.

Christopher shook it as he entered a series of giggles. "Are you a real pirate?"

"Christopher!" Elizabeth scolded. "I'm sorry, sir. I'm afraid he listened too much of the sailor's stories on the voyage."

"Oh, that's alright," Henry said looking up to Elizabeth. He turned back to Christopher. "I'm something like that, yes. But I'm a lot nicer than the other ones you'd meet," he said. He stood up and returned his attention back to Elizabeth. "I plan to leave tonight to get your daughter back. You are all welcome to stay at my estate if you wish."

Elizabeth gritted her teeth and thought for a moment. She glanced behind her shoulder at Meghan's, where a pirate was escorting a lady of special services inside. Then she looked back at Henry, the man who had kidnapped her daughter. *What was the lesser of two evils*? she rationalized. "Thank you."

"Master?" Norton said, coming out of the tavern with numerous other spectators who were curious about the commotion going on outside the tavern window. "I thought you would have left by now to find the miss?"

Miss? Elizabeth thought. *They actually call her Miss? Dirty, disgusting pirates using formality?*

"I was planning on it," he said, forcing himself to smile as he faced Norton. "It looks like we have Adelina's family as guests for a while."

Norton greeted everyone with a single nod. "Well, I saw Michael, Sir Huntington's messenger boy, inside. I can ask him to give me a ride back if you'd like to use the other horse," Norton offered. "He brought the carriage in for repairs, so I can take their bags to the estate with me."

Henry nodded and pulled out more loose change from his pocket. "Yes, please. It'd be easier. And here, give this to Michael for his services."

Mary stepped forward with the bags. "I'll stay with the luggage, mum."

Elizabeth nodded. "Thank you, Mary."

"Mister pirate man, can I ride with you?" Christopher asked with a wide smile and hoping eyes.

"Sure." Henry laughed. "Just let me help your mother on first."

It was a much slower ride back to the manor than what Henry had originally anticipated. He didn't expect the extra company to delay his plans. Christopher rode in his lap and persisted in asking questions about dreaded pirates and lost treasure, which Henry had endured with a distracted smile. His thoughts were elsewhere.

He didn't mind Adelina's mother and brother here. *It would be a pleasant surprise for Adelina when she returns. It would have saved me the trip back to England. It's Brandon—the incompetent fool—who I don't want anywhere near this island.* Henry sighed. *He's here to take back Adelina...my Adelina. As much as I don't want to admit it, he is her betrothed and I have to respect that. I'll have to be the better man.*

"Brandon, where are your business associates?" Henry called to the man on the horse next to him. The last thing he needed was Lord Ellingsworth and Wexford ambushing him.

Brandon didn't answer. He simply turned his attention elsewhere.

"We don't exactly know," Elizabeth muttered. "My husband told me everything—about how he cheated you. Several weeks ago he told me how he cheated an executive of the King, but his plan was exposed. The next morning, he, and everything we owned was gone. I was told to leave the country."

"I'm sorry, milady," Henry offered. He was surprised when he actually felt that he had meant it.

"Oh, no, don't be. Jonathon wasn't at all concerned about Adelina. Just money and revenge," Elizabeth said, pressing a fingertip to the corner of her eye.

"If you don't mind me asking, how did you afford your passage here?" Henry asked.

"Oh, I had already bought the passage for the four of us before he left." Elizabeth smiled. "A young man gave me your name before he passed away."

Henry hung his head thinking of Mark. He knew the lad wouldn't have betrayed his confidence if he didn't think it was for the better. *I will have to send patronage to his parents.* "Brandon, did you share this information with your associates?"

"She wouldn't tell me where we were going," Brandon mumbled. "Despite my attempts."

Henry smiled to himself. "Then what are you doing here?"

"Brandon is here to take Adelina back to England with Christopher and Mary," Elizabeth paused. "I hope…to give you my life for my daughter's."

Henry nodded, admiring her nobility.

A few minutes later, they turned onto the pebbled drive. Catherine was waiting out front, looking curiously at the new visitors. As everyone dismounted, Henry introduced them.

"Brandon is going to go with me to rescue Adelina," Henry said sarcastically, forcing himself to sound cheerful.

Catherine noted the disappointment and sadness hidden in her master's eyes, despite his attempt to hide it. "Don't worry, Masta. *Ye'll* get her back. Jest wait and see."

Henry shrugged. "Well, the sooner we get on our way, the better."

Brandon nodded and handed Catherine a small bag that he had kept with him. "These are my clothes. See that they get to where they need to be."

Henry took the bag from Catherine before she could move. "How about showing the Ellingsworths' where they'll sleep. And then we'll meet you at the dock."

Catherine smiled. "This way, milady and young Masta."

Brandon shook his head. "You shouldn't be too nice to the help like that. They start to think that they run the place."

Henry shoved Brandon's bag into his chest, pushing Brandon back a step. "She does. Let's go," he said, turning to leave. He didn't wait to see if Brandon would follow.

Brandon grunted and chased after Henry. "Shouldn't we be going back into town?"

"No," Henry said, feeling himself starting to get annoyed.

Brandon snorted. "Sure, Henry."

Henry sighed, realizing that a headache would probably develop soon. He led Brandon through the kitchen door. "This way," he gestured as he made his way to the dock.

Billy was waiting for them where the dock met the sand. He looked at Brandon's attire and grinned. "The coxswain is tied at the end. Who's the pansy?"

"Brandon, this is my quartermaster. Billy—Adelina's betrothed," Henry said, taking a deep breath. He continued walking to the end of the dock. He waved to his men waiting on the ship.

"Is that your ship?" Brandon asked.

"Billy, why is the bow facing the other direction?" Henry asked.

"Oh, um, while you were, uh, napping, I had the men take the ship into port to clean the keel and bring it in reverse so it's easier to leave," Billy stammered.

Henry turned and looked at Billy. He said nothing for a moment. With a smile, he nodded. "Thanks."

"Geez," Brandon sighed as he stepped past Henry and Billy. He put his hands on his hips and looked at ship. "How long was your nap?"

Henry hanged his head and took a deep breath, ignoring the sudden feeling of pushing Brandon into the water.

"Alright, Sweetheart, say your goodbyes now," Elizabeth said, approaching from behind.

Christopher ran down the dock, not heeding his mother yelling at him to stop. Brandon got down on his knee and opened his arms, ready for Christopher to charge into him.

Henry turned to the *North Star*, giving them a few minutes of privacy for their farewells. Something ran into the back of his legs, nearly knocking him over. Henry looked down to find Christopher holding on as if his life depended on it.

"Please bring back my sister, please?" he asked as his eyes filled with tears.

Henry lifted Christopher into his arms, letting him cling to his neck. "I promise you that I will," he whispered as he felt tears well up in his eyes too.

Christopher nodded and Henry sat him down on his feet. "Thank you, mister pirate man." He smiled as he walked back his mother.

"Christopher—where's my goodbye?" Brandon asked, still on his knees with his arms spread.

"Bye!" he called over his shoulder.

Brandon waited for a moment. When Christopher reached Elizabeth, Brandon shrugged and stood up. "Bye! We'll be back soon."

Laughing, Henry stepped into the coxswain. "Come on, Brandon. We're leaving. Bye, Catherine."

Brandon got in and sat down, holding his bag against his chest. Billy untied the boat and shoved off. Minutes later the boat was secured to the *North Star* and the three stood safely on the quarterdeck.

"Alright, men! Raise the hook, set the sails. Let's get the hell out of here!" Henry ordered. The men immediately set to work pulling ropes and raising and lowering different sized sails. Smiling, he turned to Billy. "It's good to be back."

Brandon looked around and eyed all the various men. He noticed the wide assortment of tattoos, piercings, and the two men who had lost a limb. He couldn't help but stare at them while he clutched his bag a little tighter to his chest. Then he became aware of a few of them staring back, sensing his fear.

"You really are a pirate, aren't you?" Brandon mumbled.

"You knew that when you met me," Henry said with a smile as he walked to the helm.

"Henry—" Brandon began.

"Captain Roark," Henry corrected. *I'm not about to let this man walk all over me on* my *ship.* "You refer to me as Captain Roark."

"Where am I to stay?" Brandon mumbled.

Henry pointed toward the bow of the ship. "This way," he said. He climbed down the ladder that led into the forward hold. He found an empty hammock amongst the sleeping crew and sat on it. "Here."

"Um…no, Henry," Brandon said, shaking his head.

"Captain Roark," Henry corrected. "Now, if you want to save Adelina on *my* ship, you do it *my* way."

"Did you make Adelina sleep down here?" Brandon asked as he moved his bag under his arm.

"No," Henry said, "that'd be wrong."

"Well, where did she sleep?" Brandon inquired.

"With me." Henry grinned. He stood up, seeing that Brandon had shifted the bag around so he could reach for his weapon. Henry pulled his sword out and laid the blade along Brandon's shoulder. "Don't try it, Brandon."

Brandon took a breath and nodded. Reluctantly, he sat down on the hammock, still clutching the bag.

Smiling, Henry moved toward the ladder. "You coming?"

"Why?" Brandon asked.

"Because you're not getting a free ride," Henry said sternly as he climbed up the ladder.

Brandon rolled his eyes and followed Henry up the ladder to the quarterdeck. Henry waited for him with a sponge and bucket in hand. He called for his men and they immediately gathered around him. "Listen up! This man, here, is our newest addition. Make him feel…welcome."

Brandon took the sponge and bucket. He gulped when several men whistled and snickered. "Thanks, Captain," he said sarcastically.

"You begin over there, with Patches. He's the one missing an eye. He lost his eye patch a few months ago, so try not to stare," Henry said with a slap on Brandon's back before he went to take over the helm from Billy.

Billy approached him. "Any idea where to find her?"

"Not a clue."

Chapter Eleven

"Damn you, bitch!" Jack screamed down to her. "You hear me, wench? Damn you!"

Adelina hid in the darkness with a plank of wood to protect her. She knew deep in her heart that it wouldn't do much good against a party of enraged pirates, but it still offered her some comfort.

It was far too late to change what she had done. About nine days into their voyage, the winds died down, leaving them completely stranded in the ocean. Against his shipmaster's advice, Jack ordered to strip the square sails and put them in the forepeak for storage. The next day, he had his men rig the lateen sails, determined that they would catch more wind. Despite Jack's attempt, they continued to float adrift for a week in the hot Caribbean sun with nothing to do but sit and wait. Adelina covered her ears so she couldn't hear Jack whipping his shipmaster for his bad advice. Last night, a slight breeze from a developing storm floated through the air and Jack ordered his shipmaster to bring up the lateen sails in the morning.

Not caring whether she lived or died anymore, Adelina used a discarded nail to shred the sails beyond repair. She smiled at the men when they came down to fetch the sails and even helped them lift them out of the forepeak, none the wiser to the damage she had caused.

Jack must have just released them.

Adelina heard Jack above her, instructing everyone not to send any food or water down to her until he decided what to do with her. If anyone broke his order, the person would be keelhauled, then fed to the sharks.

Thankfully, Adelina had thought of that. For the past week and a half, she took the fresh water she was given and poured it into one of the barrels. She even kept the food in a small crate, well protected from any hungry rats. She knew that if she rationed out how much she ate and drank, her supply would last her, hopefully, for another week.

All she had to do was survive Jack's wrath.

A light knock sounded at the door. It was so soft that Henry didn't even hear it in his dreams. When it sounded again, this time a little louder, it was enough to wake him.

"Come in!" Henry shouted as he sat up. His head pounded behind his ears, making his vision blur for a second.

Thomas entered. "It's morning, sir."

"Thanks, Thomas," Henry mumbled. He waited until Thomas had left before he struggled to stand up, fighting to keep himself balanced as he dressed. He splashed some cold water onto his face and stepped from his cabin, heading for the helm. He passed Brandon, dressed in dark trousers and a large cotton shirt, using a belaying pin to secure a rope to its hold.

Billy was there, minding the wheel. "Morn'n, Cap'n."

"Good morning, Billy," Henry greeted. "How close are we?" he asked as he shuffled through some map charts.

Billy sighed. "It should be right up ahead."

Henry picked up the scope and looked around, slowly scanning the horizon. After completing a full circle, Henry made a fist and brought it down on the railing. "Damn it. It's been two days now."

"Well, they couldn't have gotten far," Billy offered. "Don't worry, sir. We'll find her."

"Still…" Henry mumbled. He picked up a map and began analyzing the charts. "Well, let's try again. The wind started picking up about two—maybe three days ago. That's how we got here so quickly." He pointed to a certain spot on the map.

Billy nodded. "Uh-huh."

"So, let's say that they were here—where we are now—three or four days ago, when the wind picked up," Henry said as he marked an X on the map. "They wouldn't have been able to go far before hand."

"Yes," Billy said.

"It's been blowing north-northeast pretty much the whole time," Henry stated. "And if Burton is going to the colonies, whether for settlement or supplies, he'd have to catch the same wind we are using now. And don't forget, he's also in a barquentine."

"A barquentine?" Billy repeated with a smile, making sure he had heard right. "Then where do you suppose he is?"

Henry did some quick calculations on the edge of the map and drew a circle covering about four nautical miles. "Here. He has to be here."

"How long until we get there?" Billy asked, stepping back so that Henry could take the wheel.

"Three or four days," Henry said. "I want two—no—three men on watch at all times."

"Aye, aye, Cap'n," Billy said as he left the helm.

"Alright, men!" Henry hollered. "Get those sails back up! All of them! We're going to whistle up the wind."

Adelina jumped when she heard the crack of lightening above her. It was followed moments later by a rumble of thunder. She hid on the top of a barrel in the dark corner, pulling a tattered sail tighter around her. She tucked her knees up to her chin in an effort to keep her feet dry as she watched the water pour through the open hatch.

It had begun raining about two hours ago, pounding hard against the deck above her. With the motion of the ship, water easily splashed off the deck and into her prison. In those two hours, the water had already reached her ankles.

To her, it wasn't the cold water that she was afraid of—it was the wind. Without the proper sails, it was near impossible to steer and control the ship over the crashing waves, all in thanks to her. She could feel the ship rocking violently from side to side, sending loose crates crashing into one wall and back to the other.

Huge waves bombarded the ship, spilling more water through the open sections of the hatch. She heard someone screaming and another man calling, "Man overboard."

Frantic footsteps sounded above her, but they were quickly deafened over the pounding rain. Several more men screamed as the ship tilted to one side.

Suddenly a man appeared at the hatch. "This is all your fault, you stupid bitch!" he screamed down. Then he was gone.

If I don't survive, Adelina thought, *then we'll all meet at judgment.*

The clouds darkened heavily overhead. Henry didn't expect the storm to catch up to him so quickly. He had expected the storm to come up behind him, hopefully pushing him in the direction he wanted. But it came up from the south and arced west. Without warning, the heavens opened up and the rain began to fall.

"We're turning south—into the storm!" Henry yelled over the pounding rain. He sharply turned the wheel toward the port side. In doing so, he crashed over a wave, spraying a wall of water onto the deck that pushed a dozen men off their feet.

Henry watched carefully as his men tightened and secured ropes. Several pulled on ropes that controlled the main boom to keep it steady as they changed course. He looked for Brandon amongst his men, deciding it would be best to send him below deck so that he was out of danger and could do no harm. He found him approaching the helm.

"Hen—Captain Roark. I need to talk to you!" Brandon hollered over the pounding rain.

"Not now, Brandon. Why don't you go under for a while?" Henry yelled back. A bolt of lightening shot through the sky, sending deafening thunder an instant later.

"Yes now. Look, I'm not one of your men—" Brandon started.

"I know. That's why I'm sending you below," Henry said.

"No! I am a man of higher birth. I will be in your cabin until the storm blows over," Brandon stated as he moved to walk past Henry.

Henry put his arm out to block Brandon. "No, it's called the captain's quarters for a reason. If you want to retire, which is perfectly fine, go below deck."

Brandon pushed Henry's arm out of his way. "I said I am of higher birth than you. Noblesse oblige, Henry. You cannot order about as you do. I can have you hanged, Pirate."

Henry felt himself fill with anger. "Take a look around, Brandon. You don't see King George here to protect you. As long as you're on *my* ship, you'll answer to *me*—a *pirate*. Get used to it."

Brandon stood there for a moment, staring into Henry's icy blue eyes. "When Adelina gets on this ship, she and I will share your room. Until then, my friend," he said evenly.

"No. When Adelina gets on this ship, she may sleep wherever she wishes. *You* will not step one foot into my room. Got it?" Henry hissed through clenched teeth.

Brandon tightened his jaw as he spun around and marched back to the bow. Henry called for Billy to resume his position at the helm.

"I need some time alone," Henry mumbled as he gave the wheel to his first mate and excused himself.

He entered his room and shut the door behind him. With a sigh, he removed his wet clothes, leaving them in a heap in the corner of the room, as Adelina had done for him. He sat down on the edge of the bed and swung his legs between the sheets. With another sigh, Henry turned onto his side.

On the night stand, Henry spied a book. He reached up and tilted it so that he could read the title.

"*Troilus Criseyde*," Henry muttered. He remembered how Adelina loved Chaucer and it pained him to hold his work in his hands. He saw himself throwing it across the room, breaking the weak binding and watching the torn pages flutter in the air.

He placed it onto the pillow next to him. *She might want it to read on the way back*, he thought as he drifted off to sleep.

A rumble of thunder woke him up less than three hours later. Henry climbed out of bed and dressed into dry clothes. There was a dull ache in the back of his head, but he continued to ignore it. With a groan, he left his room.

"Hello, Billy," Henry greeted as he took the wheel into his hands.

"It wasn't much of a storm," Billy said. "The rain's already beginning to let up."

Henry nodded. "Good then. You can rest now, if you'd like."

Billy nodded. "Thanks."

"Wait," Henry called Billy back. "Where's Brandon?"

Billy snorted. "That pansy refused to take his eyes off you until you went into your room. He crawled below the deck with his tail between his legs."

"Good. Then that means I won't have to watch over him," Henry said, evenly.

"Yeah, I don't see how Adelina can put up with him," Billy muttered as he left for his room.

Henry nodded and looked up into the sky. Billy was right. The pounding rain had reduced into a slow, steady mist. The lightening and the thunder were growing steadily farther apart. *It wasn't as big of a storm as I thought.*

"Cap'n!" Thomas called, running across the quarterdeck with his scope in hand. He slipped in a puddle and the scope went flying backward. Thomas got up, retrieved the instrument and carefully walked to his captain's side.

"What is it, Thomas?" Henry asked.

"There's a ship!" Thomas said, face beaming as he handed Henry the scope. "It's over there—on the port side."

"Jake—here, take the wheel," Henry ordered as he jogged toward the bow of the ship. He brought the scope to his eye and slowly surveyed the horizon where Thomas had pointed.

Something is out there all right. He could vaguely see the dark outline of a shape in the distance. When the mist cleared for a moment, Henry announced that it was, indeed, a ship.

"Is it the *Blood Water*?" Thomas asked eagerly.

Henry squinted. "I can't tell. The sails are badly damaged—it might just be an abandoned ship. Let's check it out anyway."

Thomas nodded, trying to hide his disappointment. "I guess it wouldn't hurt. It might have supplies we can use or something."

"Wait…hold on," Henry paused, leaning over the railing as he adjusted the scope to read the lettering inscribed on the back of the ship. "It's the *Blood Water*."

Everything above her went deadly silent. Even over the pounding rain Adelina was able to hear men hollering and calling to one another. When the rain turned to the wet fog, she could still make out bits and pieces of conversation. Then, all at once, everything stopped.

Was something wrong with the ship? Were they sinking? Did everyone abandon ship? Adelina put a protective hand to her abdomen where she was certain that after forty-five days after her last monthly, she was carrying a baby. *What will I do? I can't let anything happen to Henry's child.*

Adelina stood up, leaving the sail on the barrel. She shuffled through the cold water that reached halfway up to her knees until she stood below the open hatch. "Hello? Is someone up there? What's going on?"

Jack appeared above her aiming a pistol at her through the hatch. "Don't say a word. You scream, I'll kill you."

Fear finally sunk in. Adelina grabbed the wooden plank and splashed through the water back to the barrel. She crawled under the sail and strained her ears to find out what was happening.

Henry stood on the quarterdeck and waited impatiently for his men to gather around. "This is the ship that we've been looking for," he paused as a few men whooped and cheered. With a smile, Henry waved for them to stop. "Now, as everyone can tell, the ship looks deserted. But we're going to board it anyway and hope for the best," Henry paused again. "So, here's the plan…"

An explosion sounded and a loud splash followed it. The thick, bitter stench of gunpowder quickly filled the air, making Adelina gasp and cough in her prison. *Cannon fire! Maybe it's Billy coming to save her!* Adelina thought happily. Her excitement grew, eager to be rescued. But then her heart sank. *That's impossible. Without Henry to lead them…maybe it's another pirate ship. Besides, who else would attack a pirate besides a pirate? Maybe it's the British coming to save me. Doesn't matter anyway. If my name has been ruined, then it would not stop the British from doing what pirates do.* Adelina gripped the wood tighter, sure that her fate was doomed.

It took almost two hours for the *North Star* to come side-by-side with the *Blood Water*. Henry had fired a warning shot over the bow of the ship, but there was no response. With his eyes never leaving the ship, he ordered his men to throw grappling hooks to the *Blood Water* so that the two ships could be secured together for boarding. He had a dozen men armed with swords and pistols line up against the adjoining railings ready for any foul play.

Cautiously, Henry stepped onto the deck of the *Blood Water* first, followed by Billy, Brandon, and another thirty men, each with their swords drawn and ready. The rest of Henry's men remained behind to protect the *North Star*.

The deck of the *Blood Water* was deserted, all but for three dead men propped against the railing and one leaning on his side against the main mast. Henry noticed that each man had fresh blood on his shirt and had his sword just barely out of his grip, as though they were killed in battle. Henry paused next to the man by the mast, carefully monitoring his face as he kicked away his sword.

Brandon followed close to Henry as he moved about the ship. The sun broke through the parting clouds for a brief moment and he shielded his eyes. "At least the weather is clearing."

Henry leaned forward and brought the blade to the dead man's neck. Without a word, he slit the man's throat, spraying blood in a wide arc that landed on his shirt and Brandon's clean shoes.

Brandon jumped back several feet and began to dry heave. "That was a little overkill, don't you think? He was dead already for goodness sake!"

Henry shook his head and stepped away from the man whose throat he just slit. "Dead men don't blink."

"What?" Brandon asked, growing irritated.

"To arms," Henry yelled, raising his sword.

At that instant, the other three men reached for their swords and scrambled to their feet. One of them shouted, giving the signal to the other fifty men hiding below deck. In moments the rest of Jack's men came pouring onto the deck, swords drawn and ready. They gathered themselves on one side of the ship, eyeing Henry's men as they aligned the other.

This was exactly as Henry had anticipated. He raised his sword over his head. "Let's send 'em to Hell!"

Adelina gasped at the first clash of swords and shifted her grip on the wooden plank, sending a splinter into her palm. Whimpering, Adelina pulled it out and wrapped a piece of cloth around her hand. She grabbed a second discarded rag and wrapped the base of the wood to keep from further injuring herself.

There are more men above me now, Adelina was sure of that. *And there is definitely a battle going on for one reason or another.* She heard an additional amount of footsteps shuffling on the deck and twice as many voices. She thought she heard Henry's voice once or twice, but dismissed it as a figment of her imagination.

The clatter of swords was almost deafening. Pistol shots echoed through her prison, filling the air with gray, acidic smoke. She heard men screaming and others shouting words of encouragement to each other. A couple of cannons rang out, and Adelina fought to keep from screaming as she felt the ship quake from side to side and wood blasting apart.

But who else is up there? Adelina thought. She was convinced she didn't want to know. *What will happen if they found me?* She wrapped the sail around her and hid underneath its folds.

Henry spied Brandon hiding behind the mizzenmast. He was half hidden by the helm and well out of danger of the battle. Again, Henry found himself wondering why anyone would want to marry this man.

The man in front of Henry raised his sword with full intention of swinging it into Henry's neck. With ease, Henry sank his blade into the man's stomach, causing him to gasp and drop his sword. He pulled his sword out of the man's body and watched him drop to the ground, clutching his mid-section.

Henry began to make his way to Brandon, but became distracted when he spotted Patches out of the corner of his eye struggling to duel two men. Henry turned and dodged several attempts on his life as he made his way to his surgeon and ran his sword through the back of the second man he was fighting. Relieved of the extra threat, Patches knocked the other man unconscious with the handle of his sword. He gave Henry a grateful nod and went to find his next victim.

Henry turned back to Brandon, surprised to find one of Jack's men behind him, lunging his sword at him. Henry ducked away with seconds to spare, leaving the man to run past him into the back of another one of Jack's men. Henry watched as the two men clutched each other in tears, waiting for death. With a deep breath, Henry turned and headed to Brandon's side.

"Get up and fight, man!" Henry ordered as he knelt down near Brandon, glancing over his shoulder at the battle behind him.

"Please, Henry. They'll kill me," Brandon begged.

"This is against the Articles. If you were one of my men, I could maroon you for this," Henry said, grinding his teeth. He looked into Brandon's terror-filled eyes and pitied him. "Well, make yourself useful then—see if you can find Adelina."

Brandon nodded, still reluctant to move.

Henry rolled his eyes and marched proudly back to the battle. He caught a glimpse of Billy's large frame above the crowd of men. He stood at the far railing of the *Blood Water*, grabbing one of Jack's men after another as they charged at him and threw them overboard. Billy would look over the railing and laugh at the men as they hit the water before he would turn around and reach for another.

"Well, look who it is!" a man called to him from the bow of the ship. "Damn, I thought you were dead."

Henry turned in the direction of the voice to discover Jack, with his sword on his shoulder and his foot on the hatch that led to the forepeak. Henry smiled as he moved toward Jack. "I'm just full of surprises."

"I'm just full of surprises," Jack mimicked in a high voice. He stepped away from the hatch and raised his sword off his shoulder and swung it around in front of him. "Ready?"

Henry slid the blade of his sword against Jack's, accepting his challenge. "Always."

Together, they moved in a circle, each waiting for the other to make the first move. Jack advanced and raised his sword over his head to bring it down on Henry's shoulder. Henry took a retreating step backward and to the side, narrowly missing the blade.

Henry took the opportunity to move behind Jack and use the moment to lunge at Jack's back. Jack spun around in defense and ricocheted Henry's sword a moment before it reached his skin.

"Good try, old friend." Jack laughed.

Henry grunted and pulled his arm back to swing the sword into Jack's stomach. Jack stepped back and Henry continued in a circle. When he faced Jack again, he barely had enough time to bring his sword up to block Jack from bearing down on him.

"Before I kill you," Henry wheezed, "where is Adelina?"

Jack laughed. "I tossed that wench to the sharks a while ago…right after I bedded her."

Henry brought his boot out from under him and stomped heavily on Jack's foot. Jack yelped and stumbled backward a few steps, bracing himself against the railing to keep from falling. "Wrong answer. Now, where is she? I'm not going to ask you again."

Jack put his hands out as if he was holding something. "She was a good ride. Had a nice, tight little—"

Henry raised his sword and sunk it easily into Jack's left shoulder. Jack cried out in pain as Henry removed his blade. "Try again."

Henry stepped back, giving Jack a moment to analyze the damage on his shoulder.

Grinding his teeth, Jack raised his sword. A wild sort of anger flowed through him and he ran toward Henry. Henry dodged the sword, but not before the blade cut deep into his left arm, right above the elbow.

Henry took a sharp breath as he quickly examined the cut. It was deep and he knew he would need about half a dozen stitches. But there wasn't time to agonize over that right now. Jack stood in front of him, laughing. Rolling his eyes, Henry closed the three steps that distanced them and ran his sword through Jack's stomach.

Jack screamed, drawing everyone's attention from the battle. He pulled out Henry's sword and dropped it with his own. Clutching his stomach, Jack staggered backward a few steps, watching as dark blood reddened his fingers as it escaped his wound. The back of his legs hit the raised hatch, causing him to fall backward, landing on the portal that led to the forepeak. The thin planks guarding the portal couldn't support his weight and he fell silently through the wood.

Adelina heard the wood breaking above her and the distinct thud of a body hitting the floorboards, followed by splashing as the water moved about. Slowly, she peered out from underneath the sail.

She saw Jack's body lying in the middle of the floor surrounded by broken pieces of wood. Carefully, she crept from her hiding place, with the plank of wood raised high above her, ready to strike if she saw any movement. As she stood over him, Adelina could see Jack's shoulder and stomach wounds, where the blood slowly dispersed into the water, turning it bright red.

Holding her breath, Adelina nudged Jack's limp leg with her foot. When he didn't respond, Adelina breathed a sigh of relief. Her tormentor was dead.

Without looking away from Jack, Adelina returned to her barrel, hidden in the shadows. She sat on top of the sail, still clutching the plank.

Who is up there?

Chapter Twelve

With their captain dead, many of Jack's men immediately surrendered. A few men attempted to be heroes and be brave, taking command, but their efforts were in vain. Within the hour, all of Jack's surviving men were tied up and secured in the *North Star*'s stockade.

"How many?" Henry asked Billy as he finished stitching and bandaging his arm.

"Just three. Patches, Thump, and Petie," Billy mumbled.

Henry nodded, saddened for the loss of his men. "How many did we gain?"

"Fourteen. All pledging their services for their lives. I had them sign a copy of the Articles already." Billy looked up with a smile. "Cowards."

"And Adelina?"

Billy's smile faded and he glanced at Brandon, still hidden by the helm. "No sign of her and no one is talking…yet."

"She has to be on this ship," Henry paused. "Unless what he said was true."

"I'll have a search organized before we depart," Billy offered.

Henry thanked him and turned to walk to the stern of the ship. Brandon stood there, still rooted to the spot. "Get back to the *North Star*. We're leaving soon."

"What about Adelina?" Brandon mumbled.

Henry shrugged. "We're still looking."

Brandon's lip quivered, but his face grew stiff with anger. "You'd said we'd find her."

"I'm sorry, Brandon," Henry offered, his own heart breaking.

"You'd said we'd find her!" Brandon repeated, yelling his words. He stepped forward and pushed Henry. Baring his teeth, Brandon brought his sword in front of him.

"Now, where was this an hour ago?" Henry asked. Other than raising his weapon, Henry turned and walked toward the bow of the ship.

Running footsteps sounded behind him and Henry barely managed to jump to the side before the blade could sink into his back. Henry drew his own sword and waited for Brandon to turn around and face him.

"Stop it!" Billy shouted as he stepped between them. "You're both on the same damn side!"

Henry carefully slid his sword into his sheath, his eyes never leaving Brandon. "He started it."

"Billy? Is that you?" came a weak voice.

Everyone went silent.

"Billy? Please—answer me?" the voice came again.

Brandon, closest to the open hatch, peered into its pending darkness. Eyes straining, he saw his betrothed standing almost up to her knees in water. "Adelina!"

"Brandon?" Adelina mumbled, shocked with disbelief.

Henry glanced around him and found a rope ladder slumped to the side. He picked it up and handed it to Brandon, letting him be the hero. After a few minutes, Adelina's head emerged from the forepeak. Brandon knelt, nearly dragged her to her feet and immediately enveloped her into his arms.

From behind, Henry silently inspected Adelina. Her arms hung limply at her sides, with her bleeding palms facing him. Her hair was in complete disarray, wet, dirty, and tangled like he'd never seen before. The gown was completely shredded below her knees, displaying the blotches of dirt that covered her numerous cuts and bruises along her legs and bare feet. Her dress was no longer the sea foam color he last saw her in, but a mixture of browns and blacks. *She's beautiful.*

"Oh, Adelina, how I missed you so," Brandon said, hugging he close. "I came all the way over here to save you—you should have seen me. I killed two dozen of those dirty scoundrels who took you. But I found you."

"Brandon…" Adelina murmured, still in disbelief.

Henry watched as Brandon rubbed her shoulders. He fought the sudden urge to run over to Brandon and throw him overboard after what he had tried to do to Adelina before he had kidnapped her. Henry knew deep in his heart that if Brandon takes Adelina to England, not only would he never see her again, there would be certain danger for her. He wanted to keep her with him, to protect her and love her. But there was naught he could do.

Brandon took a step backward and cupped her chin in his hands. "Look at you, my dear. You look a sight. But that's alright. I still love you just the same. We'll get you cleaned up and properly dressed in no time."

Henry shoved his hands into his pockets. "I think she looks wonderful."

Adelina spun on her heels. "Henry!" she nearly screamed. Laughing, she ran into his open arms.

"Oh, Adelina, my love," Henry whispered into her ear as he held her tightly. He forced himself to swallow the lump in his throat. *She's finally in my arms again. I can protect her now.*

"I thought I lost you," Adelina murmured, tears spilling down her cheeks.

Ignoring Brandon's questioning stare, Henry leaned down and softly kissed her lips. "I missed you so much, my love."

"I missed you, too, Henry." Adelina smiled, putting a hand to her stomach. "I need to tell you something."

"What is—" Henry began.

"What's going on here?" Brandon asked as he approached them. He put a hand on Adelina's back, expecting her to step next to him. She didn't move and Brandon found himself growing agitated.

Henry clicked his tongue against the top of his mouth. "How about we get off this ship and go home?"

"That sounds like a nice idea." Adelina smiled.

Adelina looked up at her betrothed to find him gazing out to sea. *What can I say to him?* Before she could speak, he stalked to the railing, leaving Adelina alone.

"I'll be right back," Henry said, almost regretting leaving her side. "Will you be alright while I'm gone?"

"I'll be alright for a few minutes," Adelina said with a smile.

She stood there, unsure of what do to when a gurgling sound came from behind her. Adelina turned to find Jack crawling out of the forepeak. His skin was white and his shirt was stained red from his blood. He hunched over on his knees and spat blood onto the deck. He looked around and spied a discarded sword lying a foot away from him. Groaning, he lifted it and stood up.

Adelina watched in horror as Jack faced her, blood still dripping from his lips. He began to limp toward her, but his steps quickened. Adelina screamed as he approached her, drawing Henry and Brandon's attention, but they were too far away to help and Jack was too close.

Adelina took several steps backward until the railing pressed against her back, preventing further escape. *Run!* her mind screamed, but her legs did not obey.

"Now I got you," Jack said as he gasped for air. He raised the sword at level with her chest with a bloodcurdling snarl. Just as Jack lunged forward, Adelina rolled onto her side, barley managing to dodge the weapon.

"Umph," Jack groaned as his stomach hit the railing, pushing out the air from his chest. He spat a mouthful of blood into the water.

Biting her lip, Adelina moved behind Jack and lifted his feet. With all the strength she could muster, she lifted his legs over her head and pushed Jack overboard. She heard him hit the water and she rushed to the side of the boat, expecting to see him treading water, waiting for her.

But there was nothing. Just several ripples that circled a series of bubbles that surfaced. Then the water stilled.

Henry ran to her side and took her into his arms, rubbing her back as she cried into his chest. "I'm never going to leave you alone again. Let's go home," he whispered near her ear. He put an arm around her waist and led her back to his ship, carefully helping her cross onto the *North Star*. He gave the orders to separate the two ships and set fire to the *Blood Water*. Without glancing back at Brandon, Henry led Adelina into his cabin.

He left her standing by the door as he opened the trunk at the foot of the bed. Smiling, Henry pulled out a peach-colored dress and a package wrapped in brown paper. Inside was a pair of matching slippers, a bottle of perfume, a bar of scented soap, and a hair brush. "I knew Catherine would do this."

Minutes later, Thomas entered with fresh water to pour into the bathtub. "I thought she would like to freshen up a bit," he said, giving Adelina a grin.

"Thank you, Thomas," Adelina said. "I would like that very much."

Thomas beamed and left the room with a smile. Henry followed out to give Adelina privacy, walking backward so that he wouldn't have to take his eyes off her.

Adelina undressed and climbed into the cool water. It might not have been a hot bath, but at least she could clean herself.

After an hour, her body and hair was rid of every single dirt particle. Almost reluctantly, Adelina stepped out of the water and dressed. She brushed her hair until every tangle and knot was gone. Feeling the best she had in weeks, Adelina left the cabin.

She found Brandon at the bow, watching the waves break alongside the ship. "Brandon…"

"What?" he asked, plainly.

Adelina sighed. "I want to apologize…"

"For what?" Brandon asked, turning to face her.

"Things weren't supposed to turn out this way," she offered.

"But they did," Brandon stated.

Adelina was silent for a moment. "Is there anything I can do?"

Brandon reached out and grabbed her by her wrist, pulling her into him. His other hand fondled her breast. "I want to bed you. You owe me that much."

Adelina gasped as he groped her. She pulled back her free hand and slapped him across his cheekbone. "No!"

Brandon snorted and released her. He touched the red cheek and glanced away for a moment. "Then let me keep your dowry, considering your father already gave it to me before you were, uh…inconvenienced."

Adelina nodded and cautiously stuck out her hand. "Deal."

Brandon shook it and turned his attention back out to the sea without another word.

Adelina breathed a sigh of relief and went to find Henry. He was at the helm. "Well, I talked to him."

"You didn't—" Henry started.

"I wanted to."

Henry didn't say anything for a moment, waiting for Adelina to finish. "And?"

"He'll be alright." Adelina smiled.

With one hand on the wheel to keep it steady, Henry reached out and pulled her against him. "Then you're all mine?"

Adelina nodded. She stood on tiptoe to plant a kiss on his lips, but his mouth opened and his tongue danced wonderfully on hers.

The journey back to Barbuda was far less aggravating than the journey to find Adelina. Or, at least, that was the way it seemed to Henry. In Adelina's mind, it was maddening torture. She couldn't wait to be on dry land, eat fresh food and sleep in a bed.

By mid afternoon on the fifth day of their return voyage, the *North Star* sailed through the tall cliffs and into the lagoon. Adelina raced to the jib of the ship and waved to all those waiting on the deck. She was shocked to find Michelle standing in the crowd, as though waiting for the ship to return. Michelle spotted her and crossed her arms before turning around and stomping back toward town.

Carefully, Henry steered the ship through the narrow channel that led up to his estate. Adelina remained by the railing at the bow of the ship, watching the scenery as they slowly sailed by, waiting for the first glimpse of Roark Manor.

About an hour before sunset, when the sky began to grow pink, Adelina spotted the dock protruding into the water. She ran back to Henry with a large smile on her face and continued to pace between Henry and the jib until the anchor was lowered and she could board the coxswain.

"All that jumping will make the boat flip over." Henry laughed as he pulled Adelina into his lap.

"I know. I just can't wait!" Adelina smiled as they rounded the bow of the ship.

"Adelina!" a woman shouted from the dock.

"Mother—Christopher—Mary!" Adelina called out as she attempted to stand up and wave.

Henry reached up and pulled her onto his lap. "You'll flip us all, woman!"

Billy couldn't secure the dinghy to the dock fast enough. He stepped out first and turned to help Adelina out of the boat seconds before she jumped out herself. Brandon clumsily pulled himself onto deck and stood up. He brushed himself off and shoved past Elizabeth, marching toward the house.

Adelina threw her arms around Elizabeth. "Oh, Mother, I missed you so much! And, Mary, how are you? Christopher, my how've you grown," she laughed. "Where's Father?"

Elizabeth smile dropped. "He couldn't make it, dear."

It was true after all, she thought. "That's alright. Let's go inside. I long for a hot bath. Did you get my letter?" Adelina asked. She glanced back over her shoulder at Henry, who followed them at a distance.

Henry snorted behind them.

Elizabeth nodded and took out a folded piece of paper. "I have it right here."

"So…" Henry paused. "What else was in that letter?"

Adelina gave him a small smile. "I told them where I was, who you were, and that you were captain of the *North Star.*"

Henry reached out and took the paper from Elizabeth's hands and opened it. He read the fancy script and shook his head. Expelling a long sigh, he tore it into a dozen pieces and tossed it into the air. "No more correspondence."

Adelina smiled. "I never expected everything to change."

In the kitchen, Catherine gave Adelina a welcoming hug, blaming the oncoming tears as a reaction to the budding flowers. With a smile, she announced that she was going to prepare a feast, so it was time for everyone to leave the kitchen so she could begin. Elizabeth and Mary volunteered their services, seeing that they were guests, and Catherine gratefully accepted. Brandon, on the other hand, stalked away to the parlor and helped himself to a bottle of liquor.

"If you don't mind, I think I will freshen up a bit before dinner," Adelina said excusing herself.

Henry agreed. "I think I shall too."

"Oh, sir," Elizabeth paused, waiting for Henry to turn back to her. "About my daughter—"

"There's no need," Henry said with a wave of his hand, cutting her off. "But you are welcome to stay here as long as you wish."

Elizabeth smiled, fighting the oncoming tears. "Thank you, milord."

"Now, if you don't mind, I could really use a good soak. My pardons," Henry said, excusing himself as he followed Adelina upstairs. With a soft smile, she departed into her bedchamber.

Adelina was thankful to find the hot bath waiting for her. She undressed and poured a good amount of cold water into the tub, fearing that the hot water could possibly harm the baby. In her nudity, she touched her tender breasts. They seemed to have grown slightly larger in the past month, indicating her present state. Sighing, she stepped into the water and sank into its depth. Again, she looked up and realized that she had forgotten the scented oils.

"Henry!" she called, barely loud enough to go beyond the bath chamber.

"Yes?" he asked from the doorway.

"I didn't see you. How long have you been standing there?" Adelina asked.

"Long enough. I told you I wasn't going to leave you alone," Henry answered as he took off his shirt and approached the bathtub. He pulled up the wooden stool and brought it behind Adelina. He sat down and began to knead her shoulders. "You look different."

Adelina smiled. "I feel different."

Henry took a deep breath. Rage began to fill him as he thought of Jack's hands on Adelina. "Did he do anything? So help me that if he—"

"No, Henry, he didn't," Adelina reassured him.

Henry relaxed a little. "Then what?"

Footsteps sounded in her bedroom. Adelina looked up to find her mother and Mary in the doorway.

"Oh, my—" Elizabeth muttered, spinning around to leave, bringing Mary with her.

Henry sat up and rubbed his palms over his eyes. He handed Adelina her towel and helped her put on her robe. When she was decent, he donned his shirt. Together, they stepped into her bedroom.

Elizabeth sat on Adelina's bed with her back to them. Mary busied herself by searching through the closet for a dress her mistress could wear.

Adelina sat down on the bed next to her mother and reached for her hand. Henry moved out of earshot to the other side of the room, giving the two women their privacy.

"Now I know why Brandon was in a bad mood when you returned," Elizabeth mumbled, not able to bring herself to look at her daughter.

"I told him to keep the dowry," Adelina whispered.

"Is this what you want?" Elizabeth asked, barely able to keep her voice from breaking. "Do you love him?"

"I do. More than I could ever love anybody—even Brandon. Especially Brandon," Adelina put a hand to her stomach. "This is exactly what I want."

Elizabeth saw the gesture and gasped. She slid her arms around her daughter and held her close. "I thought you looked…different. Does he know?"

Adelina beamed and shook her head. "I'm still…not exactly positive."

Elizabeth nodded and stood up, wiping a tear from her eye. "Come, Mary. We'll wait for them downstairs."

Mary left a dress on the bed and followed Elizabeth out of the room, carefully shutting the door behind her.

Henry watched carefully as Adelina dressed in the gown and pulled her hair back with a ribbon. "Is everything alright?"

Adelina nodded. "Actually…yes."

Henry nodded, waiting for her to continue. When she didn't, he shrugged and opened the bedroom door. Adelina followed him out and allowed him to escort her down the stairs and into the dining room.

Everyone finished their conversations and moved to their seats. Henry sat at his usual place at the head of the table, with Billy to his right, followed by Thomas. On his other side sat Adelina, Christopher, Elizabeth and Brandon.

"Let's eat," Henry commanded after Elizabeth finished saying grace.

"I was thinking," Elizabeth said to her daughter. "This is such a nice area, I was debating about whether I should get a townhouse or a small cabin."

"Oh, Mother, that would be wonderful. But what about England and Christopher's schooling?" Adelina asked.

Elizabeth waved her hand. "There's nothing left for us back in England after what your father has done. And besides, I could probably hire a private tutor for Christopher."

Henry nodded. "That's a great idea. I'll even help out with the finances."

Elizabeth thanked him, glad that the whole ordeal was over. She didn't expect the man who kidnapped her daughter to be so generous and charming. She could see how her daughter had fallen in love. *He would definitely make her a good husband*, she determined.

Catherine entered the dining room from the hallway. "Masta, it's Mizz Deb—"

Michelle pushed the older woman aside and barged into the dining room with Mayor Ramsey right behind her. "There she is! Arrest her!"

Henry banged his fist on the table and stood up. "What's the meaning of this?"

"She assaulted me. You were standing right there, Henry. Now she's going to pay for it!" Michelle yelled, crossing her arms.

Adelina stood up but before she could respond, Henry was there in front of her. "Mayor, there was no such thing."

"What—" Michelle gasped. "She—she—hit me!"

Elizabeth gasped behind them.

"She was provoked!" Henry yelled, his anger rising as he clenched and unclenched his fists.

"Ah—I remember this young lady and what happened, despite what everyone may think," Ramsey said.

"Then what are you going to do?" Henry asked as he slipped a hand around Adelina's waist.

"I know more about what is going on in this town than what you give me credit for, Henry. This is nothing more than a domestic dispute and rivalry over the same man. I suggest you two ladies work this out yourselves," Ramsey said with a yawn. He turned to Michelle. "I can't believe you woke me out of bed for this."

"But...but..." Michelle stammered.

"Goodnight, Henry," Ramsey said. He gave Michelle a heavy look as he left the dining room.

Michelle stood there, rooted to the spot, watching Ramsey leave. She turned back to Adelina. "You conniving little—ugh!"

"Oh, be quiet, Michelle," Adelina spat. She turned to Henry. "But she's right. I did hit her. She deserved it, but I did hit her."

"That she did." Henry smiled.

Michelle snorted.

Henry pulled Adelina closer to him. "I love you, Adelina Ellingsworth. I thought that I had lost you once. I could never lose you again. I want to keep you by my side forever."

"Wh—what are you saying, Henry?" Michelle asked from behind.

"Marry me, Adelina," Henry begged. "Be mine forever."

"Oh, Henry, I will!" Adelina cried as she stood on tiptoe to kiss his lips.

Michelle shrieked and was suddenly between them, pushing them apart. She faced Adelina, cheeks red with anger. "You'll never have with him what I had, wench," she said with a grunt. She stormed out of the room, slamming the dining room door behind her.

Adelina followed her with Henry on her heels. "Michelle," Adelina called after her when they reached the foyer.

Michelle stopped and faced her. "What do *you* want?"

With a smile, Adelina walked around Michelle and pulled open the door. She put her free hand to her abdomen. "I wanted you to know that I already have that…and much more."

Michelle gasped, realizing what her foe had meant. Without another word, she stormed out the open door. To Adelina's shock, Brandon passed by her and followed Michelle out the door. He shared some words with her and got into Michelle's waiting carriage, offering no excuse or an explanation.

Adelina watched the carriage speed away before she closed the door. Smiling, she turned and found Henry staring at her, with his head cocked to one side and his arms crossed. "What?"

Henry took the step between them and placed an open palm on her stomach as he nuzzled close to her ear. "Oh—and so much more."

Printed in the United States
93475LV00004B/238-300/A